A WORLD OF VAMPIRES

VOLUME 1

To Travis,

Long live vampires!

Dani Hoots

DANI HOOTS

A World of Vampires
Volume 1
© 2014 Dani Hoots
ISBN for paperback: 978-1-942023-15-9

A World of Vampires:
Hooh-Strah-Dooh
© 2014 Dani Hoots
ISBN for kindle: 978-1-942023-02-9
ISBN for nook: 978-1-942023-03-6

A World of Vampires:
Baobhan Sith
© 2014 Dani Hoots
ISBN for kindle: 978-1-942023-06-7
ISBN for nook: 978-1-942023-07-4

A World of Vampires:
Strigoi
© 2014 Dani Hoots
ISBN for kindle: 978-1-942023-11-1
ISBN for nook: 978-1-942023-12-8

A World of Vampires:
Jiangshi
© 2014 Dani Hoots
ISBN for kindle: 978-1-942023-13-5
ISBN for nook: 978-1-942023-14-2

Content Edit by Desiree DeOrto
Final Edit by Justin Boyer of A Bibliophile's Workshop
Cover Design Copyright © 2014 by Daniel Somerville
Formatting by Marcy Rachel of Backstrip Publishing

Hoon-Strah-Dooh

AS I WALK THE BUSTLING streets of either Boston, New York, Chicago, Philadelphia, I am quite intrigued by all of the flashing lights, the countless stores and ads telling me what beauty is, what to consume, what not to consume, whom I should vote for, the list goes on. Everyone wants your attention, everyone wants your money; it doesn't seem to matter where you go now because everyone is trying to draw your attention. It's unbelievable how much has changed in the past eighty years, how much the world has suffered, how much everyone has suffered. But life never stops. Nothing ever quits.

The thing that really strikes my attention, though, is the countless ads for stories of vampires. These stories exist across many fictional genres in books, including teen drama, romance, and horror. Basically, the myth has spread throughout every genre I can imagine, beyond just those three. They are everywhere: in bookstores, on the TV. There are clubs and bars with horrific themes that not even I would ever want to attend.

In all these modernized, frilly vampire stories, young girls dream wasteful, tired dreams of being saved by a brooding creature of the dark, in the hopes they can spend an eternity with the one they think they love. And maybe, at one point in my life, I believed in the same thing, falling in love with Brian MacAuliffe at a mere age of seventeen. But the truth is that there is no happy ending to my story.

And every day I will live with that fact.

I have been running ever since that day and I will never stop. I can never stop running now. Not to enjoy life, not to smell the roses, and not even to enjoy friendship or love. The stories that say life as a vampire is every person's dream come true is an utter lie. Not only will you suffer in the end of this supposed dream, but you will never perish unless you get caught, and believe me the end result isn't pretty.

So I'm writing this to let people out there know the truth about us vampires, to let them know the pain that we must endure. Even though we want to end it once and for all, our desire to survive overpowers it. We are created to endure such unimaginable agony, but nothing is more painful than seeing the years go by and not be able to stop them for a second to savor. Life keeps going, and you are stuck in a never ending loop for an immeasurable eternity, or until you can't take it anymore.

I will agree, being a vampire does has its perks, including being able to see things in a new light. Then there's the speed, the energy given when blood trickles down your throat. But none of these enhancements have been worth the torture. My story is a cautionary tale for any of those who go looking for people like me to turn them, or somehow improve the outlook or story of their lives. Those who think they can handle it. I can tell you now, at least, you won't be able to.

It all started on a warm, summer day. It was mid-July, 1931 and the city of Boston was roaring with life. Prohibition was still intact and many gangs made it their business to smuggle, steal, and sell wherever they could for a quick buck. There were robberies, shootings, underground parties happening all over the city; it was all a part of the time, and it was an interesting time indeed.

I was living in the southern part of Boston, where the Irish mob had the most control during that time, both MacAuliffe's Gang and the Gustin Gang. Up until that point, I had nothing to do with the mob. I had only heard the news of robberies, shootings, and of course of all the speakeasies they were involved with. Most of this I overheard at the market or sometimes from my mother and father. If any of it hurt them financially or was posed an inconvenience in their lives because either a road or shop was closed, I was, of course, to blame for these isolated events, beyond my control.

It wasn't until my brother, the idiot that he was, had gotten himself involved with MacAuliffe's Gang that things changed drastically for my life. He thought joining their gang would be way of attaining easy money, and he hoped he could make our parents proud. Of course, that didn't happen, for he was always an idiot. And, to make matters even worse, he had stolen from Mister MacAuliffe, thinking he would somehow get away with it.

We hadn't seen him for almost a week. Either he was dead in a ditch somewhere or the gang leader MacAuliffe had locked him up somewhere undisclosed to the rest of his gang. Although I hated my older brother, I hoped for the latter. I didn't need our parents blaming me for his failures, as they usually did.

My father's belt came down on my arm again. "Don't you dare defy me again, you hear me? You go out and you find my son, you worthless piece of filth." The belt struck me again.

"Stop, please!" I screamed as he hit my ribs. "I will go look for him. I'm just saying I don't know what I can do to get Mister MacAuliffe to release him. Daniel was stupid to steal from them."

"Don't you dare talk about your brother like that!" he yelled as the belt missed my arm and slapped me across the cheek. I felt it slice into my skin. I held back the tears, knowing they would just make matters worse. I hurried out the door before he could hit me again.

"And don't come home until you get him released! Do whatever it takes!" he yelled then slammed the door shut behind me. I glanced back to find our neighbor, Miss Havington, staring at me with concern. I diverted my gaze to my feet, not wanting to show my tear-splotched face to her. I felt ashamed of how weak I was and I didn't want her to see, looking so pathetic.

I hurried off towards Mister MacAuliffe's office.

I loathed to go home empty-handed and didn't look forward to returning there ever again, either way. I was never given mercy nor love, I just always returned to a metaphoric prison. I should have run away when I had a chance, but I had nowhere to go and life could be worse if they ended up finding me. My body was already covered in bruises from refusing to go out and search for him the night before. Today's beating left me feeling even worse than usual.

The heat hammered down on me as I made my way through the busy streets of southern Boston. I held up a dirty, week-old newspaper to shield my face from the strong sunlight beating down on me. I really had nothing else and the temperature was almost unbearable. It had been a while since it was this hot.

I dreaded going down into the area where Brian MacAuliffe had his headquarters. Being a young girl of seventeen, it wasn't one of the safest place to go alone, but I had no choice. Not if I wanted to survive the day.

The walk was long, at least a good four or five mile walk from my home. I hadn't had anything to eat yet that morning, since my parents only let me out of the closet before they eventually made me head out to track down my brother. I had refused to go out the night before and my father wanted to remind me just who was in charge of the family. If he cared so much about his son, he should have gone out and retrieved him himself.

This is where the more exciting part of my story begins. I had arrived to the headquarters of the infamous Brian MacAuliffe, taking a moment to wonder what possessed me to go there in the first place. Brian had a reputation throughout the city of being one of the most ruthless killers, not caring who or what stood in the way of his rising underground empire. Both he and the Gustin Gang ruled these streets in southern Boston together, giving all the other gangs a run for their money.

After taking a deep breath, I stepped towards the simple building that matched every other building on the block. Red bricks, wood, and concrete meshed together by some contractor who had no imagination, and had just wanted a building there so he could get paid. The only thing that stood out about this building was that it had a different number for the address compared to those around it.

That and the bullet holes.

I entered the building, the door creaking as it swung open. The fans were going, but it didn't seem to keep out the hot, humid air. A girl at a desk used a folded paper to try to keep herself cool. From how red her face was, it didn't seem to be working.

"Need help miss?" her East coast accent was heavier than most. Her hair was cut in a short bob and her dress matched her eyes-a dark green.

I held my head up high, knowing I could show no weakness, even though I could feel my legs tremble beneath me. I had heard stories of these men from my brother and what they would do to those who defied them. They were worse than what our parents did to me, or at least it sounded that way. He could have been exaggerating, since even after all those stories, he still was an idiot and went and got himself in trouble anyways. Glancing back and finding two guards at the exit did not help my confidence. I gulped, seeing their revolvers set at their sides and the scars on their face.

Turning back to the girl, "I need to talk to Mr. MacAuliffe." His name came out in a nervous squeak.

She impatiently tapped her pencil against the table. "Got an appointment?"

"No, I don't. I just need to talk to him. My brother hasn't come home for days and I need to find out what has happened to him," I explained, trembling. I rubbed where I had been hit with the belt. It still burned and reminded me that I had to get my brother out of there or worse things would be waiting for me at home.

She gave me a look, as if I wasn't worth the time. "Look, if you don't have an appointment or good reason to see Mr. MacAuliffe, I can't help ya. I would lose my job if I let in every pretty brunette just because they wanted to talk."

"But it's not like that, he has my brother and if I don't return home, my father..." I stopped, not wanting to divulge my entire life story to a stranger. The woman took another look at me and must have noticed the bruises on my arm and the scratch under my eye.

She sighed as she started fanning herself again. "I will see what I can do for ya, sweetie."

"Thank you," I watched as she went back to the other room. I glanced back at the two men guarding the door. They simply stared at me with guarded expressions. I didn't want to think about what they would do to me if they saw me as a threat. A few moments later, the woman came back out of the office.

"He's got one minute. Make it quick."

I nodded quickly, tears of relief forming in my eyes. "Thank you so much."

"Yeah, yeah," she stepped forward so that only I could hear her. "If he asks though, just tell him you had an appointment a while back that got shifted today."

She winked and I understood what she meant. She wasn't supposed to do this for me, but thankfully; she understood my situation. I looked at the door that led into his office. My heart raced and I thought about running, but I wasn't one to let fear control me. Not when worse was waiting for me at home. I straightened my skirt and I entered his office with my head held high.

The office was surprisingly dark, all the window shades closed and the fans on full blast. Through the shadows, I could make out a desk and a couple of chairs. My skin felt cold, even though it was still hot in the room. After a few moments, my eyes adjusted to the light and there stood Brian MacAuliffe. I squeezed the newspaper that was still in my hands.

At that second, I understood why he was the most feared man in all of Boston. Not only was Brian handsome, but he also had the eyes of a murderer, someone who never took no for an answer, someone who would be feared even after his death. His hair was a shaggy brown mess and his eyes were the color of the deep sea that surrounded the city. Even now when I look out at the ocean, I feel him watching me. I know that is impossible, but I like to think maybe it's not and that all that happened had been a dream.

I stood there in silence, waiting for him to say something. I didn't want to be the first to speak, fearing that I would say something wrong. I rubbed my bruised arm with my palm, waiting for a response. He stood there, examining me as if I were some kind of prey. I didn't want to be there, but I had no choice. This was better than going home empty-handed.

He motioned half-heartedly to the wooden chair closest to me, as if not wanting to bother with me. "Take a seat, miss..."

"Anne Fitzgerald, sir."

A grin appeared on his face, as if my name answered all his questions. "Ah, I see. You are here about Daniel Fitzgerald, I take it?"

My heart hammered in my chest. I hoped for my sake that he was both alive and was just being held prisoner somewhere. "I am. Is he alive?"

Brian sat down and leaned back in his chair. He was quiet for a moment, making me fear the worst. Then he finally spoke. "He is. Gave him a good beating and locked him up for a while, let him understand that people don't steal from me."

I thanked God he was still alive, otherwise I had no idea what I would have done, probably start crying in fear of going back home with the news. "Is there any way you will let him go?"

Brian rubbed the scruff on his face. "I don't know if I should, I'm not quite done with punishing him."

"I didn't say he didn't deserve whatever punishment you are going to give him," I started bluntly. Why I did that, I didn't know. For some reason I felt calm around him, at least calmer than I should have been. My hands still shook when I was around him, but I felt that he wouldn't hurt me. Not like my father did.

I knew my brother and he got into more trouble than he was worth, which meant very little to me. "But if I don't come home with him, I will be blamed for anything and everything you do to him....the worthless girl that I am." I whispered the last part under my breath, I hadn't meant for it to come out, but

I had heard so much at home that I couldn't help but repeat it sometimes.

Something about Brian changed at that moment. He didn't seem to be that menacing, as if suddenly the switch between being a mob boss and a gentleman came to him. He grinned and I watched as his eyes examined me. "Miss Fitzgerald, you look anything but worthless."

I shook my head. "My family doesn't believe so. And please call me Anne, I don't like being called by my family name." I didn't want to be reminded of them.

He steepled his fingers, examining me. "You are a lot calmer than many I have talked to. Usually by now, I would have made someone cry. Or maybe, I'm just losing my touch." I didn't say a word as he examined me again. "Well, Miss Anne, I don't think I can let your brother go. He tried to disgrace me and I can't just let someone like that go free."

I stood up and placed my hands on the desk. I couldn't go back empty-handed, it would be worse than anything Brian could do to me for speaking out after he made a decision. I had been locked up in a closet the entire night, nothing he could do to me would be worse. "Please, I'm begging you, you don't know what they will do to me if I don't come back home with him."

"Then your brother shouldn't deal with men like me if he cares so much for his life," he sharply barked back.

I flinched from his tone, the harshness of it reminding me of my father's. The tone before the belt came down. But I didn't give up, contrary from what I learned at home about talking back. He wasn't my father, he was a nicer man. "My brother's a stupid son of a bitch, I know, but that won't change how I will be affected. If you have any heart, you will listen to my plea and let him go."

Brian slowly stood up and circled me, like a lion with his prey. My heart raced, but I didn't move for fear of what could happen. He stopped behind me and I could feel his breath on my neck. I closed my eyes, expecting that moment to be my last. Strangely enough, I didn't really mind.

"I have heard worse cases than yours, Miss Anne," he whispered into my ear. "Mothers have come in here, cold and hungry, crying for their children to be let go from my clutches. Wives, children, all of them have come to me with, frankly, better reasons than yours. I never let someone who betrays my trust go, it's bad for business. You must understand this."

I turned to face him and said probably my third worst mistake in my life. "Then take me in his place."

He raised an eyebrow. "Excuse me?"

"I will be your personal servant, I will do anything you say. Dishes, laundry, cooking, cleaning, escort, whatever you want... Just let him go." Everything happened so fast that the words seemed to be pouring out of my mouth and I had no control over them. I was an idiot to say this and would end up being in a worse situation than I was already in. But I was desperate to escape, so I took the first escape route that I found and unfortunately this was it.

He narrowed his eyes. "You would give your freedom up for him?"

"This decision is more freedom than I have ever had in my entire life."

Brian grabbed my chin, his lips inches from mine. "You will do anything I ask?"

My heart was racing in my chest and for a moment I wanted to run, cry, and just fall apart. But I couldn't, so I said the one word he wanted to hear. "Anything."

He watched me closely as I said the word, biting his lip. I could feel my body shaking, fearing what he would do to me. The world was spinning around me, everything felt out of my control every single day of my life. But I felt that this was my decision and I would stick to it.

"You're strong and confident, I like that. Or you must really want to get away from your family. Either way..." He let go of my chin. "Fine, I will take your trade. You are forever mine, Miss Anne. Would you like to say your goodbyes to your brother?"

Did I want to see my brother again? The brother who had caused so much misery in my life? "No, can you just have your men tell him I'm never coming home."

He chuckled as he scribbled on a piece of paper. "That I can. As for now, Jessica out in the lobby will give you my house keys and one of my men will escort you to my house. Go there and start cleaning."

My mind had ran many scenarios of all the things Brian would ask me to do the moment he called me his servant. Many of them ended very poorly for me. Never did I think I would hear that word.

"Cleaning?" I repeated.

"Yes. I will be back at around three in the morning. Have some sweets ready for me. Also, take care of the scratch on your face. I don't want people thinking I would hit a young girl such as yourself."

I was about to ask if he was joking, but decided I'd rather take this than anything else he might come up with. I nodded and went to the lobby to ask Jessica for the things.

And that was how I met the poor bastard that was Brian MacAuliffe.

Brian's house was in a nicer part of town than I imagined, for South Boston that is. Brian's second-in-command Joshua led me to Brian's house. He didn't say anything as he drove me, but kept glancing over at me. I felt conscious of the scratch on my cheek and the bruises that covered my arms. I could feel his eyes linger on them, but he didn't say anything, which I was very thankful for. I didn t need to hear his pitiful remarks.

Frankly, I was afraid he was going to take me somewhere to make me disappear, but I guess in a sense he was. I belonged to Brian now, never to see my family again. That was the part of it, which I didn't feel too bad about. For too long, I had been praying for the day that I wouldn't have to see them ever again. As for thinking of the things Brian could order me to do. I didn't want to think about it and was grateful he was simply sending me to his house to clean up, at least thus far.

We finally arrived and Joshua stopped the car. "Well, this is it," he motioned to the house. "Brian gave you the key."

"Yeah, thank you for driving me over," I began to open the door.

He grabbed my wrist, his grip tight. "Wait just a moment. I'm not letting you off that easy."

My entire body froze. He reached over me and pulled the door closed again. We were alone in the car.

"First off, you need to know that Brian is a good man. If you do anything to betray him, I will *personally* see to it that you suffer. You understand me?"

I nodded slowly.

"Just do what he says and you will be perfectly fine," he let go of my wrist and smiled. "Now, get to it. You have a lot to clean before your master gets home."

I got out of the car as quickly as I could. I didn't like how he called Brian my 'master'. It was rather disturbing and I tried not to think how either Joshua or Brian saw me.

As I pulled out the key, I examined the house. It looked simple enough, a brick house, a close match to that of his office. It was quiet too, which was strange. I had thought it would have a lot more people around it, but I guess if they all feared him, they wouldn't want to come anywhere near this place. The people that were there walked around me as I stood on the sidewalk, worried as to what horrors could be awaiting me. Taking a deep breath, I unlocked the door and opened it.

I quickly raised my hand over my mouth and nose. The stench was horrible, worse than that on the back streets. Trash covered the floor, in no sort of form or order. I wondered if he knew what a trashcan was. I quickly went inside and opened all the windows on the first level, to clear the smell of rotting food away and to get a cool breeze going through the house. Other than the trash, there wasn't anything too distinct in the house. All the walls were painted a quaint beige, and he had a couch and half-full bookcases. No paintings, no sculptures or vases. There was a table to dine on as well with a few chairs sprawled out around it, at least I hoped it was a table and not just a mountain of papers and half eaten food.

I started searching the closets for something to start cleaning with, going straight to my job as Joshua said to do. For all I knew, he could be watching, and I didn't want him reporting to Brian that I was slacking off. I kept looking for a broom or something. Anything would have worked, really, the place was a mess. I had a good ten hours before Brian got back and I had a feeling it would take that long to sort all of it out. For a half second, each time I opened the door I expected a dead body to fall out. One never did appear, thank goodness. I'm not quite sure what I would have done if it did. Once I found the right closet, I grabbed the cleaning supplies and started away at cleaning.

I worked on clearing away any food that I could find, either putting it away if it was still edible or just throwing it out altogether. I ended up throwing out most of it, even the random scraps that were in the refrigerator. The stench started to leave the house finally.

After the food, I started on clearing all the rubbish and paper on the tables. Not wanting to throw away anything that could be important, I mostly separated out the paper on the table for him to look through. I didn't want to get killed on the first day on the job for something as small as throwing out a piece of paper. I tried to do my job as best I could, in fear if I didn't please him, he would hurt me. Would he kill me? Would he hit me? It wasn't like I wasn't used to pain and being told I didn't do something properly. Punishment and I were close friends. I took a deep breath, letting the thoughts of being trapped in one of these closets disappear out of my mind. He wouldn't do that, he wasn't my father.

Although I tried not to read much of the writing on the papers, it really wasn't my business, I couldn't help to notice some very explicit death threats written on them. And I couldn't help but notice the checklists Brian had made describing the robberies and heists he wanted to perform. It was all in code as to when and where, but I got the gist and started to realize what I had gotten myself into. I tried to push the thoughts of what could go wrong in this deal back in my mind but the more I tried, the more I started to fear for my life and wanted to run away.

I made my way up the stairs into the bedrooms. One was clean and empty, which I was very thankful for. The other one had to have been a guest room that was used a few weeks ago.

The sheets smelled stale, as if Brian never got to cleaning them again. That wasn't a big surprise. As for the last room, which I gathered was Brian's, I wanted to slap him. His clothes were scattered throughout the room, covered in blood. His bedding didn't look like it had been cleaned in weeks and there was not one drawer that wasn't partially open. I rubbed my forehead and started to realize why he agreed to send me here for releasing my brother. It was disgusting.

I gathered the clothes and filled the bathtub with cold water. I figured I would let them soak for at least a day since Brian had let them dry.

As I finished sweeping up and cleaning the rest of the house, I realized Brian asked me to make him sweets. I didn't know what he meant by it, not sure as to whether he wanted cookies or something else. At that moment, I truly hoped he meant cookies and decided to make simple sugar cookies since that's all he had ingredients for. Barely.

I waited for those to cook. As I pulled them out of the oven, I heard someone unlock the front door. I checked the clock. Three in the morning. Right on time.

Taking a couple of deep breaths, I went into the hallway, greeting him for the evening, or morning I guess it was by then. When he saw me he jumped. "Oh, you scared me. Lucky I already put my pistol down." He sniffed the air. "Why does it smell like cookies?"

Damn, he did mean something else. "You told me to make you something sweet."

He laughed as he hung up his hat. "Right, so I did. I was joking, I didn't think you would actually make me something. Honestly, I forgot you were here until I opened the door. I haven't had a maid in a while," he took a look around as he entered the kitchen. "Place looks nice."

I had spent over ten hours cleaning his mess and all he could say is 'looks nice'. His house was disgusting, I'm not sure how he even tolerated living here in these conditions. I glanced at the cookies cooling down. The cookies he was just joking about. I couldn't complain, at least he didn't slap me for making them wrong or something in the like. That's what would have happened if I were at home now. It did bother me, though, I had spent a lot of time on these and had to get creative with ingredients. This was my second batch and I had really worried about him liking them.

Facing him, I smiled as if it were the best compliment I had ever had, which in reality it probably was. "Thank you." That's when I noticed the blood soaking his shirt and marking his knuckles. "Are you okay? You're covered in blood."

He looked down at himself as if he had forgotten completely about it, which he probably did. Blood was second nature to him as I would come to find. "Oh, right. Sorry, I probably dripped all over your clean floors. I will take it off right now before I make a bigger mess."

I blushed as he pulled his shirt off, which made me feel strange. He got me to trade myself in as a servant for my brother's freedom. He was a mob boss, a gang leader, someone who killed for a living, yet something about him made me feel strange inside. He was handsome, I had to admit, but there was something else about him that made my heart beat faster. Something that made me want to know more about him.

No wound was found on his body, just blood smeared across it. I didn't know then how that was possible but I didn't question it any further. I didn't want to know about any of his business, I just wanted to survive. He handed me the shirt. "Here ya go."

I grabbed it slowly and took it into the bathroom where I had the other clothes. Brian followed me into the bathroom and watched as I rinsed off the blood.

"Last person I had clean this house saw all the blood and ran off," he stated as he leaned against the wall.

"A deal's a deal," I responded. Truthfully I wanted to run away too. I didn't ask what he did to the other person, in fear that they were floating somewhere in the bay or worse.

He leaned over and looked in the bathtub. "Are those the clothes from my bedroom?"

"Yes."

He smiled. "Usually I buy a girl dinner, before she gets to see my bedroom."

I didn't respond as I grabbed a washcloth and soaked it in some water. I turned to him and started to wash off the blood from his skin. He didn't say another word but simply watched me intently. My heart raced in my chest and I could barely breathe. I decided to broach the topic of my brother.

"So you released my brother?" I asked. I didn't really care if he was released or not since I didn't have to go back home either way. The only reason I wanted him alive was because I would have been blamed for his death. Now it didn't matter.

He nodded. "Yes, as promised."

"Then this blood..." I feared that all of this work had been for nothing,

Brian laughed. "Not your brother's, don't worry," he raised his fists. "This is though."

I stared at his stained red knuckles. "Why?"

"I told him that his sister gave her life for his. He didn't care so I laid it into him that he should. I guess it doesn't matter since ya won't ever have to see him again, but he should know how to treat ladies better."

I couldn't believe what he was saying. No one ever did anything for me like that. "You stood up for me?"

"I believe in manners, every man should have them."

"And the other blood?"

"Hijacked a shipment. Couple of men got in the way but I fixed that," he whispered.

I finished washing off his knuckles, which I found to have no cuts on them as well. I began to think about how he stood up for me. Not many had ever been nice to me, a handful at most. Without knowing me or needing to, he had decided to stand up for me.

I rinsed off the washcloth and let it soak with the clothes, thinking about whether or not he was nice to all people or if I was the only one. I couldn't have been the only one, there wasn't any reason for him to be nice to me.

"Come on, I have something for ya," he grabbed me by the hand and led me out the door. He pulled me up the stairs, not without grabbing a cookie first, and just smiled.

"Don't look so worried, I won't bite."

He also mumbled something under his breath. I decided not to think about what that was.

He opened the door closest to the stairwell, the one that I didn't need to clean. "This room is yours."

Truth be told that wasn't what I was expecting, but I had no idea what to expect with Brian MacAuliffe. "Mine?"

He nodded. "Yup," he pointed at the door to the left. "That one's mine and the other is another spare, but you probably figured that out already. I usually use it for my second-in-command Joshua, if he ever stays late and is too drunk to go home. Which is more often than not. Anyway, make yourself comfortable. I wake at about three in the afternoon," he checked his watch. "Usually stay up a bit longer, do paperwork and stuff.

I expect a newspaper on the dining table by then, some tea and a muffin, as well. Then the day will go about the same. Just keep things tidy until I can think of anything else for ya."

I stared at him for a long moment. I don't know what possessed me to say it, but I did. "Are you serious?"

He leaned against the doorway, his face inches away from mine. "Why, is there anything else you have in mind?"

I just stared at him, not saying a word since the last time I opened my mouth, I ended up with this job.

After a few moments, Brian moved back. "I didn't think so. As I said, just do those things for now until I think of something."

"Alright."

"Well, then, see you in the morning," with that, he left me for the night. I watched as he went down the stairs, wondering if he was serious or if I had been dreaming. I pinched myself. Nope, not a dream. Not even a dream could be this crazy. I turned into the room and closed the door.

The next day, I woke up late in the morning and quietly went down the stairs, which was nearly impossible given that they squeaked worse than a mouse. I kept looking up at Brian's door but it never opened. He must have been a heavy sleeper or just really hated mornings.

I finished cleaning his clothes, getting the blood stains mostly out, which took a good deal of time. After that, I made the muffins he had requested, again as simple as I could since he didn't have much in the way of ingredients, and then gathered the newspaper to be ready for him. There wasn't anything else for me to do that I knew of so I opened up one of the books from his shelf. *Beauty and the Beast*. I sat there and read it, finding the fairytale to be enchanting. I didn't get to read stories like this at home, only a few when I visited my neighbors when I was younger.

"Relating to the character?"

I looked up to find Brian standing in front of me, smiling as if he had found my reading to be entertaining. I jumped up and put the book on the table. "I'm sorry, I finished with everything you needed me to do."

"You have nothing to worry about, I'm up a little earlier today than normal," he took a seat at the dining table. I quickly got him a muffin and placed it next to him. "Thank you," he nodded.

I started back towards the couch and he motioned to the table. "Why don't you join me, I haven't had someone to eat with in this house for ages."

I did as he said and sat down awkwardly, staring down at my hands in my lap. Every time I glanced up at him, I found him studying me.

"You seem nervous," he ate some of the muffin. "I said I wasn't going to bite."

That was the second time he brought up biting. I fidgeted with my skirt, not sure how to respond to it. I still expected him to hit me or throw me in some box for doing something wrong.

He watched me with a careful eye. "You also have nothing to worry about while you're here, this house is one of the safest in all of Boston."

I stared at him. After reading all those death threats that had been on the table, I didn't quite believe him. "Really?"

"Yup," he took another bite of the muffin. "My men are always around."

I didn't notice anyone when I had come the day before. "None of them did anything when we arrived yesterday."

"Called ahead, but if you did try to leave, they would have stopped you."

Simple enough, wished he told me though, I would have felt a bit better after reading his mail. It also explained why he didn't fear that I was going to run away. I couldn't. "Ah, I see."

He opened up the newspaper and started reading. "I also would never hurt you, so you don't have to worry about that either."

"Never crossed my mind," I lied.

"Says the girl with bruises on her forearms and ribs."

So he did notice the bruises. The ones on my forearms were apparent and I usually wore a long sleeved shirt to hide them, but it had been so hot the day before. As for my ribs, I had no idea how he knew about the bruises there. I moved a strand of hair back behind my ears. "How did you know?"

He kept flipping through the paper, as if this conversation was no big deal to him. "The way you stand and hold things. I'm used to seeing people in pain, I can tell. It's exactly why I sent your brother home in a bloody mess."

I didn't know what to say, but stared at him for a long moment. "Thank you."

He shrugged it off. "As I said, he needs to learn how to treat a lady. Speaking of which, why are you in the same clothes as yesterday?"

Was he really that naïve? I had moved here without going by my house to picked up any of my meager possessions. I had nothing with me. "Because I have no other clothes."

Brian pulled a wad of cash out of his pocket and placed it on the table. "Knock yourself out. Also, get some groceries on the way back."

I stared at the money. Never had I seen so much cash in one place. "I can't take that money..."

"Why not? You're my servant and I don't want to be seeing the same damn shirt and skirt every day. So go get something nice, please!"

I glanced back at the book lying on the table. A young girl trapped in the home of a beast. Maybe I could relate to that story, after all.

I bought myself some clothes, mostly just simple skirts and blouses. With how much Brian had given me, I could have gone all out, but that was never my taste. I liked simple clothes and that was that. Even now, I just wear tanks and jeans and a coat if need be. I never understood fashion and why someone would pay so much for clothes they would only wear once.

On the way back, I also gathered some groceries. Brian didn't give me a list, of course, so I just got things I liked to eat and some variety of sweets to cook. Deep down, I did fear that he would be mad that I didn't get what he wanted though. I tried to push that fear back, he wasn't my family, and he was nicer than that, at least to me.

As I ventured through town, I stayed away from areas I knew my family frequented, not wanting to cause a scene. Although, I figured they were probably relieved not to deal with me anymore and that they had their 'perfect' son back. I was glad to be rid of them, even though I wasn't quite sure what to make of my situation as of yet. Brian had showed me compassion thus far, but I had no idea if that would last any longer and whether it was just a temporary thing. I wasn't yet used to it and feared that if I did, it would go away.

I arrived back to the house and plotted out Brian's strange work schedule. I figured it would be easier to sleep while he was at work and wake up when he arrived back, that way I could have everything ready for his next day of work. And any errands he wanted me to do, I could do in the morning before he wakes up. Deciding this to be the best plan of action, I set my alarm for two in the morning.

I awoke just as planned and put one of my newly acquired dresses on. It felt good to have new clothes, ones that weren't second hand or something sewn by a neighbor who felt bad for me. It made me have a little more confidence in myself and I hoped that maybe Brian would think they looked nice on me. I didn't admit to myself that I found him charming, but I did enjoy his company. He made me feel as if it was possible for someone to care about me.

I was wrong about that because what I didn't know was that Brian already had his eyes on a woman that night. He rolled in about a quarter to three with a girl wrapped around him. I stood there in the entryway, jaw dropping due to the shock of the situation. I had misjudged him.

"Oh, right, you're here," he said. I almost slapped him for that, acting as if he forgot I was there. He knew damn well I was there, awaiting his arrival.

"Who's she?" the woman pointed at me.

He kissed her on the lips. "Just a maid, don't worry love," he turned to me and handed me a piece of paper. "These are things that need to be done when I wake up," he picked the girl up and headed up the stairs. "G'night!"

I shook my head. After all those things he said about respecting women, I thought he was different. Nope, he was just a pig like the rest of the men I knew in life. After shaking my head disdainfully, I unfolded the note to reveal it only having one word. 'Cake'.

Rubbing my forehead, I realized that he had acted surprised when he saw me, so how did he have a note for me? I wondered if the note was actually for me or if he just happened to have a note for someone else and realized he could give it to me to do. Rolling my eyes, I started on his cake.

It took Brian a week to remember I was there. He would come back with some girl, all different I might add, act surprised I was there, then give me some random task to perform. Sometimes it was to cook something, other times it was to deliver a letter or package to some stranger. I didn't ask questions but did as he said, even though it crushed my heart all the while. Though, being ignored was a lot better than the alternative. It wasn't like I had anywhere else to go and Brian gave me money for anything I needed. All I had to do was what he said, which really wasn't much.

A month went by, Brian coming back early in the morning with either blood all over his clothes or with a woman in his arms. I didn't know which one I preferred. It was probably the blood because then at least I was the one who got to undress him, and have a conversation that wasn't just, 'oh, ignore her she's my maid'. The more I hated seeing him with other girls, the more I began to realize I had feelings for him.

In the mornings, I got to spend time with him. The girls usually left before he ever got up and I would always open the door for them on their way out. It was nice spending time alone with him, hearing him talk about his enterprise. He was a genius, knowing when to use fear and when to use politics but this story isn't about his empire, this is about something far darker.

It was in August when he woke me up late one night, a never-ending knock on my door. I blinked my eyes, waking myself from a heavy slumber, and realized it was not even nine at night. The sun was just going down.

"Anne!" he called through the door. "I need you to do something for me."

I stumbled out of bed and opened the door. I still just had my nightgown on, I didn't really care. It was unheard of a man to see you in a nightgown in that era, but truthfully, so was living alone with a man you weren't married to. I couldn't ever get him to look at me in that way, or at least that was what I thought then. Now I knew I was wrong. "What is it?"

He handed me a dress. "Get changed, I'm taking you to your first party."

"What?" is the only response I could come up with in that moment. I didn't have much experience in how to react when a man wakes you up in the middle of the night and hands you a dress.

"The Wallace brothers are having a party down on Old Colony avenue, I do hope I can enjoy your company."

I thought about replying 'you're crazy' and be mad that after all this time he finally acted like I existed more than just some maid hired to clean the house, but decided that I should be happy that he wanted me to leave the house with him for once. "I have to get ready first."

"That's fine, I will wait downstairs."

This was definitely a development in working for Brian, even though I didn't quite understand his reasoning behind it. Personally, I just wanted to get out of the house. I got ready as fast as I could, knowing I couldn't let him wait for too long, he wasn't a patient man I had gathered from the stories he told of what he did to men who made him wait too long. I didn't want to be that person in the story.

Brian had picked out a long red dress, the cut in the front a little lower than I would have liked. Fortunately, most of the scars I had were hidden still by the dress. My arms were still freckled with some, but I had grown used to people seeing them. The injury on my cheek had almost healed too and I covered the rest up with makeup. I put on some lipstick to match the dress and hurried down the stairs. Brian just stared as I spun around in front of him. His eyes seemed to glitter as he watched me and it made me blush.

He clapped his hands together. "You look dazzling. Are you ready?"

I nodded and wrapped my arm around his. A car was waiting for us outside and Brian held the door for me. After he entered behind me, the car started towards Old Colony avenue.

"Thank you for the dress," I said.

"Not a problem, you have been working hard. Thought you might need a night out."

I smiled, glad to find that he still thought about me, contrary of what it seems when he brings different girls home every night. "How did you know my size?"

He laughed. "Years of experience."

I didn't want to think as to what he meant by that comment and decided to leave it alone. God only knew how many women Brian had measured up over the years. I didn't know if I should be impressed, concerned, or jealous.

A crowd was beginning to form outside of the Sportlight, guys dressed in suits and hats and women dressed in fancy gowns such as the one Brian had bought for me. The building was covered in brick and wood, small lanterns lining the exterior. I had never seen so many people trying to get into a venue, although I actually didn't have an experience in the matter. Brian ushered me out and the crowd parted as he led me into the Sportlight.

Tables were scattered around, but most people stood and chatted away as a jazz band played in the background. The bar was filled with people holding cash out, trying to get their drink ordered. Others held cigars and cigarettes, blowing smoke without even thinking about the consequences. I had never been to a place like this and I didn't know how to take it all in. I had actually expected something a lot smaller and didn't think so many people could fit in such a small building. I was wrong.

"Is this party legal?" I questioned as we stepped up to the bar. It was a stupid question, really, but I wasn't used to going out with Brian and seeing exactly what he does. I usually only saw the aftermath.

"Anne, is anything I do legal?" With a smile, he ordered us two drinks. I was going to refuse the drink, since I hadn't ever had a taste before, being illegal and all, but I decided not to bring the matter up. So I took a sip.

And I swore I about died.

The drink burned as it went down, my mind feeling like someone hit it with a sledge hammer. I didn't understand how someone could drink the stuff. Brian downed his with one gulp.

"Another," he slapped his hand on the counter. I didn't understand how he could do it, I could barely take one sip at a time. I smiled at him as he enjoyed everything going on. It made me happy to see him not as stressed, and not with another girl.

After the bartender gave him another drink, Brian held out his arm. "Shall we?"

I accepted his arm and we ventured through the crowd. Women glared at me and I received more winks from men than

I would ever care to remember. I tried to ignore them, look the other way and such, but I had never had so many people notice me before. I knew my face had to be red so I tried to just look down at my feet.

"Ah Brian, glad to see that you could make it," a man greeted Brian with a handshake. His hair was a curly brown and his eyes revealed more horrors than I would ever care for in a lifetime. "You must introduce me to this lady of yours."

Brian wrapped his arm around me. "This is Anne. Anne, this is Frank Wallace."

Frank grabbed my hand and kissed it. "Well, Miss Anne, I do hope you like the party, and bravo to you for being able to put up with this man. I've heard many stories about how much of a monster he has been. I do hope you can do your best to keep him in line."

I gulped, wondering how bad Brian could be if a fellow gang leader called him a monster. I hoped he was just teasing. "I try my best."

"You must be doing well if Brian brought you here, I haven't ever known him to bring a girl here, usually he just leaves with one."

"Oh, he does that too," I commented as I took another sip of the drink. I about had a coughing fit.

Frank laughed. "Sense of humor, this one. You better keep her close, Brian. You don't want this one stolen away."

"Don't get any ideas, don't want our parties to have fighting because of some girl," Brian added. I glanced at him. What did he mean by some girl? And why did he act as if I wasn't there? I thought about saying something but decided to hold my tongue in such company.

"The thought never crossed my mind," Frank's attention turned away for a moment. "I see that a client has arrived. Brian, it has been a pleasure as always."

Brian raised his glass to him as Frank ran off to the other side of the speakeasy.

"How many maids have you had?" I whispered.

"A few. None have lasted as long as you, great job by the way. I was sure that you would have left by now."

Did that mean he didn't want me around? Truth was I didn't have anywhere to go and I sort of liked living somewhere that I felt safe, as ironic as that was. "And where would I go?"

Brian shrugged. "Anywhere I suppose."

Easy for him to say, he had money to go places. If he wanted, he could run away from all this, though I doubted he ever would. People treated him like a king here and I was pretty sure it made his ego flair up even more than it already was.

We mingled around with other groups at the party, Brian talking to different men about the latest shipments, deals, and trades he was open to. He also talked to Joshua, his second-in-command about plans for the next week. I half listened, mostly not wanting to know exactly what he was up to during the evenings when he was out. I didn't want to think about it too much. After a while of talking, he turned to me when we were finally alone.

"Anne, will you be a dear and get us some more drinks?" he nodded towards the bartender.

"Sure, I will be right back," I took his glass and headed towards the bar. After asking for another drink just for Brian, I really didn't want another, I turned to find Brian talking to two women. I frowned. They had their hands on him, flirting away. I could feel my cheeks start to get hot. That was why he wanted me, to make women want him even more. I just stared in disgust, shaking my head. He must have noticed because he excused himself and headed over to where I stood.

"What's wrong?" he asked as he grabbed his drink.

"You just brought me to make girls jealous and want you more, didn't you?" I accused.

He took a sip. "Yeah, your point?"

I couldn't believe what I was hearing. I had thought he really wanted to take me out. *Me*. But I was just another way to get a woman to go home with him. It was pathetic. "That's disgusting."

Brian laughed. "What, are you jealous?"

"No, I just thought..." I shook my head. It was stupid, I shouldn't have thought I was special, that he cared for me when he taught my brother a lesson for hurting me. "I don't know."

"I just thought maybe you wanted to get out of the house and go out somewhere fun," he said honestly. "This was just a plus to it all."

"You are just using me then? To get a girl in your bed? That just seems a little low, doesn't it?"

Brian stroked the side of my cheek and moved a piece of my hair out of my face. I could feel goose bumps forming on my skin. What was he doing? I held my breath. He leaned in closer. "Did you want me to sleep with you?"

I could feel the blood rush to my cheeks. "I didn't say that!" I snapped back.

He laughed as he stepped back and took another drink. "Well then, doesn't this arrangement seem fair? You get to dress up and come to parties such as this, but nothing after."

"It's fair," I lied. I still didn't want to agree to it, but I also didn't want him making more comments about me wanting to go to bed with him. Although, I admit, the thought did cross my mind.

"Alright then, whenever you're ready to leave, let me know and I will call a taxi for you," he headed back towards the girls, leaving me standing there alone.

I turned to the bartender. "I'll take another."

I didn't stay that much longer, hating the feeling that was gathering in my stomach as I watched Brian with those girls. But I couldn't say anything, I couldn't let him know how I truly felt, not if I wanted to keep my job and stay away from home. No, I didn't want things to truly change because I knew it could end things in a much worse way.

Brian called the taxi just as he promised and the driver took me home. I could feel tears forming in my eyes as I sat there, alone. I wiped them away. I would just have to deal with the pain and realize I wasn't anything special. I never was.

An hour or two later he arrived with both of the girls he was flirting with. I ignored them as he took them up to his room. I had already changed into my regular clothes and begun my usual day of running errands and keeping the place clean. I wasn't going to get anymore sleep knowing what was going on in the room next to me.

This charade went on a couple nights a week for a month. I was introduced to all sorts of men that before a few months ago, I would have been afraid to meet. Now I knew just not to ask questions, stay around Brian, and I would be fine. Although initially I was furious with Brian, it still was less pain than I had endured for a long time. I had started to resent working for Brian. I hated how he used me to get girls to surround him. I never said anything, though, and held my tongue when he asked how I was doing. I just smiled, as he wanted, and told him everything was fine.

It wasn't until a night in September that I said anything to Brian. It was the same night that I found out the truth.

We had arrived to the event just as always, I think it was the Sportlight again. It was a popular venue in south Boston, everyone that was someone in south Boston hung out there in the evening. I had begun to remember people's names, whom they were associated with, who to look out for while running the random errand for Brian during the day. I had learned more than I ever would have expected in the business and Brian began to teach me how to read a person's expression and how to tell if they were lying. It would come in handy throughout the years and I was very thankful he had decided to teach me such things, even before what was about to happen.

After talking to one of the Wallace brothers, both Frank, Steve, and James, whom I could never keep straight, I excused myself to use the powder room. I caught a glance at him before I went inside. He was already hitting on a new crop of girls. I rolled my eyes and pulled out my lipstick. As I fixed a smudge in the mirror, a tall older woman came in. She had beautiful red hair cut short as most did at that time. She pulled out her lipstick as well.

"I see that you came with Mister MacAuliffe," she said. At first, I didn't realize she was talking to me. Then her eyes flickered over at me in the mirror.

I nodded. "Yes, I did."

She snapped the cap back on her lipstick and looked at me with her bright green eyes. "So tell me, what's it like to be his whore?"

It took me a moment to process what she had said. Then I realized what she had accused me of-being, which was that I was like her and just wanted to get in his bed. I wanted to slap her. "Excuse me?"

"He pays you to come, does he not?" she let the words linger in the air, her voice sounding so sweet but her words so bitter.

Again, slapping her was my first thought. "I... No."

"Well, that's not what I hear. I hear that you do whatever he says," she leaned in closer. "Satisfy any needs."

"I'm not a prostitute," I snapped back.

She shrugged, a sly smile still plastered on her fake face. "I'm just telling you what I hear. Why else would he want you around?" she spun on her heels and left me standing there in the powder room. Alone.

I glanced at myself in the mirror, my cheeks burning red. At that moment, I had so many questions running through my head, and a few not so friendly things to tell Brian and where he could put the gowns he bought me, including the shoes and the makeup. Taking a deep breath, I knew that would be a mistake and that I would probably be punished severely if I did say that. I closed the cap of my lipstick and hurried out of the powder room. Although I had calmed down a bit, I still needed some fresh air and to get away from the people who looked at me as Brian's whore.

I started for the door, my head down, ignoring everyone around me. I could feel their eyes creep across me as I walked past. I hated the feeling as it made my skin crawl knowing the truth as to what they saw me as. Before I could get to the door, though, Brian had stopped me.

"Where are you going? What's wrong?" he asked, eyes darting back and forth between mine. I thought his words to be lies, in that he didn't really care about me in any way whatsoever.

I shook my head, still mad at him but not wanting to make a scene. "What am I to you?"

He didn't seem to understand, although we had discussed this a few times before that night. "What are you talking about? You know you just work for me, nothing more."

"Then why does everyone here see me as your whore?"

"What? Who said that?" he glanced around the room.

"It doesn't matter, I have to get out of here. I need some fresh air."

"Let me call the driver..." he began.

"No, I need a walk. I will find a way back to the house."

Brian tried to say something, but I shoved past him and out the door. I know now that I should have listened to him

I stepped out into the dark, dank September night, wrapping my arms around myself. I had left my coat inside and I didn't feel like going back and getting it. People were still lining up to get in the speakeasy so I hurried off in the opposite direction, hoping to find some peace and quiet at last.

A couple of blocks later, I found myself alone, with only the partial moon filling the night sky. Clouds hid away the stars, along with the city air. I kicked at any rock that was in my path, imagining it as Brian himself.

As I walked further, I heard a car creep up behind me. I glanced back to find bright lights nearly piercing my eyesight. The car stopped and I watched as the doors opened.

"Hey miss!"

I stopped dead in my tracks, my heartbeat echoing in my ears. I was in deep shit and I knew it. I cursed under my breath, words I had learned from both my family and from Brian.

"You're that lady who's always with Mister MacAuliffe, aren't ya?"

I tried to get a better look at the man speaking to me but his car lights masked his identity well. But from the voice alone, I could tell he wasn't one of Brian's friends. He was probably an Italian from up north. "Maybe."

His laugh was deep, throaty almost, and eerie as hell. He started walking towards me and I could make out another man getting out of his car, who had some type of gun in his hand. "I wonder what he would do if his lovely girl went missing."

I turned around and started running back towards the Sportlight, even though I knew it to be a waste. Nobody can run in heels, I swore. He caught me in a matter of seconds. One can't even begin to describe the fear that had taken over my thoughts, my body. I can tell you this much, I never wore heels again after that night.

"Somebody help me!" I screamed before he placed his hand over my mouth. I tried to escape his grasp, but it was no use. I wished Brian taught me how to fight at that moment. I don't know why it never crossed his mind to give me a weapon with how many enemies he had. Maybe he thought he could always keep me safe, and I guess in a way he was right.

"Let her go!"

I looked up to see Brian standing in front of the car. I couldn't believe my eyes and wondered if he had followed me from the party. He had to have, really, it was a stupid question to think up.

The man that held me pulled out a knife and placed it under my throat. I swore my heart stopped beating right then and there, I had never been so afraid. I would have been shaking if it weren't for fear of making the knife go into my throat. "No, Brian, this is how it's going to go down. I'm taking this girl and am sending you a ransom. You pay that ransom and she won't get hurt. You fail to do so," the man pushed the knife against my skin a little harder, I thought it was going to pierce my skin. "You can say goodbye to your sweetheart."

Brian stared at the man for a long while, as if contemplating what his next move would be. I just prayed he would help, that he would care enough to save me. Was it because he cared about me or was it because he saw me as his property? It didn't matter, either way I didn't want to die.

"Anne, close your eyes," he said in a lot calmer voice than I thought he should be having at that moment.

I tried to say 'what', but it came out as a muffled, "Mphm?"

His eyes didn't leave my attackers and I had sworn they changed color. Goosebumps covered my skin. Something was going to happen and I just hoped I would survive it all. "Trust me, please. You don't want to see what is going to happen next."

"What are you going to do?" my attacker asked. "There's nothing you can do without me slipping my knife across her throat!"

"Close your eyes now!" Brian demanded.

I did as he ordered and I had no idea what happened. All I heard was a swooshing sound and the screams of the two men that had attacked me. I couldn't imagine what Brian had done to them, I had no idea. It sounded like something out of the horror movies that were to come in the following years. I remember shaking as I slowly opened my eyes. I knew I wasn't supposed to open my eyes until Brian said something. But after the man let go of me, I felt the world spinning around me. If I didn't open them, I probably would have either fallen down or thrown up, most likely both.

And what I saw made me wish I had kept my eyes close.

Brian stood over the two men, his demonic eyes glowing yellow, nothing of this world could compare. His teeth were fangs, long and sharp and blood dripped from them down out of his mouth and onto his clothes. He breathed heavily, as an animal did after an attack.

I just stared at him, my hand covering my mouth. I didn't understand what was going on, I didn't know what to do. I had never seen anything like him before in my life. I was frightened as to the creature I was looking at.

He looked over at me and saw that I was watching him with fearful eyes. "I told you to close your eyes."

"I..."

He started walking towards me. I quickly stood and started running away from him.

"Anne! Don't!" he called out, but I ignored him and ran off, far away from the horrors I had just witnessed. As I ran around a corner, I felt arms wrap around me. I began to scream.

"Shh! Anne, it's me."

I looked up to find Joshua smiling.

"Joshua, I don't... I don't..."

Something caught his attention behind me. I turned to find Brian standing there. I hid behind Joshua, not wanting to get any closer to the beast. Brian saw how I feared him and stopped, frowning.

"Take her to the country home. I will be there by the end of the week," he ordered. His eyes started to turn back to their normal color and his teeth didn't seem as sharp as they did minutes ago. For a moment, I wondered if I had imagined it all, but the blood was still there.

He nodded and grabbed my arm, very tightly I might add. Neither of them wanted me to leave their sight and I accepted that because, frankly, I didn't have anyone to run to.

"Come on, you're fine," Joshua led me down the street. I didn't say a word as he ushered me into a car and drove off out of the city.

I imagined this being my last car ride, to never return to the city. I would be the girl that disappeared one night and no one would know why. I really doubted anyone would have noticed, but I still worried that would have been me. Joshua didn't say anything as he drove for an hour into the dark night. I stared out the window, shaking in my seat. I still had not yet understood what I had seen. I understood what a vampire was but it was just a fairytale, wasn't it? Like *Beauty and the Beast.* I couldn't make sense of it. I thought about asking Joshua more of what had happened, but I couldn't ever get the words to escape my mouth. I also wasn't sure if Joshua was one, so I just wrapped my arms around myself and curled up in a ball in the backseat of the car.

As we approached Brian's country home, an older man, his greying hair reflecting the grey of the moon, stood outside the doorway. And by country home, I meant a manor that could hold at least three full-sized families. I couldn't believe Brian didn't just stay out here all the time. It was beautiful, the large white pillars greeting guests as they arrived, no neighbors for miles, only full grown forest and all that dwelled in it. It seemed like paradise to me.

Joshua helped me out and brought me to the older man. I didn't like him touching me, flinching at the initial feeling. My body shook with fear. I looked at the old man. He seemed harmless enough, like a grandfather that cared about his grandkids. One that would give you cookies when you were feeling down.

"This is Walter, he is going to be watching you for a bit. Make yourself comfortable, Brian has things to finish before he can come out here and deal with what happened," Joshua explained.

I didn't answer, I really didn't know what to say. I also didn't want to know what he meant by 'deal with'. For a while, I thought Brian was going to kill me, but realized he would have just done it in Boston if he had been planning to do that.

"I have to get back as well. Walter is going to look after you," he took a step closer, not letting Walter hear him. "And if you try to run away or tell anyone, I will kill you. If you try to hurt Brian in any way, I will kill you. You understand?"

I nodded my head yes.

"Good. With that, I take my leave," he turned to Walter. "Don't let her leave, don't let her out of your sight. Get her anything she wants. Brian will send her clothes tomorrow."

"Yes, sir."

Joshua drove off and I simply stood there, staring at the road, realizing I was trapped there for God-knows how long. Although the place was nice, I still shook at the idea of being trapped and waiting for how I was to be dealt with. Having a member of a gang say that about you was never a good thing, I knew. I had read notes in how they dealt with people and it was never pretty. Most of them just disappeared which was my fear.

"Well, madam," Walter held out his hand. "I will show you to your room."

I nodded but didn't say anything as he led me into the house. The entry opened up into a large, almost ballroom-like area, staircases going up around both sides towards what I figured to be the lodging areas. Walter took me up the stairs and, I swore, picked a random room for me to stay in. There were so many, I doubted anyone stayed here often. Was he here all alone? I understood his loneliness if he was. A candle was already burning inside on the nightstand, flickering away and letting little light into the room.

Walter switched on the main light and I could make out the blue design that the room was decorated in. A chair and table took up the corner, the bed in the middle, and a small seat next to the window. A door way on the other side must have led to the closet. I stood in awe for a moment, then went back to my shivering self. I wasn't a house guest, I was a prisoner here. I couldn't leave without people trying to kill me. In fact, I might be killed here soon too.

"Well, I will leave you for the night. If you need anything, just call for me," Walter said. I was glad he was the one watching me, not Joshua. Joshua had always scared me, even from day one. He wouldn't hesitate to kill me, I knew. He hated seeing me around Brian. Whether it was from jealousy or pure suspicion, I didn't know.

I nodded again. It was like I had lost my voice that night, I didn't have anything to say.

"Goodnight," he closed the door behind him.

I sat down on the bed and held my hand over my mouth, trying to stop myself from screaming.

A week passed, I didn't hear anything from Brian or Joshua other than they had sent my clothes over from the townhouse. I mostly sat and read. Brian had a lot of books stored here, ranging from fairytales to history and poetry books... I found it strange how he had so much more here than he did in the city. I never figured out which was the real him, the minimalist or the man who had to show off. Maybe it was both.

Sometimes I would sit and play on the piano he had, letting my thoughts drift away with the notes. Walter tried to talk to me, asking a little about my past or just questions to get to know me, but I usually answered with minimal responses. I had too much processing through my brain to want to talk.

Walter let me take walks through the woods, accompanied by him of course. He walked a few paces behind me, as I enjoyed the serenity. I hadn't ever been outside the city, all of it was new to me. It was beautiful, I felt at peace for once in my life, at least if it weren't for the fear of Brian finally deciding to kill me for what I knew.

Then, finally, after the longest week of my life, I heard a car pull up to the house. I was at the piano when I hurried to the window to find Brian getting out of the car with Joshua. I waited in the entryway, fiddling with my sleeves. So many emotions were running through me. Fear, anger, worry. All of it was coursing through my veins, but only one of them overpowered the other.

The door opened and I ran straight to Brian, wrapping my arms around him. He just stood there confused and probably in shock. I could feel Joshua and Walter staring at me and was sort of surprised neither of them tried to stopped me, for all they knew I could have been trying to attack him. I guess no one expected me to respond in that way and, frankly, neither did I know I would react in that way. I just felt that it needed to be done.

"Thank you," I whispered in his ear.

He wrapped his arms around me and just held me for a brief moment. He nodded to the others to leave us. I heard them enter the library and we were alone. The moment felt like it could have lasted forever, and I wished it did. Even though he didn't treat me fair, even though I was pretty sure he didn't have feelings for me, I knew that I loved him for standing up for me, for caring enough to let me hold him like this.

I moved back. "I'm sorry, I didn't mean to make you feel uncomfortable."

"That's alright," he motioned to the parlor. "Please, let's talk. I believe I owe you an explanation."

I followed him inside the room and took a seat. I watched as he poured us both a drink. During this entire week, I had drunk more than I ever thought I would in a lifetime.

He handed me the drink and I took a large sip of it. "Do you know what I am?"

"I know of things you could be, but those aren't..."

"Real?" he laughed as he sat across from me. "The name is hooh-strah-dooh, it's a creature from Wyandot folklore. You might know them better as vampires."

My eyes widened. So it was true, all the stories. All the legends. My mind raced, thinking about what other creatures could have existed in the world.

"I," he laughed again, as if it were some kind of joke. I think that was how he dealt with it all, looking at his life as some joke for the God that had let him come into existence. "I did something I probably shouldn't have. It was a war, though, and I got too involved. I killed a lot of people, a lot of innocent people, or at least that's what they say. Well, I pissed off the wrong people and when they captured me, instead of killing me, they decided to curse me." He took a sip of his drink. "The curse was creating me into a creature, the hooh-strah-dooh. Then they buried me alive in a way they thought I would never escape from. Big metal box of some sort. I craved blood and flesh and the hunger was unbearable," he paused as the memory came back to him. "The want... the need. I can't even describe what it felt like, the realization of what I craved," he took another sip as

I listened further. "I also couldn't die and would suffer for what they thought was an eternity.

"A few years later, a grave robber found me and dug me up. Joke was on him when he opened my coffin and reached his arm inside. I grabbed it and drank his blood. Poor fool didn't know what happened. Then I went to find the people who did this to me. The Wyandot."

I didn't say a word as he replayed everything back that was swimming in his mind. I wondered how many people he had told this to over the years. I never did ask, but I had a feeling it was very little. First off, people would think him crazy, and second, when they understood he was telling the truth, they would run off screaming.

"So I murdered them," Brian stated as if death no longer had any meaning. "The people who did this to me. Every single one I could get my hands on. A couple got away and have been trying to kill me ever since," he smiled. "I think now they wish they had just killed me instead of making me into this. They are the ones suffering now, I made sure of that."

It was a lot to take in, I had to admit. But there is one thing that Brian did not explain. "When did you become this?"

"1677."

I just stared at him. That was almost 250 years ago. That couldn't be possible, it just couldn't. None of what he was saying seemed real, yet I had seen what he did. He was telling the truth. He had no reason to lie anymore.

He grinned. "I know, I don't look a day past a hundred."

"How is that possible?" I asked.

Brian shrugged. "A little magic, a little luck. I fought in the Beaver Wars initially, and have fought in some other wars as well. I've almost died a few times, but after a while you figure out how to stay away from places that will get you killed."

He must have seen so much, I couldn't even grasp what that must have been like. "So you became a gang leader?"

"Yeah I got caught up in a fight with the Gustin brothers and they saw how well I fought and offered me a job. After a while, I broke off and started my own gang. It's the perfect job for me, I can kill and drink blood without anyone noticing."

I felt like I was going to be sick. That was the blood I cleaned out of his clothes, that was the blood I cleaned off his skin at night. I covered my mouth.

He brushed his finger against my cheek. "Do you fear me, Anne?"

I didn't answer because at that moment, I wasn't sure. I had known him to be a nice man, but that didn't mean he still wasn't a creature that fed on humans just like me. It didn't mean that he still wasn't going to kill me. When I didn't answer, Brian stood up and knelt down in front of me.

"You have nothing to be afraid of," he said, his thumb stroking my hand. "I would never hurt you, okay? This doesn't change anything, I would be a killer either way. How does this make me any different than the gang leader you knew?"

He had a point, he still killed the people he would have killed as a gang leader. It actually explained a lot, sleeping during the day, how smart and quick witted he was, why he couldn't take too much seriously. All the pieces were beginning to make sense. "It doesn't."

He placed his hand in mine. "Now that's what I wanted to hear. Why don't you get ready for supper? I brought a special treat." I stared at him, a little wide-eyed. He sighed. "No, it's not a body."

"I knew that, just wanted to make sure."

"Good," he said. I started to get up. "Oh, and Anne?"

I turned back to him to find that his face had darkened.

"A deal is a deal, you promised to serve me until I decide otherwise. With this information, I can't ever let you go. No one knows the truth except the four of us that are in this house. If you tell anyone, I will kill you and if you try to run, I will kill you. Do we have an understanding?"

I nodded slowly. He smiled, returning back to his cheery self. He was always good at that, which made him ever the more frightening. "Good, now go get ready for supper."

I thought before that there was no turning back. It wasn't until that moment did I truly understand what no turning back was.

A couple of days went by and the four of us stayed in the house together. I didn't say much, still not quite sure as to how I should react to all of this. I gathered I should be afraid or scared for my life, but it actually felt good to me. It was interesting, it was an adventure. Nothing was as it seemed anymore and I wanted to learn more. Maybe that was why I didn't talk much, because I knew the way I responded wasn't normal, or maybe I was still processing everything and how exactly I fit in to the equation. I just knew I had nothing to worry about being around Brian. No one could hurt me, other than Brian of course. But even then, I had received more pain growing up than Brian ever had given me thus far. I regretted ever thinking that.

I started to feel more comfortable around Brian. I started to see him as a friend, as someone who actually cared about me. And, I hoped, he saw me the same way...

It wasn't until late one night when I awoke to the sound of a violin playing. I followed the music down the stairs and into the parlor. I was surprised to find Brian playing the wonderful music. I didn't think he was someone who would be good at music. I watched and listened. He was playing *Mary, Young and Fair*. His back was to me and he didn't know I was standing there. I smiled as I listened, knowing he thought he was only playing for himself. Some of the most wonderful music is often played alone.

Quietly, I took a seat at the piano and followed the music as he played. As I started, he paused and turned to me. He just smiled and started playing again as I played along. The song was beautiful, definitely one of my favorites. It had an upbeat melody to it, but you could also hear the love that the composer had for the girl. It was all too sweet.

At the end of the song, Brian took the violin away from his chin. "You play the piano?"

"Ever since I was little, yes. My parents would leave me at the neighbors and she would teach me. No one ever knew in my family, but when I was older I would sneak over and get lessons. Luckily I never did get caught."

Brian laughed at my rebellion towards my family. "That's brilliant. What other songs do you know?"

"Anything you have sheet music for I can play. I just happened to know the song you were playing by heart."

He opened up a chest and pulled out some sheet music. "Do you mind? I haven't had someone play this piano in a very long time."

I looked at the sheet. *Home Sweet Home*. I started playing it without asking as to why he wanted that song. He sat down next to me and listened, his eyes following the sheet music. After I finished, he would say again. This went on for at least thirty minutes, him never getting tired of the song.

"Alright, that's enough," he grabbed my hand and helped me off the bench. He kissed my hand. "You played like an angel. Go get some sleep."

I went back up the stairs to bed and heard him start playing his violin once more. That was the moment I realized he wasn't the monster he thought himself to be.

They kept me at the house, as Brian and Joshua moved back and forth between Boston and the country home. I wondered if I would ever be allowed back into the city or if he was just testing to see if I would run away. Walter didn't watch me as closely as he did before, which I was thankful for. I got to stroll through the woods on my own, although I did swear I felt I was being watched sometimes but I never did see anyone.

Then one night, a storm came to pass, trapping all of us in the house. Rain poured, wind howled, and the sky flashed light. Hours passed as I watched the storm from the parlor. Brian looked anxious, more anxious than normal. I had no idea what was going on with him as I watched sweat pour off his skin. He paced around the room, running his hands through his hair. Joshua and Walter were both silent as Walter went about his daily chores and Joshua sat across from me.

"What's wrong?" I finally asked.

"Nothing," he snapped and stopped pacing. He pointed at the piano. "Play some music."

For the most part, Brian had always kept his calm around me. He never got mad at me but also talked to me with kindheartedness. Tonight was different, tonight there was something very wrong.

As I played, he began to pace again. He muttered under his breath as he wiped away the sweat. I tried not to stare at him as I played. I felt bad and had no idea what I could do for him. So I did as he said and played the piano.

The wind howled even louder and the power suddenly went out, darkness flooding everything around us. Lightning flashed around the house and the silhouette Brian created sent shivers down my spine. Quickly, I got some candles and lit them in the parlor. I went back to playing, to soothe the beast. Walter and Joshua didn't say a word as I continued to play while Brian continued to pace around the parlor.

Suddenly Brian slammed his fist down on the table. "When will this storm be over with?!"

"From the looks of it, not for a good while, sir," Walter answered as he entered with a tray of refreshments.

He grabbed one of the drinks and threw it against the wall. The drink stained the wall and floor where it had splashed down to. I jumped, startled, and stopped playing for a moment. Brian's eyes shined yellow and he breathed heavily. His fangs were extended and I could tell he was trying to calm himself down but nothing was working. I think it was at that moment I understood what was wrong with him.

"Did I tell you that you could stop playing?" his voice was low, almost like that of some predator.

I spun back around and started playing again. But instead of playing from the sheet of music, I listened to the storm outside and tried to match the rhythm of nature. I let my heart guide me. The tempo was gentle, but strong and demanding a listener's attention. I had never been one to make up songs as I went but with the tension growing in the house, I knew I had to do something.

Brian didn't move but just stared at me with his glowing yellow eyes, the candle light reflecting back in an eerie monster-like way. I glanced back once or twice, but dared not to meet his gaze. I didn't know what to do other than to play.

An hour passed before Brian said anything.

"That's enough."

I stopped and turned to him. Sweat still poured down his face, his clothes soaked.

"Are you alright?" I asked.

He shook his head. "No, I'm not."

I glanced at Joshua. He still didn't say anything but he looked more concerned as the night progressed.

"You're hungry, aren't you? For..." I hesitated. "Blood."

"Bingo," Brian coughed. "I can't get anywhere in this storm. I was supposed to go out yesterday but yesterday was bad too. The roads are flooded," he coughed again and looked at me with his predator-like eyes. I held my breath, not even able to move as he looked at me. "I'm going to my room. Walter, please lock it until the road is clear."

"Yes, sir."

Walter followed Brian up the stairs, leaving Joshua and I alone. I hated being alone with Joshua. It didn't seem that he ever had anything nice to say to me and always saw me as some kind of threat to Brian.

Joshua leaned forward and nodded towards the stairs. "You should go up there and give him your blood."

I was right. Never had anything good to say. "Excuse me?" I asked.

"He saved your life, took you in when no one else would," he began. I narrowed my eyes at him. "You owe him. Not to mention you are his servant, the girl he keeps around for only God knows why."

"You think that I would just go up there and give him my blood?" I said. He was asking me to give my life up to Brian just because he hadn't gotten any blood for a few days.

"Yes. You wouldn't be the first girl to. You saw the way he was looking at you, he needs blood."

"Why don't you go up there and give him your blood then?" I shot back.

"Because he craves *your* blood. Why do you think he went upstairs? He couldn't handle the temptation anymore. He desires you and you just flaunt yourself in front of him. He has given you so much, so much you don't deserve. He won't kill you, he just needs to stop suffering. Don't you want him to stop suffering?"

I glared at him for a few moments. Brian had given me a lot, even when he didn't have to. But what Joshua was saying was scary. I didn't want to die, I didn't want to be in pain anymore.

But neither did I want Brian to be in pain.

Slowly I stood up, still glaring at Joshua, and headed up the stairs. The stair way was dark, only a few candles that Walter had lit brought any light to the area. As I got to Brian's bedroom, Walter was still next to the door.

"What are you doing, dear?" he asked.

"I can solve this simply, I owe it to him."

His eyebrows furrowed. "He can't control himself like this, I've seen what happens before. You would be risking your life."

I thought about listening to his request of not going in, but the thought of Brian in pain and how he had risked his own life to save me, I couldn't just walk away. "Then I better be quick before he gets worse."

Walter nodded, a look of concern still on his face, and unlocked the door.

"I will be fine," I tried to ease his worry. "I trust Brian won't hurt me."

It was dark inside, only one candle in all the room lit. Shadows flickered around the room and I could barely make out any of the furniture in his room. All of a sudden, Brian was standing in front of me. I jumped back, mostly from surprise and the fact he looked more horrible than he did downstairs.

"What are you doing in here?" he demanded.

"I thought I would give you my blood, help you through this storm."

"No."

"You saved my life, it is the least I can do."

He shook his head. "I said no."

I didn't move, whether it was because of fear or I really wanted to be there I wasn't sure. "I'm not leaving here until you take my blood."

He shoved me against the wall, his fangs exposed and inches from my face. He took a slow breath, the air tingling against my skin. I felt my heart racing in my chest. I had never seen him so dangerous, so beast-like. This was dangerous, I realized, but after everything Brian had done for me, I couldn't just let him suffer.

"What about now?" his breath was hot and made me shiver, but I wouldn't budge. My breaths were coming fast and my mind was racing, worrying about what could happen.

"You aren't going to scare me away if that's what you think," I whispered.

He leaned in closer, his yellow eyes inches from my own eyes. "I don't scare you?"

I took a deep breath. "No."

He just laughed. "But I will. Trust me, if I don't kill you, you will fear me."

"I couldn't fear you Brian, not after everything you have done for me."

Brian was silent for a moment, battling the urge to drink my blood. "I don't want to kill you."

"Then don't."

It was taking everything for him to hold back, I could tell by the way he shook and how his eyes shifted back and forth. "You don't know how strong this hunger is, I don't know if I will be able to stop."

I placed my finger on his lips before he could refuse. "Then I will stop you, okay?"

Brian's eyes drifted to my hand that was in front of his face. Slowly he wrapped his fingers around my arm and pulled my wrist to his mouth. I could feel his tongue against my skin, which was a weird sensation, to have a man lick you. Then the piercing pain of his fangs entering my skin came. I held back the scream, I held back the tears. Pain was second nature to me, but this was entirely different. This was sharp pain, like a knife. Not blunt like I am used to. Not only that, this pain was brought on by someone who cared, someone who didn't necessarily want me to hurt. And that single thing was keeping me from breaking down.

I could feel the blood seep out of my skin as he drank it, his tongue slurping up each and every drop. I was glad it was dark, I did not want to see what was happening.

Brian let go of my wrist, still taking deep breaths, his eyes still looking like that of a predator.

"Brian, was that enough?" I asked.

He didn't say a word as he brought his face close to mine.

"Brian?" I whispered.

He grabbed the back of my neck, squeezing and not letting go. I couldn't move my head. He leaned in and slowly bit into my neck. I screamed this time, knowing full well I wouldn't be able to stop him.

"Brian! Snap out of it!" I tried to push him away but he didn't budge. With each second passing, my body started to feel even weaker. Flashbacks from all the beatings I had, all the times pain was brought down on me. I shook, cried, and screamed. Nothing was stopping him. If he had cared for me, he would have stopped. Maybe I was just another girl to him, one he could just use. Nothing made sense anymore and the pain was overwhelming. Everything was spinning around me. I closed my eyes.

"Brian, please..."

Tears were rolling down my cheeks. Without reason, Brian stopped, drawing his fangs out of my throat. He touched his cheek where one of my tears had dropped on to him. He looked at his hand then at me. I didn't say a word but knew I had a look of fear. He still had one hand holding me in place and I didn't know if he was going to bite me again.

He let go of me and stepped back from me. "Anne, I'm sorry, I'm so...so sorry," he reached for me but I flinched, prepared for more pain, pain that would keep coming no matter where I ran. He drew his hand away from me and shook his head. "I can't begin to repay you for this. I'm sorry."

Brian hurried to the door. "Walter, let me out of here! I need to get Anne bandages now!"

The door opened quickly and Brian left. I slid down the wall and collapsed on the ground. My body didn't feel as if it could move again. It was weak and I didn't have the strength. Whether it was from the loss of blood or from my mind snapping and the memories of everything flooding back, I wasn't sure.

Walter came in and helped me to my bedroom. He laid me in my bed and began to wrap up my injuries. I stared up at the ceiling, my eyes dry, no more tears being able to escape any more.

"Are you alright, Miss Anne?" Walter asked as he washed away the blood.

I shook my head. "No."

He grabbed my hand and stroked it gently. "Brian told me about your past. You came from an abusive family, is that right?"

I nodded.

"He lost control, didn't he? And hurt you. It felt like you lost all trust in him, that if someone whom you thought cared about you could hurt you, what is stopping the rest of the world from hurting you."

I glanced over at Walter. He was right, that was how I felt. The emotions were swirling inside my mind, frustration, confusion, but more importantly anger at myself for trusting him to not be different. I hated feeling it, knowing that it wasn't his fault, that he wasn't even human, not anymore.

"Anne, you have to understand that he didn't want to hurt you. That was why he locked himself in there, because he couldn't stand being in the same room as you. No one should have suffered as you did, but you also have to understand he can't control the hunger, especially when it is someone he truly cares for. It's why he can never get close to someone, why he hasn't been close to someone for so long. You are the first he has ever went to extremes to stop himself from, at least that I know of. Remember, he has been around for a while."

I pondered the words Walter had said as he finished cleaning up the wound. Did he truly care about me? That was why he tried to stay away from me. None of it made sense, and I just wanted to sleep and not think about it anymore.

Walter finished cleaning and left me for the night. I requested he leave the candle next to the door burning. I didn't want to be alone in the dark any longer.

The storm cleared the next day and Brian and Joshua headed back to the city. Walter wanted to know if I wanted to talk to Brian before I left and I told him no. I knew it wasn't Brian's intention to hurt me but I was afraid that if I saw him in such short amount of time after what happened, all the emotions would come flooding back. I shouldn't have thought I was strong enough to handle it, I shouldn't have lied to myself.

After I had gathered enough strength, I was able to leave my room and go down the stairs. There wasn't much to do but to work on the song I had created for Brian during the storm. It was a way I could calm myself down and forget all that happened and to remember that he was the one who brought me out of the darkness. That he had saved me from my misery that was living at home and I was thankful for that. I came to realize that it wasn't Brian's fault he had been turned into a monster. He fought it as hard as he could.

When Brian and Joshua arrived back, I was in the library reading some of the books collected by Brian over the years. I had *20,000 Leagues under the Sea* in my hand when he came through the door alone. He didn't say a word as he sat down across from me. I placed the book down and we sat there in silence for a few moments.

"I'm sorry," he said. "I didn't want to hurt you, I should have never..."

"No, it's my fault. I made you... Even though you said you didn't want to. I should have did as you said and left the room. I should have known better."

He shook his head. "After you entered the room, you couldn't have left. I may have wanted you to leave but... even if you backed down I don't think I would have let you leave without taking your blood. And I want to apologize for that. I..."

I got up and sat next to him, placing my hand on his knee. "It's alright. Stop making yourself out to be a monster."

"You don't understand, it's hard to be around you when I'm like that. I don't know if I can control myself. I took enough blood the first time I bit you, but after... When you desire someone, when you feel something, it overwhelms you and the hunger and desire combine. It is intoxicating and I couldn't resist."

I listened to his words very carefully. Was he admitting he had feelings for me? That was the reason he couldn't stop? "I don't know what to say, I just wanted to help you."

He caressed my hand with his thumb. "You are too good to be true, Anne. And because of that, I want to let you go."

I blinked. "What?"

"You are free to go. You don't have to serve me or anything. You can leave, do what you want to do. I can give you money to go get started. I don't want to hide your beauty from the world any longer."

I couldn't believe what he was saying. After everything, he was just going to let me go? I knew his secret, I could tell anyone if I wanted, not that I did. He also had just confessed that he had feelings for me. "I don't want to leave this place, I don't want to leave your side, Brian. I don't have anywhere to go. I'm not leaving."

He smiled. "Good because, honestly, I don't think I really could have let you go out that door. I would have ended up begging you to come back."

Seemed about right. I laughed, feeling more comfortable around him. I had to put the past behind me and realize that I wasn't the only one with demons in my past. Brian had suffered with this curse for hundreds of years. He understood pain more than I could ever know.

Brian leaned in closer to me. My heart felt like it was going to skip a beat. But the dumb idiot didn't kiss me that night. At the last possible moment, he turned away. My heart sank in my chest as he stood up. "I should go check and make sure Walter has started dinner."

"Alright."

Just as he stepped into the doorway, he turned to me. "And perhaps, after, I can accompany you on the piano."

I nodded. "I would like that, yes."

He looked at me a little longer. "Yeah, I don't think I will ever let you go, Anne. You better get used to me," with that, he left me sitting there alone in the library.

We did just that. Brian and I played the piano and violin through the night. I saw Joshua watch from the entryway with a frown on his face. I didn't know why but as the days passed, he seemed to hate me more and more. I wondered if he figured Brian would kill me that night, only for us to become closer. Joshua didn't like the idea of Brian having someone to love, I presumed because he didn't want him to get distracted from business.

A few days after the storm, the phone rang as Brian and I enjoyed each other's company in the library. Walter gave it to Brian and after a few minutes, Brian had a wide grin on his face. He hung up the phone and yelled in triumph.

"Yes!"

"What is it?" I asked.

He picked me up and twirled me around. "He's arrested! The bastard got caught!"

I just laughed at his excitement. "Who?"

"Al Capone! The bastard is in prison!" he laughed again and spun me around. When he stopped spinning me, he stared into my eyes for a long moment. Leaning in, he kissed me gently on the lips.

He backed away quickly. "I'm sorry, I shouldn't have done that."

I pulled him close again and kissed him harder. He wrapped his hands around my waist and ran them up my back. We parted mouths and he leaned his forehead against mine, taking in the lost breaths.

"Well," he said. "I didn't see that coming. Usually if I kiss a girl without their express permission, I get slapped."

Before I could respond, which would have been something along the lines of 'a lot of women must give you permission then,' I heard a coughing sound coming from the entryway. We both jumped back to find Joshua standing there.

"Who was on the phone?" he asked, eyeing me.

"Great news, Joshua! Al Capone is in the slammer! We must celebrate! Call the boys and invite them out here!"

"I take it that you are already celebrating," he stared at me for a moment longer then left to do what Brian wished.

"He's not happy," I whispered.

Brian shrugged. "He will get over it. As for the party tonight," he picked me up and twirled me around once more. "You must play the piano. I insist."

"I don't know if I am good enough to play in front of everyone. Honestly, the three of you are the first live audience I have ever had."

"Well, I don't believe in hiding such great things from the world. You must play more."

I agreed to it and helped Walter begin to clean for that night's festivities. A few hours later, car after car started arriving. Al Capone had been causing the Irish mob a lot of pain in the past years, not only in Chicago but throughout the east coast. He had gotten away with the Saint Valentine's Day Massacre, many murders, thefts, and when he was captured for something such as tax fraud, well, there wasn't an Irish soul who wasn't celebrating the man's suffering.

Brian moved the piano into the ballroom and I played pretty much every song that was requested, and people danced all around us. They laughed and cheered and I was glad I was a part of it all. I had gone to quite a few parties with Brian and never did I see so many smiles on everyone's face.

As I played more, I watched as people mingled in the room and throughout the house. After a while, I lost track of Brian. Presuming he had many people to talk to that night, I didn't think about looking for him, at least not until Joshua came.

"Hey, Brian has been looking for you. I think he is in the library," Joshua said. "I can get someone to take over for you in the meantime."

He seemed a lot more cheerful than normal. I should have gathered something was up, but I had been too distracted from all the things going on. I finished up the song and got up. "Alright, thanks."

"No problem," he smiled as I left. I headed through the hallway and into the library and that's when I saw him. Brian, sitting with a woman whose lips were against his and her hand moving up his thigh. I just stood there, in the doorway, my hand over my mouth. I couldn't believe after everything he said that he would still go after another girl.

Brian looked up and saw me. "It's not what it looks like."

I shook my head and left the room. I could hear him calling after me but I didn't bother stopping. He grabbed my wrist. "It's not what it looks like, I swear."

Like I hadn't heard that one before. "No, I get it. You were just using me again. None of it meant anything to you, I should have known. Just like earlier," I pulled my hand away from him.

"Anne, wait, please," he begged. "It's not like that, let me explain."

"I'm going out and getting some air," and with that, I left him standing there. Quickly I grabbed a jacket and ran out into the crisp autumn night.

Looking back on it, this was probably the second worst mistake I had ever made in my entire life. The first was still yet to come, unfortunately. I ventured into the night, alone, tears falling from my eyes. Brian had broken my heart once again. He had showed me so much compassion the past couple of weeks and after the kiss that morning... I really thought he had loved me. I was just another girl to him. I didn't even want to give him the chance to explain himself, it probably would have just been another lie.

The air was cool against my exposed skin. I tried to stay as warm as possible because I didn't want to go back to that house. I didn't want to be the fool that believed someone could love me any longer. I didn't want to be manipulated anymore and I didn't want to be lied to. I had thought I had escaped a home full of pain only to find even more.

As I pondered on the thought of where I could go to leave everything behind me, I heard a howling noise. I stopped in my tracks and listened. The howl echoed around me, I couldn't make out as to where it had come from. My heart started to race in my chest and I held my breath in the silence.

I was in deep trouble and I knew it.

I slowly looked back at the house. It was a small light in the distance and I didn't know if I could make it in time. At least that time, I wasn't wearing heels, as I promised never to do so again. I started to hurry back when I heard the growls start to encircle me. I really should have never left Brian's side because everything bad seemed to happen if I ran off from Brian, or if he went off alone.

Making a straight sprint back towards Brian's house, a dark object leapt out from the bushes and on to me. I barely had even got five feet before it knocked me down to the ground. I screamed and kicked at the creature's mouth. It exposed its sharp teeth and its piercing eyes looked at me with intent to kill. A wolf. I tried to get up and kick the wolf in the muzzle. It snapped at my feet as I moved. The creature's teeth sank into my ankle and I screamed again. I could feel the sharp fangs rip away at my flesh. It pulled me down to its level and bit my side and stomach. I tried to kick it off but it was no use. The wolf was stronger than me.

Something moved in the shadows like a flash. Suddenly, the wolf moved off of me and growled at the object. I tried to move, but the pain shooting through my body was unbearable.

"Somebody…help me," I whispered into the night. "Please."

I heard the sound of footsteps coming to me. "Anne!"

It was Joshua.

He knelt down beside me. "Oh, God, Anne. What happened?"

"Wolves. They came out of nowhere," I tried to move but the pain swept over me. "Ow!"

Joshua placed his hand gently on my arm. "Don't move, don't move. Brian knew something was wrong and sent me out here. He's fighting off the wolves right now."

I couldn't believe what I was hearing. "What? Is he crazy?"

"The wolves have been after him for a while. They are part of the tribe he massacred. They are shape-shifters."

"I don't understand," I began.

"It's not important now, we have to get you medical attention immediately," he tried to move me. I cried out in pain.

"My stomach, it hurts," I hadn't looked down and I knew I didn't want to.

"Oh, God," Joshua said. "Anne, I can't move you, I can't get you out of here."

I heard more footsteps. "Anne!"

It was Brian. I tried to look up at him but the pain was overwhelming. I grimaced and my head fell back. Everything was beginning to go blurry and I could hear voices but none of them were making any sense. My body started to feel numb and I could barely breathe.

Brian knelt down beside me and did one of the strangest things I had ever seen someone do. Brian bit down on his wrist.

"What are...?" I began, everything was spinning around me.

"Shh, don't talk," he placed the blood to my lips. "Drink it."

The red drops came off his wrist and into my mouth. My mind was screaming, every wound was screaming, but the moment the blood touched my lips, the world was silent. I couldn't hear anything. The pain shooting through my body fogged my mind and I drank the blood pouring out of his wrist.

And I couldn't stop myself.

Brian pulled his arm away from me. I couldn't see anything but red, not being able to feel anything but the fire that dwelled in my veins. I had no idea what he did to me but it felt magnificent. No more pain, no more fear. It was all gone. For once, I felt alive and strong. For the first time in my life, I felt in control.

Then everything went to hell again.

A wolf leaped out of the bushes and attacked Brian. All I could see was the large hairy creature leaping over me and onto Brian, growling and snapping its jaws at him. I saw Brian try to reach for his gun only to drop it. Everything was blurry still. Joshua pulled out his own gun and shot at the wolf. It lied there, dead.

Another wolf jumped through the darkness at Joshua. He screamed. I tried to blink away the blurriness of my sight. I had to help them, I knew I had to do something.

I grabbed the gun that Brian had dropped, and rubbed my eyes. I shot the wolf on top of Joshua. It whimpered and fell to the ground. I swore I saw it start to change shape but once I knew it was dead, I didn't have time to delay. I ran after Brian and shot the wolf that attacked him. The wolf went down.

Brian was slumped over. I hurried to his side. "Are you alright?"

He shook his head. "Not quite," he moved his hand to reveal his arm covered in blood. "Can't heal from their bite."

"What?" I looked at the wolf again but here was no wolf, only a man lying on the ground dead, his dark hair crusted with blood. I dropped my gun and covered my mouth. "How?"

"The Indian tribe I pissed off was part of the Wolf clan. After turning me into what I am, I escaped and slaughtered many of them. Those who survive called upon the spirits of their ancestors and, well, the spirits answered. They taught them to turn into wolves and one bite from them," he grimaced. "Can kill a hooh-strah-dooh. They've been after me for years. Looks as if they finally won, that is if you count this as a win for them."

Kill a hooh-strah-dooh? No, that couldn't be possible, I couldn't let that happened. I rushed to his side. "What do we do? What can I do?"

He shook his head and placed his hand on my cheek. "There isn't anything we can do, the only way to heal me is with the blood of another hooh-strah-dooh..." he collapsed and fainted.

Joshua limped to us. "What happened?"

"He got bit and said it's going to kill him," I started shaking. "He said only blood of another one of his kind can heal him. What do we do? How do we find another? Are there even other creatures out there?"

Joshua stared at me for a while. I didn't know what was running through his mind but I knew it wasn't good.

"What's wrong?" I questioned, stepping back from him.

"He said the only way was the blood of a hooh-strah-dooh?"

I nodded. "Yes."

He raised his gun at me.

"What are you doing?" I asked, jumping back.

"I'm sorry, but he has to live," with that, Joshua shot me.

And that was how I died.

I awoke a few hours later, with the worst headache in my life. My head was pounding, shooting pain throughout my body. If I didn't know better, I swore I just had a hangover and everything had been a dream. But unfortunately that wasn't the case. I glanced around to find myself back in the house. Everyone had left, leaving trash that I would have to clean up. But why did everyone leave? I couldn't remember. Slowly, things started to come back to me. The image of a gun pointed at me came into my mind. I touched my head to find blood crusted in my hair.

"What the..." I began as I looked at my hand. It was covered in blood.

"About time you woke up, I was beginning to worry it wouldn't work," Joshua said. I turned to find him sitting across from me.

I thought back to the last thing I remembered. The wolves had attacked us, if they were wolves, and then I shot them. Brian was hurt. Then... "You shot me."

"Killed you actually. With Brian's blood in you. I recalled that's how he was made into a hooh-strah-dooh."

"A hooh-strah-dooh... You made me... No," I shook my head. "No, that's impossible."

Joshua stood up. "It's the only way to save him, I had to make you into the same creature. You had his blood in you, it was perfect. Luckily Brian told me all about the process when he was drunk one night. Looks like the information paid off." He pulled out a knife and slashed his hand. "Now you just have to drink my blood for the change to be complete."

I shook my head. "I can't, I will not! Walter!"

"He's not here, I sent him out to take care of hiding the bodies of those wolves. And what is your problem with taking my blood? You took his blood without hesitation. This is the only way to save him, I know that you love him."

"But he doesn't love me. He was with that girl," the thought of what I had seen still made my heart ache. He had betrayed me.

"He didn't do anything with that girl. I hired her to make it look that way so you would be mad at him. Honestly, Brian hasn't touched a girl since you were brought here. I don't know why, but he thinks he loves you."

I stared at him. Everything, all of this heartache, was because of him. "Why would you..."

"Because he doesn't need his priorities complicated! He is the greatest gangster there is and if he gets distracted something bad will happen, like tonight. It was your fault he was out there. He went after you, knowing that he would risk his life to do so. You owe it to him to complete this change and give him your blood."

I frowned. Everything he said was true. I was the reason he was out there, I was the reason he could be dying. Although the reason I was out there was to get away from what Joshua had set up. Everything was a blur and my head was pounding.

I stared at Joshua's hand, the blood dripping seductively down to the ground. The hunger was there, the hunger that I would discover soon seemed to never end. I had to do it, I had to help Brain. I cared for him, I was completely and utterly in love with him. With this I could save him, with this I could be strong and finally stand up for something I believed in.

I grabbed Joshua's hand and drank the blood that spilled out of his hand. The warm liquid filled my mouth and instantly everything was clear. My headache went away, my senses were heightened a hundred fold. I felt more alive than I ever knew possible. And the taste of human blood, nothing could come close to how satisfying it was. Nothing.

My body felt like it was transforming, every sensation magnified tenfold. I felt as if it had awoken from sleep, every sense became heightened. The insatiable hunger began to grow in the pit of my stomach.

Joshua pulled his hand away and for a moment I forgot he was there. I forgot I was drinking his blood, a living being. The only thought I had was about the drink itself. I licked my lip, not wanting to waste a drop.

Joshua looked at me as if I was a monster. He wrapped the wound up and nodded to the stairwell. "He's in his room."

I nodded and headed up the stairs. The creaks echoed through the empty house. I could feel my heart beat in my chest. I was changed now, I was no longer human. The thought echoed in my mind. No longer human. I couldn't believe it. Everything I knew about life was gone and only a mystery remained. An eternity remained.

And that scared me, but at least I didn't have to face it alone, at least not at that moment. I wondered how Brian could have done it all this time.

I opened Brian's door slowly. Something crawled into the shadows as light flickered into the room. I quickly shut the door behind me.

When I turned, Brian was in front of me. This time I didn't jump.

"You shouldn't be here," he whispered, his eyes a glowing yellow. Blood was splattered across his face and his wound on his arm seemed to be getting worse.

Placing my hand on his cheek, I leaned in and kissed him. He tried to push me away but I didn't let him. I pulled his mouth down to my neck. He bit down but this time there was no pain, this time I could feel everything without the pain. I ran my hands through his hair. The feeling was haunting, as I could sense my blood being taken by him. It was the closest our kind could be to one another, sharing each other's blood.

Moments passed as he drank my blood, he was not hesitating as the hunger trapped him. I didn't stop him, knowing full well it would not kill me. It was strange, being able to compare being bit as a human and as a hooh-strah-dooh. My body was so much stronger now.

When he backed away from me, his eyes widened and he shook his head. "No, no, you can't."

I placed my finger on his lips. "Shh."

"He killed you, didn't he? After I gave you blood. He did this to save me!" Brian tried to open the door but I grabbed him and pulled him close. I kissed him on the lips, my teeth biting down and drawing blood.

And it tasted fantastic.

Brian wrapped his arms around me, forgetting about everything that had happened. I loved him, and I wanted to forget the rest of the world. I wanted to forget where I had come from, the gangs, the wolves, and the people wanting to kill him. I wanted to forget that life was happening outside those doors; I wanted to forget it all and to forever be in his arms. And for a brief moment, I thought we could.

Brian pulled me to his bed, unzipping the back of my dress. I unbuttoned his shirt and pushed him on the bed. I licked my blood-stained lips. Nothing was as satisfying as the taste of the blood of the one you love. With someone who felt the exact same thing. I jumped on top of him and bit down on his neck like a savage animal.

I woke up alone in Brian's bed. I could still smell his cologne on the bed sheets and for a moment I lay there and took it all in. Everything seemed right in the world, insofar that we overcame everything and nothing could stop us.

At least I had hoped.

I heard shouting coming from the floor below. Quickly, I grabbed some clothes and hurried down the stairs to find Brian and Joshua arguing.

"You had no right!" Brian shouted, throwing one of his antique vases at him. I really liked that vase, too.

Joshua ducked out of the way. "I did it for you, it was because of her you almost died!"

"You turned her into a creature just like me! Did you think I would be happy about that?" Brian threw another vase at him.

This time the vase hit Joshua in the chest. He flinched as shards went in every direction. "Why do you care? She is just one of your servants!"

Brian grabbed him by the throat. "I care because I love her! Do you understand that? Apparently not since you have been trying to sabotage it from day one!" He kept his hand around Joshua's throat and wasn't letting go. I could see his face starting to turn color.

I placed my hand on Brian's arm. "Let him go, Brian."

Brian's eyes didn't leave Joshua. "He did this to you, don't you understand that?"

"I would have done it willingly. You could have died because of me and I wouldn't have been able to live with that. Not when you saved my life more than once."

He glared at Joshua a moment longer, then let him go. "Go now, head back to town. I will be there later this week. Just get out of my sight."

Joshua didn't say a word as he opened the door and left. I shielded my eyes from the light coming in, blinking a few times to get the pain to go away.

"How do you go outside?" I asked rubbing my eyes.

"Years and years of practice," his eyes were still at the door.

I leaned in and kissed him.

"What was that for?" he asked.

I smiled. "You said you loved me."

He kissed me again. "Well, I do. You are the best thing that has ever happened to me since getting turned into this creature. I'm sorry that the misfortune has fallen to you as well."

I shook my head. "No, this is the greatest thing that has happened to me. I feel strong for once, as if I can do anything," I stepped forward. "And we can finally be together."

He grinned and placed his hand on my cheek. "Tonight, it is just going to be you and me. I have something to show you, I think you will like it. Then we will return to the city," he kissed my forehead. "And I can train you in the ways of a hooh-strah-dooh. Meanwhile, you relax. I would stay out of the light, you aren't strong enough yet to endure the sun."

"How did you manage it?"

"I have had a couple of centuries to figure it out. Mostly I just stay out of the sun, if you haven't noticed. That's why I get up so late in the day."

"Here I just thought you were lazy."

"Anything but," he nodded back up the stairs. "Go get some more rest, I will come get you when twilight falls."

I did as he said, the light did cause me to feel a bit dreary. It was strange to not be able to look into the light without pain. To forever live in the darkness. I didn't feel that I would miss the light. To be honest, I had always been in the dark. Now I was strong enough to fight back.

I lay there for a while, staring at the ceiling. I couldn't fall back to sleep, realizing everything that had happened. I was now a creature, a monster of sorts, but I felt somewhat the same, still me. Granted, the confidence and strength were there, but for the things I enjoyed, the things I loved, they were all the same. I was still me. And I would be me until the day I died, if I ever did. I had an eternity now, an eternity with Brian.

That night, Brian drove me to the coast. It wasn't that far, probably just a few minutes in the car. The moon was half full, bringing some light to the sandy beach, but I didn't need it to be able to see. I could see everything fine then. A predator's eyes could see in the darkness.

Brian parked the car in an abandoned area. No one was around, being so late into the night. It felt invigorating to have the place to ourselves. The normal fear of the darkness was gone and there was only excitement to start life anew in its place. I followed him out onto the beach.

I never realized how serene the night was until then. The dark waves looking like a never ending pool of black ink, the sand a shadowy mess of shimmering glitter in the moon light. Shadows engulfed us and I felt at home for once in my lifetime.

"What do you think of this gem of a spot?" Brian asked as he watched my eyes light up.

"It's beautiful, I can't believe I had never noticed how gorgeous the night is."

He laughed. "Glad you think so, for we are forever trapped in it," his face became stern as he grabbed my hands. "Anne, this isn't a curse I ever would put on an enemy, let alone someone I cared about. Please don't think I would ever want you to endure this pain as I have for over two centuries."

I shook my head. "I don't blame you and I'm happy to be able to share this."

"You may one day regret it, and I have to tell you there is no way out."

He didn't smile and I began to worry as to what he meant by it. No matter how much pain we had endured and wanted to end it, an internal instinct of survival inside fought it. We could never take our own lives, no matter how much we wanted to. That was our curse.

I kissed him on the lips. "I don't want a way out. I just want you."

He grinned and hugged me, holding me there for a long moment. His embrace was warm and I felt I could let him hold me forever. After a while, he stepped back and got down on his knees. "Anne, will you spend the rest of eternity with me? We can run away from this place, go overseas. I heard Paris is lovely."

I couldn't believe what was happening. I covered my mouth. He wanted to leave everything behind to be with me. I stood there, speechless. After the roller coaster of the last few days, running away from it all seemed like a brilliant plan. "You want to run away with me?"

"Yes. Just let me finish up the year, making Joshua in charge of my gang. Then we can leave, at Christmas. I will get the tickets and we can leave this place behind forever. Just you and me, we will forever be free."

I nodded quickly. "Of course, Brian, I will run away with you."

He stood up and kissed me, his soothing lips warming my own. His smooth hands ran through my hair and I pulled him closer so our bodies weren't apart. I knew I wanted to be with him for that measure of time. We stayed on that beach all night, talking of all the things we were going to do in the future. I wanted those things so much and it breaks my heart when I remember everything that was said that night.

We went back to south Boston later that week. I hadn't been back in over a month and surprisingly I had never realized the stench of city air until that day. I didn't know if it was my heightened senses or if I just was always used to it. It took me a while to get used to this new hypersensitivity to smell.

As promised, Brian taught me everything I needed to know to be a hooh-strah-dooh. The pros, the cons, the secrets, the ways we can die, the ways we couldn't die, all of it. I don't think I would have survived this long if it weren't for those two months of learning how to fend for myself, to find victims that I could drink from, how to fight, skills just to survive in the world.

I thought about going to my home and showing my family what I had become, let them fear me just as they had made me fear them. But I decided against it. That life was behind me and I didn't want to remember it ever again. There was no reason to dwell on the past when I had eternity for a future.

Thinking back on it, those two months were the best of my entire life. It felt so short, only a fleeting moment in my memories and if it weren't for the biggest mistake I ever made in my life, maybe it would have been better then. Maybe life wouldn't be so lonely now.

Brian had gotten us tickets for December 23rd to sail to France. We would celebrate the New Year in Paris, just as we had discussed. It was going to be a new start for the two of us. No more gangs, no more fighting, just adventures. It would have been perfect, but, as I know now, nothing can be perfect.

The night before we left, Brian got a call from Frankie Wallace. They had just hijacked an important shipment from the yards that day and the gang leader up north, Joseph Lambardo, wanted to cut them a deal. 'Normal business transaction', I had found that was what they called it. Frankie wanted Brian and a couple of his men to come with them for back up, they never knew how those things would go down. I begged Brian not to go, a feeling in the pit of my stomach telling me it wasn't going to end well, but he said it would be his last meeting and that there was nothing to worry about. So I waited for him to come back, our suitcases ready to go.

Letting him go was the worst mistake I would ever make in my life.

As I waited, the silence in the house was eerie. I felt as if it haunted me while I waited for Brian, echoing in my mind that he was never to come back and I was forever alone. I didn't know why I was so afraid, in only a few hours we would always be together. We could finally not have to think about anything except for ourselves. And that would have been a first for me.

I daydreamed about the places we would see. We had the entire world to explore. Europe, Asia, Africa, it was all there just for us. I wondered if there were others like us that we would run into while we traveled. I didn't know if that would be a good thing or not and figured it wouldn't happen. It would have been interesting, though, if we did.

Out of nowhere as I sat in Brian's house, bullets rained through the windows, glass flying in every direction. I ducked and waited for the attack to stop. I wouldn't necessarily die from getting hit by a bullet, but I knew it would hurt like hell. Whoever it was stopped shooting and kicked down the front door. Hurrying around the corner into the entry, I surprised the attacker and slashed his throat with my nails, a trick Brian had taught me and one that I would use more often than not. As he lied there, dead, I took a good look at him. Italian. Part of the gang Brian was to meet that night. At that moment, I knew my fear had been correct and Brian was in deep trouble.

I ran outside to find three more men waiting. Bullets poured out of their guns at me, but I was too quick for them. I had learned to anticipate where they would shoot and they couldn't get a hit. I slashed each of their throats and stared at the blood that began to seep out of their throats and stain the concrete beneath.

The sound of clapping echoed through the streets behind me. I spun around to find Joshua standing there, smiling. "Bravo, Anne. Brian has taught you well."

My heart pounded in my chest. How could he have just stood there while I was being attacked? Unless... "What did you do?"

"What am I doing? The better question is what you two are doing?" he held up the tickets. "I found these on Brian. You two were leaving for good, weren't you?"

I didn't say anything but focused on the blood that covered the tickets. My heart felt as if it sunk into my stomach. It couldn't be true, I couldn't have lost the one I loved. Every emotion in my mind shut off as I stared at the blood. I could smell it, it was Brian's. He wasn't lying to me.

My body started shaking. We were supposed to run away together, we were supposed to start anew, finally, after all this time. All this pain. There was supposed to be happiness at the end of the tunnel, not complete and utter darkness. "Why?"

"He lied to me. I asked him about this and he lied. He said he would always be here and he would never leave. Until you came and destroyed everything!" he held up a stake. It was made of the wood Brian told me about. The only wood that could kill us. Red-bud.

"You killed him," I stated. "You *killed* him! You bastard, you are going to die!" All I knew then was that I was going to rip Joshua into a million pieces for what he took from me. My blood turned hot and I was beginning to see red. Nothing was going to stop me from ripping him into pieces.

"He deserved it! He lied to me!" he started for me. "And now it is your turn."

I started to back up when I heard the sound of growling. I turned to find three wolves behind me. "The Wyandot," I whispered.

"Yes, they were very happy to find Brian's whereabouts. I mean, I knew I couldn't kill Brian alone and I happened to come across one of the wolves that survived the night a couple months back. I also let them know of you and how you were also one of those creatures. They were more than happy to help me kill you."

I ran towards the house. I knew exactly where Brian kept the gun to kill the wolves, the ones lined with silver. I barely made it through the door as one of the wolves jumped at me, hitting the door as I slammed it shut. A few pounding sounds later and the door was open again. I ran up the stairs, the monsters biting at my heels. I couldn't let them get one bite or I was dead. Without Brian, I had no one to save me.

Grabbing the gun, I turned back on my attackers. The three wolves growled as I pulled the trigger. None of them got close enough to stop me. I watched as they slowly turned into the men they once were.

"Well, that went surprisingly different than earlier, but I guess killing you myself will have to suffice," Joshua stepped over the three bodies. I raised the gun at him. He simply laughed. "You are out of bullets, sweetie."

I pulled the trigger. He was right. I threw the gun down and stared at the stake he had in his hand.

"Funny, I would have never known about this wood if it weren't for the movie earlier this year. *Dracula*, do you remember it? Brian took me and laughed at the things they used to try and stop the monster. He said, though, a stake made of red-bud would indeed kill him, but that was the closest that movie ever got to the truth. I wonder if that movie didn't come out, if I still would have been able to kill him."

"You bastard, he was your friend!" I yelled.

"And it was you who ruined it all. It was you that brought this death upon him," he raised the stake. "And now it's your turn to die."

I wanted to die that night, but as Brian always said, we were never that lucky. With a simple flow of motion, I smacked the stake out of his hand and grabbed him by the throat.

"Don't you dare think you can kill me that easy," I bent down and picked up the red-bud. It burned in my hand, the smell of burning skin filled my nostrils but it was worth it. I rammed it through Joshua's chest. Blood splattered out of his mouth as I let him fall to the ground.

Then I did the only thing I could do. I ran.

I don't know what possessed me to do it, but I had to go by and make sure Joshua was telling me the truth. As I came up to Hanover Street, people crowded around, looking at the damage that was done. Glass was shattered, blood draining into the gutters. I shoved past everyone, even the cops who tried to pull me back and that's when I saw him. My one love, with a piece of the red-bud stabbed through his heart.

Tears falling from my eyes, I ran to his body, repeating the word 'no' over and over again. I didn't think it to be true, I didn't think it to be possible. We were ready to live an eternity together, we were ready to be happy. I bent down and collapsed next to him. My heart ached as if it had been sad and I truly wished I had been. Life was over and from then on I lived like a shadow, never existing and never truly gone.

There is no happiness in this life, I have come to find. I have been on the run for almost a hundred years, some members of the Wolf clan still searching for me, and other people who have noticed something suspicious as they watch me go about my day. I still visit Boston more often than not, security getting stricter as the years go by to leave the country. It was hard to use my old passport, no one believing me to be the age I was, so I had to live in the shadows, waiting for something smart and strong enough to kill me. One day, I hope to find my match so I can stop suffering and pray that there is a heaven where my love is waiting for me. Did creatures like me get salvation? I had no idea.

But there is always hope, right?

A WORLD OF VAMPIRES

Baobhan Sith

Beauty. Of all the things that people nowadays got right, at least in Western cultures, it was those monsters' beauty. With their long blonde hair, emerald green eyes, skin as pale as the moonlight, the Baobhan Sith were not something you wanted to come across during the lonely nights that were a natural part of traveling through the Highlands. Their faces had to have been chiseled by the gods themselves, if there is a god that is. After seeing what I have seen in my lifetime, I tended to think that there wasn't.

No human could ever compare to the Scottish vampires that I had met that night in 1746. Their allure and beauty had even surpassed that of the love of my life, Alice, and she was my one true love. She alone is what makes this story a hard one to tell.

In the cold dark nights, I swear that I can feel her arm wrapped around me still. It isn't until I open my eyes that I realize it was all just a dream, that time had passed and she was no longer with me. Time always seemed to go by, I damn wished that it would stop for an instant and take me along with it.

I've watched as centuries go by, observing countless other men's lives disrupted by those demons of beauty. They hunt and kill each and every one of them as if it were just part of some disgusting game to pass the time. To partake in such acts just to survive, it's barbaric, yet... I cannot stop myself. And that is what makes this living hell so much harder to deal with.

In recent years, or at least in this last century, stories of the creatures of the night, of vampires and the like, have made their way to the theaters and on each and every bookcase. I spit at these fantasies, of these so called vampires that have a heart, that have feelings for the living. They have no such thing, I promise you. They would never die for a person, never stop to think of how their actions affect others, and never drastically change for the love of a mortal. Those are all what they are made out to be: fiction. The real story is that these monsters only care for one thing, and one thing only.

Themselves.

Or at least that is what the Baobhan Sith care about, only themselves. I can't speak for the rest of vampire kind, presuming that other species exist. I believed that they did and that I wasn't the only unlucky soul that had to endure this life as long as time itself. I just hoped, for their sake, that they didn't have to live a life as unhappy as mine.

It all started back in April, 1746. We, the British Army, had just defeated the Jacobites in the Battle of Culloden and were ordered to lodge near Glen Coe in the Highlands on the way back to England. Never had I seen a battle so bloody, the Jacobites losing most of their men. It was a slaughter, a slaughter that I would remember until the end of time. I wasn't as lucky as the others, who had died in battle, and therefore did not have to endure the tormented nightmares. No, they were the lucky ones. I had seen far too much death throughout the centuries.

I was Captain back then of a small group of men, who obeyed every word I would say. I tried to keep all of them safe during the battle, but some suffered the fate that all fear in war: death. My heart dreaded that moment when I would have to report their deaths to their families back in London and elsewhere in England. It was all a part of the pattern of war, and I had to put up with that sore fact.

Due to some misunderstanding between me and my Colonel, he pretty much told me to go to the wrong town, my men and I were the last to leave Culloden, a small village east of Inverness. Our next stop was the King's Inn, a mandatory stop that the Commanders had given us to let our men rest. I had agreed to this stop, knowing that my men needed to take a break from all the traveling we've been doing for weeks on end.

Nevertheless, I shouldn't have stopped.

It was stormy that night as we made our way through the Highlands of Scotland, towards the King's Inn. There wasn't anywhere else out there to stay, really, so our choices were limited to that one little inn. Desolate didn't begin to describe this lifeless place, since only farmers or hunters seemed to be the predominant type of inhabitants in this area for miles and miles. I never understood why someone would want to live in such a place like this, unless they were trying to punish themselves for some horrible sin that they had committed in their past. It was the only way I could understand someone staying out in this place.

The wind was whipping through the valley, howling almost like a shrieking banshee. I had never heard anything so sinister in my entire life. It was no wonder men created banshees in the first place to represent their fear of this type of weather, although it wouldn't have surprised me if they were real.

Rain came from every direction imaginable, soaking through both my red regiment coat and plain shirt underneath. My light ginger hair clung to my scalp and forehead. I wiped away the excess water from my eyes. I could barely see the road in front of us, and as the water poured harder and harder, I feared we wouldn't find the Inn in this storm.

All I could smell was both the freezing rain and mud that had seemed to cover everything that we possessed. I had lived in England all my life until this war and never had I seen a storm so vicious as this. It was as if nature itself was fighting against us that night, wanting to take our lives or make us suffer even more than what we have suffered already. All the odds seemed stacked against us in those Highlands.

My poor horse was as cold and miserable as I was, while my men and I made our way down the military route. Her brown hair was wet and matted, adding to the horrid smell that the rain brought all around. She was a brave horse, enduring these past few weeks without any clear complaint, and I was very lucky to have her at my side. Even after how brave she was throughout the battles we've fought in, I could still feel her flinch as the wind howled once more.

I patted her on the side. "Easy, girl. It's just the wind. Nothing to be afraid of."

I could feel that her body was still tense, but she didn't become startled as the wind howled once more. In the far distance, I could hear the sound of thunder rolling in. The storm was worsening.

"Captain Williams," George, my cadet, moved closer in order for me to hear him. His thin, short hair seemed to be gathering rain drops more so than the men who had long hair. His coat was as soaked as all the rest of ours were, and he held his hand up as if he could block the rain that was coming from every direction. "This storm seems to be getting stronger. Shall we stop and take cover?"

I glanced around. There were no trees within sight, I had no idea just where he thought we were going to take cover. There were reasons why he was a cadet and I was a captain, and it wasn't just because he was a physically unfit lad due to all the biscuits he consumed during meals. "Don't you worry, we are almost to the inn. We will be out of this in no time. Keep the thoughts of a warm fire and biscuits that will be waiting for us."

George mumbled something about biscuits and went back to his spot in line. I watched as the sky began to darken even more, like a witch had cast a spell in these parts. Lightning crashed, and thunder echoed through the highlands. It wasn't my first storm in the Highlands, and it certainly wasn't the last, but something about it stood apart from the others. It was stronger, and more sinister, than more generic storms, if that was even possible.

Crash.

My horse raised its front hooves as the lightning hit the grass right in front of us. Miraculously I didn't fall off as she spooked me as well. I pulled on the reigns, trying to keep my balance and not be bucked off. All I needed then was to be covered in mud and even more bruises than I obtained during our last battle. "Calm down, girl. It is all right."

The horse was still jittery, not wanting to move forward, but at least she had stopped bucking. I didn't need another creature being afraid of the darkness, I already had all my men to worry about. I made a clicking noise, trying to let her know who the master was, although most of the time she let me know she was in charge. She was just like my Alice.

As I calmed down my horse, I glanced forward to find a figure in the distance. Rain and fog made it hard to distinguish much, but I could see her as clear as day. A woman, at least it appeared to be a woman. She wore all white and the aura that surrounded her seemed lovelier than any woman I had ever met, even Alice. I watched her in awe but also in confusion, wondering what she was doing out in a storm like this, and how she could seem so perfectly still with everything that was going on.

Another flash of lightning hit the hillside nearby, destroying my ability to see for a moment. White spots filled my vision, making me blink until they were gone. As my eyes adjusted to the darkness, I found no trace of the woman. I glanced all around, but she was nowhere to be found.

Strange, I swore I had seen someone.

I dismissed the entire thing as being a figment of my imagination. It wasn't like someone would be out in this mess, especially not a woman. I had heard of sailors doing the same thing at sea, imagining mermaids and the like. I probably was just turning into an old sea dog. It was about time I retired from this life, it wasn't one I ever wanted anyway.

I felt as if I couldn't move any longer, my body frozen by the chill of the stormy wind, but I pushed on nonetheless with the rest of my shivering men. I couldn't let my men see me in a state of vulnerability, not when they needed to know it would be alright. I just hoped that the inn was near. The innkeepers knew we were coming, and if it weren't for this supernatural storm, we would have arrived already. Maybe, they would come searching for us.

One of our carts broke, the wheel getting stuck in all the mud. Ralph, one of my cadets and the most hardworking man of my brigade, was the first one to leap off of his horse to assist with the broken wheel. His brown hair and clothes were soaked but that didn't stop him as he started moving the material from the wrecked cart to the other carts. I watched as other men joined him, knowing that I didn't need to assist any of them. They had it all under control.

Andrew and Percy also stayed on their horses, Percy too proud of a man and Andrew just too selfish to care. I would be happy when those two were out of my hair. At least with Andrew, he was still a rebellious youngster due to troubles he had as a child. I knew his parents and they weren't the nicest of folk. As for Percy, well, he just couldn't climb off his high tower to think of others. I thought about talking to him about it, but in reality as long as we got to London, I didn't really care anymore. A new captain could deal with him.

Rounding the last bend, I could see a flickering light in the distance. It was a candle coming from the King's Inn. I thanked the Lord we didn't have to travel any longer in this God-forsaken storm. I saw the relief on my men's face and they saw the same on mine. They hooted and hollered as we made the last stretch of the journey. None of us wanted to push any farther than we had to, not after making it through that last war.

As fast as we could, we hurried to the inn, the owners saw us in the distance and came out to help us put away our things. Thankfully, they had some stables to retire our horses in and get them out of the rain. We quickly put the horses away and gathered our gear. Everything was soaked, but luckily the inn keepers, Duncan and Fiona McGregory, already had a fire waiting for us. Each of us huddled up close to it, trying to get rid of the feeling of being chilled to the bone. After everyone had time to warm up, we took turns laying our things out to dry.

There were nine of us, all huddled in the room, trying to stay warm. The room wasn't that big, nor did it have much to it, but we made it work. The McGregorys had retired for the evening, leaving us with some food and water and some dry wood to keep the fire going.

Looking around, I saw the disappointment in my men's eyes. They wished to be home, away from this treacherous place. Everyone was quiet, wallowing in their own misery. As a captain, it was my responsibility to get them to forget their worries.

"What are you all looking forward to when we reach London?" I proposed a question to get them thinking of events awaiting them in the near future.

Each one of them glanced at each other, uneasy with the question. It was like I asked them to put down their horse.

"Come on men," I stood up. "What in London makes you smile? What will be there waiting for you?"

George was the first to talk. "Better food?"

I raised an eyebrow at him. Of course he always thought with his stomach. "I'm sorry George, but English food isn't that grand."

He leaned back, as if mad I had shot his answer down. "Better than Scottish food."

Rolling my eyes, "Anyone else?"

"Having a real doctor's office," Jonathan, our medic, sighed. "Where I can actually work on the sick instead of the injured." He ruffled his hand through his greying hair and beard.

I clapped my hands together. "Good, good, come on men, we all have someone waiting at home for us."

Ralph shook his head, flinging water in every direction like a wet dog. Andrew was the first to hit him.

"Watch what you are doing," Andrew said as he smacked Ralph on the side of the head.

"Enough," I said before Ralph could say anything to make Andrew any angrier. "Ralph, why don't you tell us what you are looking forward to."

He shrugged. "Not all that much at home, except my mother. She will be happy I guess, needing me to work the dairy with her."

"Mommy's little boy," Percy commented. Ralph stood up, as if to fight him or something stupid like that.

I held out my hand. "No, sit. Percy, you lost your turn for sharing."

He shrugged, probably not caring either way.

"I'm looking forward to getting home to my wife. We had a little girl just before I left, I can't wait to go home and see her," Michael smiled warmly. He was a man I could always count on in seeing the good side of things, always keeping a positive attitude about everything.

"That is great, Michael, congratulations," I patted his back. The other men congratulated him as well. "Thomas, you have anything you are looking forward to?"

Thomas was an older man, at least in his fifties, the oldest in our group. He had lost his wife a few years earlier and joined the military to get away from the memory of home. He shook his head. "Just looking to be shipped out again."

"What about you," Kenneth asked, his curly red hair and freckles making him still look like he was a young boy. "What's waiting for you at home?"

"Don't you know?" George smacked me on the back. "This lad has a lass waiting for him to come home."

All of my men whistled and made suggestive comments. At least they seemed to be cheering up, even though it was at my expense. I motioned for them to settle down. "I do have a girl waiting for me at home. Her name is Alice."

"And what are you going to do with dear Alice when you get home?" Ralph smiled as he took a sip of some whiskey.

"I... am going to make her my wife," I stammered.

Each of the men congratulated me on the news. I hadn't made it known that I had planned to marry before we went into battle, fearing that I would curse myself and be killed in battle. I figured now there wasn't anything bad that could happen. I would be with my wife until the day I died. The thought of her made my blood began to heat up and I felt warmer. As long as my cheeks weren't turning red, or then I would suffer the embarrassment of being teased by my fellow men. I couldn't help it, I just loved her that much.

"We plan to open a pub back home," I went on, wanting to tell everyone of our plans, even if they didn't care. "And I am going to retire from the Royal Army so I can be with her. Once our pub is up and running, you all are invited for a free round of drinks."

George held up his drink. "I can drink to that! To Henry and his bride-to-be Alice! Let them love each other for the rest of their lives!"

The men cheered and for once in a long while, I felt happy, as if I could finally enjoy a moment of peace. Each of the other men told their stories, each of which involved a woman of some sort or a good pub and drink, not the crap we had been sipping on for the past few weeks. After a good while, we settled back down into silence.

I stared into the flames, thinking about the lady I had seen out there in the storm.

She had seemed real enough. I wasn't one to hallucinate when I was tired or hungry, but her appearance seemed otherworldly, like an angel sent from Heaven itself. I had heard of men in war sometimes having seen such a divine presence, but that was usually during a battle, not after one. Was she real, or was she just in my imagination? I shook away the thoughts. It must have just been the lightning. There was no way any sane being would be out in that storm if they weren't lost.

After a bit, the rest of the men retired for the night, wanting to catch up on some much needed sleep. God knows they deserved it. I sat there on the wooden rocker, not having any desire to go to sleep for the night. Too many thoughts were running through my mind. The blood shed on the field. Men falling down beside me as I kept on fighting. Not being able to do anything for them except to fight on. It was the hardest thing I ever had to do, and it was going to take a while for me to recover from those nightmares. So I tried not to sleep, and simply stared into the fire.

The blaze of the fire reminded of the spilt blood that divided the hours on the battlefield. Friends lost, comrades injured. I was lucky that the men that slept now were still alive. They were probably going to be haunted by those gory battles for the rest of their lives. Just as I was.

I rubbed my eyes, trying to make the images go away. I prayed that once I returned home, and had Alice at my side, she would be able to help alleviate the pain I had been feeling through these past few months. She was innocent, pure, and being around her made me feel sane again. I could pretend that this war had never happened, that I didn't kill men on the battlefield. I would be able to hold my dear Alice, and also be cleansed of all this blood I had on my hands from all the bloody battles I've been engaged in over the past few weeks.

I felt a cold shiver run down my spine. I scanned around the room looking for where the draft could have come from, but didn't find anything. It must have just been my imagination running wild, making me feel cold once again. I wrapped my arms around myself, but I could still feel a cool breeze against my neck. I glanced around again but nothing seemed to be causing it.

As I gathered myself closer to the fire, I heard a voice.

"Henry..." A whisper called me. It was the sound of a woman's voice, soft and sweet. I glanced around but there was no one there. I couldn't hear anything but the storm outside.

"Henry..."

That was definitely not my imagination. I stood up and hurried to the window. Whatever it was, it seemed to be coming from outside, as if being carried by the storm. I peered out into the storm.

Wind was rushing through the few trees that were surrounding the inn. I could hear them creak and crack as the branches were pushed beyond their limit. Even in the darkness, I could see the grass being whipped back and forth and I was glad I was no longer out there in the thick of it. Lightning was striking the hillside, bringing light to all around it. I swore I had seen some figure out on the hillside. I waited for the lightning to strike again. As it did, I noticed the figure to be missing.

It must have been my imagination again. I closed my eyes for a moment, taking in all the sounds, seeing if it was all just in my head.

"Henry..."

My eyes shot open and not too far out in the distance, she was standing there like a beacon. Her white dress flowed to the ground like an angel's and she appeared to be almost floating. I gaped at the figure, confused as to its existence. She was definitely the same figure I had seen when we were coming down the Highlands, but it just couldn't be possible. How could she be out in that storm, especially appearing dry and not bothered by any of it?

As I stood there at the window with my mouth open, flabbergasted, she raised her hand towards me. *"Come to me."*

I don't know what happened, but everything around me seemed to disappear and all that was left was her. It had been her voice, it was hypnotic, I couldn't think straight. All I wanted to do was obey her every command, no matter what it was. Something in the back of my mind was shouting at me to stop, but I just couldn't listen to myself. The rest of my body wouldn't obey. I slowly stepped for the door, wanting to go to her. Her voice was like a melody, beautiful and pleasant, making you want to forget everything that was around you. She kept repeating my name, as if it were some note of a song. Even with the wind howling in the background, I had to go out there with her. I had to be with her.

I began to turn the knob of the inn room door.

"Captain, is everything alright?"

I blinked, coming back to reality. It felt strange, as if I was aware of moving across the room to the door, but at the time had no control over my movements. I stretched out my hand. I had control now and that was all that mattered. I glanced back out the window. There was no sign of the woman that had been calling me now. After taking a deep breath, thinking I had definitely begun to lose my mind, I turned to find Ralph standing there, staring at me as if I had gone crazy. I didn't like it when men a lot younger than me gave me a look as if I had gone senile.

I smiled. "It's nothing. I just thought I saw something out there."

Ralph stepped up next to me and took a look outside. "In that storm? It was probably just shadows playing tricks on you, sir."

I gave him a look, letting him know I didn't appreciate him mocking me. I was tired and irritable, making night the worst time to cross me.

He coughed. "It also could have been an animal, sir. Back on the farm, they have played a few tricks on me in the middle of the night."

"I suppose it was," I glanced out the window once more. Nothing but the storm waited for me out there. There was no point in searching for illusions. Even if they had seemed so real.

"In fact, there was this one time when our cow, Kathy…"

I gave him a look, not wanting him to go one with the story. He stopped talking.

"Have you seen anything strange lately?" I asked.

Ralph shook his head. "Nothing other than this horrible storm."

I took another moment to stare out into the darkness. It was strange, that was for sure. Whatever was haunting me, was only bothering me and no one else.

"It's about time I retire, Ralph. I bid you fair night," he yawned.

He nodded as I passed him and retired to my own room. I didn't particularly want to fall asleep, but neither did I want to stay and see if that woman would come back, and whether or not I would be able to resist her this time around.

She had known my name.

I had heard her voice; that wasn't an illusion. Or maybe it was. I sat down and rubbed my face with my palms. I hadn't gotten much sleep for the past few weeks with the war, so that could have played a part. I probably just missed the embrace of a woman, so this ghostly apparition had to be a figment of my imagination

Opening up my locket around my neck, I took in the picture of my fiancé, Alice, who was waiting for me in Nottingham. It was a cheap painting I had a friend do that didn't do her any justice, but it was at least something I could take with me when I was away. Dark brown hair, sea blue eyes, a smile that could warm up the hardest of hearts. She was perfect. I had promised to wed her the moment I came back from this war and I would uphold that promise. Throughout the battle, I had kept her in my mind and it was the only thing that had kept me going. Soon we would be together until the day we died.

I kissed the locket and placed it on the table next to the bed side. Maybe, if I fell asleep, my dreams would be filled with memories of her back home.

I didn't dream of Alice.

No, I couldn't be that lucky. Instead I dreamt of canons, gunfire, echoes of screaming commands, death and destruction. Over and over again. It was a cycle that never ended, brother against brother, men and woman fighting for freedom, for power. It made my heart sicken.

I opened my eyes to find only quiet calmness. The storm had subsided for now and all that was left was the tiny drizzle of mist that surrounded the Highlands. The clouded light beamed into my room and I watched as a dark colored bird flew past my window. I was never that good at remembering species of different types of animals, nor did I ever really care. I appreciated them, though. They brought liveliness, where sometimes we can't find anything.

We would have to spend one more night here, taking a break from traveling, before heading back to England. I didn't look forward to staying here again, but my men needed the rest, and I wouldn't mind it as well. I wanted to lie here all day, losing myself in the images I could make out of the wood on the ceiling. I slowly closed my eyes again, hoping to drift back into my thoughts about Alice and how happy I would be to see her.

I was never that lucky.

A tap sounded at the door. "Captain, are you awake?"

It was Kenneth. I rubbed my face. *What did he need now? Why couldn't I ever get some rest before one of my men needed me?* "Yes, what is it?"

"We can't find Ralph," he explained. My heart quickened.

How could you not find someone in this inn? It wasn't that big.

Kenneth went on. "We were wondering if you knew anything as to where he might have gone."

I jumped up out of my bed and quickly put on my coat. I wasn't going to lose another man, not after the battle was over, even though he probably was just wandering around outside like he normally does. He was a kid after all. But it was a bit nasty outside, I didn't know why he would want to go out during a day like this. Running my fingers through my hair a few times, I opened the door. Kenneth appeared disheveled, his hair a mess and his shirt not quite tucked in. I wondered how long he had been awake, although I probably didn't look any better. "How long have you been searching for him?"

"Since five this morning. It is seven now sir."

And they didn't wake me? Why wasn't I notified? I felt like asking this, but knew they just didn't want me to worry about something that started out as something so trivial. Now it had been two hours since Ralph was last seen and they knew they needed me to help find him. "Did he go outside in the morning? Did anyone see him?"

Kenneth shook his head. "No. No one had seen him since last night."

He had been there when I saw that woman. *Could she have been behind the disappearance?* No, she was just a figment of my imagination. There had to be something more to it. I rubbed my eyes. "No, I saw him early this morning, around one. He was checking in on me, said he couldn't sleep. I retired after that."

"So he was up and about?" Kenneth asked.

I nodded, a cool tingling feeling creeping up my neck. If he had seen the woman, he would have gone outside, just as I was about to do. "Have you searched the premises?"

"We have not yet, Captain, we were awaiting your orders," he said. Of course they were, these men wouldn't know how to lead a search party even if it determined their survival.

Buttoning up my coat, I started down the hallway. "Then let us do it."

An eerie mist had swept through the Highlands, taking away me and my men's ability to see more than a couple yards in front of us. The fog's moisture clung to our skin, chilling us straight to the bone. We separated into two teams of three, leaving both Andrew and Percy to wait at the inn, since they didn't really care nor think anything was wrong. Kenneth and George were grouped with me.

The air smelt of wet grass and mud. Although the chilliness was unpleasant, the smell of the Highlands did beat that of the city, which was an odor consisting mostly of smog from factories, sludge, and feces. If I could make enough in the countryside, I would choose it over living in the city any day. I wasn't a farm boy, though. Rather, I had grown up in the city of London as the son of a Royal Army Commander. I didn't have a choice in the field I went into, though I doubted anyone in life ever did. Alice grew up living above a bakery and had spent her entire life in the city as well. We wouldn't know the first thing about living in the countryside, so our dream was to open a pub in the city, even with all the downsides.

And that dream of a life after the war was what kept me going.

Every strange sound echoing through the hills made my skin crawl. I swore it had to be coming from something entirely otherworldly. Nothing deemed good in God's creation would have sounded like that. If hell was a place on Earth, this had to be it.

"Ralph!" I called out into empty abyss of white fog. "Are you out there somewhere?"

In this God-forsaken place, I almost added. I didn't, though, since I didn't want to shout more than I had to, for the cold air filled my lungs and mouth every time I did. It made my voice hoarse, the frigid air burning my lungs and throat. "Ralph!"

There was no answer, only the echoes of my other soldiers calling out his name were heard throughout the surrounding area. *Damn it, Ralph, where are you?* I listened closely for anything else. I heard nothing. Even the random noises of birds and wind that made up the Highlands had subsided. All that was left was the eerie sound of silence, which was worse than any other sound out here.

I glanced around, but all I could see was that familiar murky white fog. If it weren't for Kenneth and George being there, I would have felt lost and abandoned. I wasn't even that sure of how far we were from the inn any more. Such places could easily play tricks on the mind, and I just wished to be out of here as soon as possible. No one should have to suffer in these parts any longer than they had to.

"Where do you think he went off to, Captain?" George questioned. "There ain't nothing out here except Satan himself."

He had that right. "I'm not sure, George."

I glanced over at Kenneth, whose red curly hair was the only thing I could see other than the fog. His hair was like a beacon and I was slightly thankful for that. I could barely make out the concern he had on his face for his friend. Both he and Ralph were young, and they had a connection from the start. They even talked about taking a trip down to the coast together before they went back home. I just hoped we found him before something bad happened.

None of us were to stray too far from the inn, in fear that we wouldn't be able to find our way back in this strange mist. I took a mental note of the direction we were headed, but every time I glanced back, I feared we wouldn't be able to find the inn. If all else failed, we could probably call out loud enough for someone to hear, but the thought did spark a little fear in me.

"Ralph!" I called out again, beginning to think we wouldn't find anything. He couldn't have wandered out this far, we have to be almost a mile from the inn, it just wouldn't have made any sense. Maybe someone else had found him. "We should head back. Maybe the others found some clues, as to his whereabouts."

Kenneth and George both nodded, not wanting to be out in this area any more time than needed either. We were worried about him, but we also didn't know if he had made it back to the inn while we were searching for him. It was something he would do, have all of us worry, and then show up acting as if nothing had happened. As the three of us were just about to turn around, I spotted an object straight ahead. It was large and sprawled out like a human.

"Oi! Over here!" I pointed ahead near the base of the hill and hurried towards the object, fearing that we were too late. As I got closer, I recognized Ralph's red coat. We had found him, although he seemed to be passed out, or worse, dead. I prayed to God that he was still alive.

I slipped on the mud as I reached him, going down to my knees and my hands, both now covered in filth. I didn't care about the grime, knowing I needed to help Ralph. His face was in the dirt, so I carefully turned him over.

His skin was white, like that of a ghost. I covered my mouth. I had seen many dead men throughout the years at many stages of decomposition, their bodies bloating, skin lightening, and a stench coming off of them worse than anything else, but none of them had ever appeared like Ralph did. It was haunting, not like that of anything from this world. I didn't know what to say or do. Both Kenneth and George caught up with me and gasped at my discovery.

"What is wrong with his skin?" George asked, his mouth not closing as he looked at the body. He had noticed the same thing I did. It wasn't something you normally observed a dead body to physically undergo in such a quick time, even in these temperatures. I glanced at Kenneth, who was still in shock of finding his friend dead. I wanted to comfort him but first we had to get out of the cold.

I shook my head. "I haven't the faintest idea." It was puzzling indeed, and I doubted we would ever find out. I would have Jonathan, once a surgeon before joining the Royal Army, take a look at him. Maybe he could figure it out. "But we must carry him back to the Inn. George, Kenneth, help me get him up."

His body was a lot lighter as well. I had carried many a dead men through the years, never had someone felt so light. It was odd, I had no idea what to make of it. Normally a body was a lot heavier when it was lifeless. It was all quite strange. My mind raced to put the pieces together, but nothing seemed to make sense.

The three of us carried him back to the inn. One of the search parties had already beaten us back and each of the men gasped in horror upon seeing Ralph's body being carried, unceremoniously, into the inn's common room. I had to admit, it took everything for myself to not wallow in self-pity as his body laid there. He was young, had a long life ahead of him. It was unnerving that such a young spirited man could die in such mysterious conditions. I had promised no harm to come of any of my men, between Culloden and on the way home to London, and I had let them down. I probably shouldn't blame myself, especially when such unexplained supernatural forces were playing against us. Nevertheless, I couldn't help shouldering the blame for what had just happened. I was the captain and I was responsible for the welfare of my soldiers, regardless of who our enemy was.

Luckily, the McGregorys had a room that wasn't being used for anything other than storage. So, two of the men, laid Ralph's prone body on the cot, from where Jonathan would examine him further. The innkeepers tried to be as accommodating as possible, knowing that this was quite a tragic event for us. As such, they left us in peace, as we prepared Ralph's body to be examined.

Not wanting my men to endure the horror of seeing Jonathan examine the body of their comrade, I ordered them to wait out in the parlor room and keep warm near the fireplace, since the inn was a bit drafty. Sitting in the parlor, none of my men, though, appeared to pay the cold air any ounce of attention. Rather, their trembling bodies seemed more of a response to Ralph's uncertain fate, and any contemplation as to the horrors visited upon him.

I watched as Jonathan inspected the body, crossing my arms and keeping silent. He checked for any noticeable wounds and tried to narrow down the cause of Ralph's death. He didn't seem to be going into too much detail during the procedure; a normal examiner would normally cut the body open but we needed to take him back to London before anyone did that. We wanted to return his body intact, since cutting it open could cause other unwanted issues during our return home. Jonathan checked inside Ralph's mouth. Life as a surgeon had to be grotesque, I could barely imagine.

It was an hour before Jonathan came up with anything.

"Quite strange indeed," he washed his hands off with some water.

"What is it?" I asked, glad that the body was now covered and I didn't have to look at it any longer. I could have waited outside, but some yearning to know exactly what happened to Ralph kept me in this room with Jonathan...

Jonathan let out a sigh as we went into the hallway. He closed the door of the extra room behind him and glanced around to make sure there was no one nearby to overhear our delicate conversation. "The cause of death was a cut to his throat, as if by a knife, yet there was no blood near the wound, not to mention most of the blood in his body is gone. I have never seen anything quite like it."

That would explain his appearance, but it still sounded preposterous. I had never heard of such a thing. "The blood is gone? What do you mean?"

Jonathan shrugged as he pulled out his pipe—a habit to help ease the grave tension of being in such close contact with so many dead bodies. He took in a few puffs. "I mean what I say. I could cut him open all the way and there would be nothing inside of him but flesh and bones."

I rubbed my chin, trying to process this information. *How could his blood be missing? How was that possible? Who could have done this, especially to someone as kind and young as Ralph?*

Or what?

The woman I had seen yesterday, was she real? Did she do this? And if so, how could she have been out in that storm last night? None of us would ever have chosen freely to be out there, we rushed to this inn as fast as we could when out in that brutal weather. That could only mean one thing: was there some kind of witchcraft or sorcery involved with the circumstances surrounding Ralph's strange death?

Either way, someone or something had to have killed him. It was my duty to him as a Captain to figure it out. His mother was at home, waiting for him. I had to solve this if not for her, but for Ralph himself. I straightened my coat and drew up my sleeves.

"I'm going to talk to the innkeepers and see if they know of anyone nearby who could have done this, or what type of creatures live in these parts?"

"You don't think it could have been any of our men, do you?" Jonathan asked.

I glanced at him, worry in my eyes. It was a good question, but I knew my men. They were glad to be going home and, if there was any fights between them, they wouldn't have waited until now to kill him, but done it out on the battlefield where no one would have noticed. It wasn't likely any of them had done this. Though, Percy and Andrew weren't the nicest to him, I don't think they would ever stoop to something this low.

I shook my head. "I don't think so, but I will still question them, just to make sure."

I found Duncan and Fiona in the kitchen, helping the staff get ready for dinner. There was a lot of chaos going on as they prepared for the nine of us, causing me to rethink owning a pub with Alice. *Was this what it was like? Chaotic and a mess?* The chaos would be manageable, no doubt, as long as I had Alice help me with keeping things in our future pub under control. We would manage and we would be happy; we had to be or life wouldn't be worth living.

Nodding to Duncan, I motioned that I wanted to talk to him. He finished up helping the cook move a large pot of water to the stove and hurried over to meet me.

"Captain Williams," he said as he rolled down his sleeves and ran his fingers through his thinning brown hair. "Is there anything else you need? We are happy to help with anything. We are very sorry for your loss."

"Thank you. It was indeed a strange, unforeseen circumstance. I am very grateful that you are doing whatever it takes to help us get over this sudden trauma."

"Don't worry about it, I was in the military when I was younger, I understand how sick you are of death, and to have something like this happen to you when you are so close to home is horrible," Duncan explained. I watched as his eyes seemed to journey with his mind into his past. A lot of men went into the army, they saw it as their duty. I felt bad, though, when others had felt the same pain as I experienced for the past few months. It didn't seem that it would ever end any time soon.

"I do, however, have some questions I want to ask you pertaining to his death," I began. "They have to do with these Highlands. Do you have a moment?"

I noted as Duncan fiddled with the cuff of his jacket as I asked the question. That was a nervous tick of his, but he had no real motive for me to suspect him of doing anything out-of-the-ordinary. Maybe he just didn't like being questioned, I knew of men who hated being asked anything, even what they wanted to eat. It was strange but not uncommon. But that didn't beg the question that roamed in my mind; did he know more than he was letting on?

He nodded, stroking his mustache, and motioned down the hallway. "Yes, I believe I can slip away from the kitchen for a bit. Let us go into my office."

I followed him into his office, not too far off from the kitchen. It was bare, with only two chairs and a table with stacks of paper atop it filling the room. The walls were the same as the rest of the inn, white and bare. Only one painting hung on the wall, depicting the inn itself. I definitely would had found it too dull to work there, though I wondered how much time he actually spent in this room. Based on all the dust covering the furniture, I took it to be not that often.

He nodded to the chair. "Please, take a seat."

I did as requested, leaning back, the wooden chair squeaking as I did so. It seemed old and I hoped it wouldn't break like some cheap furniture tends to do.

Duncan took a seat himself across from me and adjusted himself comfortably. "Now, what did you want to ask me?"

I started to lean back, but could hear the chair begin to speak again. Not wanting to break the chair, I straightened back up. "I was curious if there was anyone else in these parts or if it was only travelers staying here, or those working at your inn."

He shook his head and smiled as if I had asked something humorous. "There isn't anyone for miles. Not many want to come up here, except for some farmers and the occasional hunter. Why do you ask?"

That's what I had thought, but I had to ask to make sure. I scratched the back of my head, frustrated as to everything that was happening over the last day, or so. It was almost more frustrating than the war itself, as everything began to pile on top of each other. "I'm just trying to figure out what happened. I wanted to eliminate any outsiders."

Duncan raised an eyebrow. "Do you think your man was murdered? What makes you believe that?"

I shrugged. I didn't know yet, for all I knew he could have killed himself, though there weren't any weapons on or near him. "It is hard to say yet, but his cause of death is strange. He was found without any blood and had a cut along his throat."

He stared at me, his eyes widened for a moment. He swallowed and took a deep breath, then went back to his normal composure. "That is quite strange indeed."

I knew he was letting me know everything that he knew, which wasn't very much. But, I knew he had no reason to hurt Ralph in any heinous way. Believing that it might have been him was my all imagination, once again. "Do you have any idea what could have done this? Are there any animals in the Highlands, capable of killing a full grown man?

He shook his head. "There are some badgers in these parts, but I've never heard of them attacking someone like that. I also don't know how they would make a slit on someone's throat."

I debated asking him about the woman I had seen. By the sounds of it, there wasn't anyone close to this place, and it definitely wasn't any of the workers residing here either. None were as beautiful as the girl I had seen. I dismissed the thought of the girl as pure fantasy and decided to start questioning my men as to whether or not they had seen anyone or anything suspicious.

I stood up. "Thank you for your help, Mr. McGregory. I will let you know if I need anything else."

He nodded and saw me out of his office. "Glad to have been of some help. I do hope you figure out what or who is behind all of this."

"As do I," I started for the common room where my men were waiting.

None of my men had seen or heard anything last night that might have sparked suspicion. All of them claimed to have been sound asleep the entire night. None of them had a plausible motivation either, which would have logically explained one of them being a likely suspect for murder. Ralph was a great guy and had gotten along with everyone. He had a family back in Sussex, to whom I would have to eventually deliver the news myself to. I didn't look forward to telling his mother. It wouldn't be the first time I had to do this, but hopefully it would be the last.

I had already lost ten men in my camp, now this was the eleventh. I would have to deliver the message to each of their families. It was the second hardest thing to do in my profession, the first being the witness of their death. I had seen each and every one of them die. I was sick of it and I couldn't wait to be relieved of my duty as Captain. I wanted to move on with my life and start anew with my wife-to-be.

All I had to do was make it back home, all in one piece.

It seemed easy enough, but I knew that was never the case. With some strange thing out there now killing one of my own, I was sure it was only the beginning of worse things to come. Life as a captain of the English army could never be easy and I was deemed to suffer through all the nasty twists of fate that came as a part of this job. Only God knew how right I was at that moment that things were about to get even uglier...

I decided to take another look around the general area where we had found Ralph's body. I brought George along, not wanting to go by myself in case I did run into the creature. I also trusted him the most, he was one of my first cadets that I had in the army. Going back out here was definitely not something I wanted to face by myself, either. And if the strange, ghostly woman appeared yet again, I would know whether or not it was just me that could see it or if others including George could as well. Hopefully, neither of us would have to test this theory of mine in this way.

I didn't want to think I was the only one who saw it, making me worry about my sanity. It had seemed so real at the moment of first seeing it with my own eyes, yet the nagging fear she wasn't real ate away at my thoughts. It scared me, made me fear that I couldn't control my own life, that this being could possess me to do anything, as it tried to get me to go outside the night before. *Could she have gotten Ralph to go outside instead?*

As we headed out into the Highlands, I grabbed my pistol, as did George. We didn't know what would be out there waiting for us, even if the innkeeper had said there wasn't anything out here. George also grabbed a scone, he said it was for in case we got lost and needed food. I noted that he had only grabbed one, but I wasn't worried we would get lost. Rather, I was worried about encountering the very thing that started all of this mayhem.

We were able to back track to where we had found Ralph's body. I had a keen sense of direction, luckily, and we were able to find the indentation in the ground where his body had lain.

"What are we looking for?" George asked as I knelt down and examined the ground. All I found was wet grass and mud, typical for all of Britain and Scotland.

"Look for anything out of place. A clue, of sorts," I explained, touching the ground with my hand.

He nodded and knelt down beside me. "Right, sir. Hopefully won't take too long, I smelt biscuits for today's dinner."

I gave him a look as we started searching the surrounding area. The rain had left the area finally, not even a drizzle, although the air still felt damp. There was nothing out there but us. I glanced back at the inn. I couldn't even see any movement inside. They must have all been in the common room still, drinking. After this was over, I was going to open a bottle of scotch myself.

I went on with searching for any minor detail that could lead us to what had killed Ralph. As captain, I had to figure out this mystery before it was too late, and the killer got away before we had to return home. I owed it to him, for not keeping him safe while he was in my care. It was one thing to lose a man on the battlefield, it was another to lose him in such an awful way. Maybe I was wrong, maybe something didn't kill him and it was just an accident, but his death was quite strange. Something had to have cut his throat and drained his blood, for some purpose. *But what? And why?*

A small indentation in the mud caught my eye. I squinted, trying to figure out what exactly it was.

"Are those goat tracks?" I pointed the strange indentations out to George.

He inspected the tracks as well, bringing his face closer to them than I. "Why, I think they are."

I glanced around. There was no sign of any goat-like creatures around, who may have left these tracks "What was a goat doing way out here on a night like last night?"

He shrugged. "I'm not sure, Captain. Maybe it was one of McGregory's goats that escaped their pen."

I had asked Duncan earlier about animals, he didn't mention anything about goats. Since goats weren't notoriously violent creatures, he may have felt including them was silly, in addition to the fact I never overheard anyone talking of any escaped goats. "Seems very unlikely, a goat committing a murder. What, did it steal a knife from the kitchen and coax Ralph into the night?" I felt bad about the joke having to do with Ralph's death, but thinking a goat had committed the murder was preposterous.

"Then what do you think it is?"

I traced my finger around the indentation, the short, stubby, identical lines. "I'm not sure." It was also strange that they were next to where Ralph's body was discovered earlier in the morning. It seemed like there were only a pair of them, not four. To be quite honest, I didn't know what to make of it. "Let us follow them and see where they lead to."

George nodded and we started following the hoof tracks. As I had thought, there only seemed to be two different hooves, not four like a goat would have. They went for a good distance, not something a goat would have done in the storm last night. A goat would have found cover and probably would have ended up back at its pin in no time.

I tried to come up with a theory of what could have happened but I was still coming up blank. Something drew him out here in the middle of the night; that was for certain. As for what had killed him and why, I just couldn't figure that out. *What could have made these hooves?* It was evidence that something was out here, but I still wasn't sure as to what exactly it was.

The tracks ended at the rocky hillside. We didn't have equipment to climb up it, nor did we know exactly where the tracks led off to. *Did the goat-like creature climb the rocky hillside?*

"Well, we know it wasn't human then, Captain. Whatever it was came out of those mountains. There's no way a human could have made that trek."

I stared up into the hill. George was right, it would have taken a skilled professional to hike that hill during that storm. No sane person would have been able to manage that kind of feat. Everything that has happened was all quite puzzling. There was something strange going on, but I hadn't the faintest idea as to what it was.

George and I returned to the inn and decided to tell the rest of men, who were gathering in the parlor, that we haven't found anything that might help us discover Ralph's murderer. I didn't need to start another search—this time for a rogue goat. That type of search would lead even further away from any strong leads for this investigation. At this point, I could only see it ending horrible, especially when all the men were already drunk, the only thing they knew how to do in a time like this. They were stuck in this building, since I didn't want anyone else wandering off, so they decided to drink.. I could smell the alcohol when I stepped into the inn. So for now, only George and

I would indulge in this mystery, if it really had anything to do with the goat, which I was sure it didn't.

Mr. and Mrs. McGregory had prepared dinner for us, some stew and potatoes. We ate in silence, as the sun went down and we were left in the darkness once again. Their food wasn't the greatest, bland and sometimes just strange, especially haggis. Although, the scones were nice, and George ate as many as he could. When he was nervous, he consumed more than anyone believed possible for one man to consume at one time, which was scary compared to his normal eating habits since he had already been eating at least two men's worth of meals.

As for my other men, most of them seemed not to be that hungry. We were all losing our appetite, thinking of the wretched event that occurred this morning. Percy ate fine, of course, he didn't care about anyone but himself. I couldn't wait until we reached London so I wouldn't have to deal with his lack of empathy. Andrew didn't seem to have an appetite either, but I wasn't sure how to interrupt that. He never cared for Ralph, they always seemed to fight, although maybe he cared more for him than I thought. Maybe, he saw him as a brother.

As for the rest of us, we were still reeling from the shock. Even Jonathan, who saw death more than the rest of us through all the autopsies he had performed, barely ate anything, and simply sat there and smoked on his pipe. I tried to think of something to say to get the men's morale up, but even I couldn't think of anything. No matter what I would say, it would just bring more sadness.

Night came, but none of us felt like sleeping. We didn't want the same misfortune to reoccur, again. For all we knew, there could be a killer out there. The wind howled like a wild animal, as if the wind was alive. I had never heard anything so vile in all my life. If I weren't a sane man, I would think this place was haunted with ghosts and demons, especially after seeing the woman, her dress as white as a ghost. At this moment, I promised myself I would never come back to this dreaded place, for as long as I lived.

Letting my mind drift away, I thought of Alice. What I wouldn't give to see her at that moment, to be able to wrap my arms around her and give her the kiss that awaited her when I returned. I pondered on the thought of whether or not she would let me take her to bed again as she did before I left. I had promised to marry her, so it seemed it was not either wrong or indecent. *Did a promise of marriage not mean the same thing as being married?* It was a promise between two souls and God, it shouldn't matter if a priest declared it or not. It only mattered what was in the heart, and that, for us, was love.

After dinner, I opened a bottle of scotch that I had found in the storage area, sharing a bit with each of the men as they gathered near the warm fire. The chill of the Highlands never ceased. It did not taste very good, seeing as how the inn's selection of alcohol was fairly limited. Nonetheless, it was still something alcoholic that we could drink to help forget all that had happened in the past few weeks. For that, I was thankful.

Sipping on the inn's signature scotch I found that it had to have been a rather young bottle. It was potent, leaving a burning sensation in my mouth and throat. All I could taste was the alcohol in it, since it didn't seem to have much flavor. I coughed as I sat the glass down, giving myself time before taking another sip. At least it would help me forget my troubles, and eventually get me to go to sleep. Maybe thinking of wedding my dear Alice and starting our future pub, somewhere far from this drab inn would help as well.

"Captain, are we leaving this godforsaken place tomorrow?" Michael questioned. He was a tall man with brown hair and one of the skinniest men I knew. His ability to remain thin throughout this entire war campaign never ceased to perplex both me and the other men. He rather looked like a hay-man sometimes, but I never said that to him. He was a nice man, religious enough and always kind to his comrades. My men all murmured in agreement, wanting to know when they could finally make it back home soon, before they were the shadowy murderer's next victim of choice.

I nodded as I took another sip of the scotch. "Yes, I plan to head out in the morning. Although none of us feel like sleeping, we probably should rest up for the journey ahead of us."

"What about Ralph?" Kenneth questioned. The rest of them looked at me, as if they all had been wondering the same thing. They should have known we were going to take his body back with us, but I presume they were wondering how.

"Luckily, the McGregorys have a large wooden box we can place him in until we find him a better coffin," I sighed. I promised myself that we hopefully wouldn't have any need of bringing back any bodies, yet here I was, doing just that. "We will have to unload some supplies, but it shouldn't be an issue. We will be home in no time."

"If we leave tomorrow, why we then won't ever solve the mystery behind who killed Ralph?" George asked as he munched on another scone. I thought we had completely ran out of them by now.

"His body will be examined more thoroughly once we reach London. There, they might be able to figure out the cause of death. As for now, we have no idea what could have happened. For all we know, it could have been an accident and we don't want to waste any more days here, figuring out one way or the other," I explained. I knew George was thinking about the strange goat tracks we had found, but it still wasn't enough evidence to narrow down who or what may have killed Ralph. It was probably just pure coincidence.

I got up from the wooden chair and stood next to the fire, watching the flames dance around. "I do want us to partner up tonight for sleeping arrangements, just to be safe. I already had beds moved around in order to do so, so everyone pick a partner."

Everyone partnered up, no one seemed to have a problem finding a partner, and we determined who would stay where. The men stumbled around, having drunk more than their body weight's worth of alcohol for most of the day, but it was all organized in the end. I rolled my eyes as Kenneth fell to the ground. He really needed to learn how to hold his liquor, but he was still young. He shouldn't have to be drinking his sorrows away like this. He wasn't the only one, though, for both Michael and Jonathan also almost fell as they went down the hall to move towards their rooms to gather their things, and move into their newly assigned room. I wondered if this was what a foretaste of how things would be every night when owning a pub, men stumbling around and having great difficult with finding their way back to their rooms. Recalling most of the pubs I had been to, it was going to be very similar to the environment of this inn, maybe with just a little more activity.

After everything was situated, everyone came back to finish up their drinks, which they really didn't need. We were all quiet as we stared at the fire's burning embers in the main room of the inn. Each of us had lost a great friend in a very tragic, unforeseen event, and no one wanted to talk about it aloud, adding to the heavy burden of our shared sorrow. We thought we had suffered enough and that it would be free sailing back home.

My eyelids began to feel heavy, causing my blinks to become longer and more frequent. I stood up and drank the last of my scotch. There was a special place in hell for people who didn't finish their scotch, and I wasn't going to join them. I set the glass down. "Well boys, it seems I have reached my limit. I bid you all a good night."

I motioned George to join me, who seemed tired as well, and a few other men retired to their assigned rooms as well. They were wobbling still, after all the alcohol they consumed, as they groped their way in the dark hallways towards their rooms. I was surprised none of them fell all the way down.

As I laid down in my bed, I could still hear a few murmurs in the common room as others decided it was late enough. George was out the moment his head hit his pillow, snoring louder than the wind howling outside. I had definitely picked the wrong sleeping buddy, and I should have remembered back a few weeks ago when we shared a tent that he was a snorer. I hit him with my pillow to stop and he rolled over, causing the noise not to be so loud.

Going back to my bed, I stared up at the ceiling. This time tomorrow, we would be on our way home. We would be out of these Highlands, meaning, we wouldn't have to face whatever was out there any longer. No more strange creatures, no more strange women outside in the storms. We would be safe and I would be with my Alice. My dear Alice.

I let my eyes close and my mind drift into the dream world.

But I swore I heard someone calling my name as I dozed off.

I woke up to shouts coming from down the hall. Quickly, George and I got up and hurried out of the door to find the bodies of Percy and Kenneth being pulled out through the doorway, leading out into the cold, nightmarish world of the Highlands. A menacing, cool breeze whipped through from the open-door, bringing shivers down my spine. Both of the men's corpses looked the same as Ralph's own corpse when we discovered him; they were both pale white with a cut through their throat.

Not only did I note the same appearance as Ralph, I also noted that each of them had their pistols strapped to their sides. They were clearly armed, yet whatever had murdered them had given them no time to even honorably defend themselves or have some kind of heroic fight to the death. They were soldiers, after all, they knew how to fight.

I just couldn't believe it. Two more men lost to whatever it was. I couldn't believe it, more death even after everything we had been through. All I wanted was to go home, to get away from this mess, but it didn't seem that good fortune was in store for me.

"Did anyone see anything?" I demanded as I looked back and forth at my men, who all looked scared out-of-their-wits. Everyone shook their heads in an uncertain manner.

"They were the last ones up," Andrew explained. "Thomas and I retired around two."

"Where did you find them?" I asked, not believing this could happen again, even with both of them.

"The same place as you found Ralph," Andrew said. "Except this time, we also found evidence of a fire having been burnt out there. Some charred wood pieces in the dirt."

I raised an eyebrow. "A fire?"

"Like a camp fire, yes."

That was impossible, unless the men themselves had made it. Even then, the wind was so strong last night that there was no way a fire could even be started outdoors, not to mention the dampness of everything out there. For the last few nights, it had been raining off and on, which was typical weather for Scotland. What would have possessed them to do such a thing? Especially, when there was a fire inside the inn where it was warm and not dark.

I grabbed my coat and pulled on my shoes. "Show me."

Yes, this was the remnants of a fire.

I bent down and took a closer look at the charcoal. I touched it, the black staining my fingers a bit. It was still warm, even though sprinkles of rain had been pouring down on it. What could all this mean? I wiped the black charcoal dust off on my pants.

"Everyone else was accounted for?" I asked as I stood back up. I wasn't getting much from the fire pit. In fact, it was confusing me even more.

Jonathan nodded. "Yes. I'm thinking we should still head out of the highlands today Captain. I don't think we should risk another night here, even if we want to solve this mystery before us. It may be completely out of our hands."

As much as it hurt to leave whatever had been killing my men out in these parts, I knew he was right. There was no way I would risk staying another night out her, especially with the added risk that more men would be killed. It was suicide. I felt as if we were betraying the three that died though, not getting revenge on whatever had killed them. But when we had no idea what exactly was causing all these problems, it was a little hard to exact revenge on the murderers of three of my own fellow soldiers.

Even though some of us didn't get along with Percy, being part of a unit was like being family. I cared about these men and something was taking their lives. Poor Kenneth and Ralph, they were both so young. They didn't deserve to die like this, not after having fought in such a battle. *What monster could have done such a thing?*

I rubbed my scruff on my chin, knowing we had only one choice and that was to leave this place. "I agree. Tell the men to ready their things. We leave before noon. I will speak to the McGregorys about our plans."

"Yes sir."

"We are again sorry to hear about your men. Do you have any idea what would possess them to leave the inn at such a dreadful hour?" Duncan asked. I had found him in the inn, preparing for the day, and told him about what had happened.

"That, I do not know. Whatever it was, it had to have been the same reason Ralph went out there as well. Unfortunately we may never know the cause of it. My men and I have decided to take our leave this day. We don't need anyone else dying from mysterious circumstances," I explained.

Duncan nodded. "I understand, but do note that a storm is making its way through the Highlands late today. You must leave before it arrives, or I fear you won't make it to the other end of the Highlands tonight."

I looked out at the clouds that were beginning to darken. "We are well aware of this storm. We plan to..."

"Just let me know if you need any other assistance. Me and my workers are at your disposal."

"Thank you, we may need help getting the horses ready, if that is alright with you."

"It is no problem, I will send out a couple of people at once."

My men prepared the horses with help of Duncan's men, we were soon on our way down the Highlands in no time. We had to place Kenneth, Ralph, and Percy's bodies all on one of the carts and leave some of the stuff that was on their behind. Michael and Jonathan volunteered to leave a lot of their things behind, along with smaller items that we didn't need. Everyone was silent as we placed the bodies on the cart and covered them up with some old blankets that Duncan gave us. Once everything else was safely packed and tucked away, we started down towards the bottom of the hills, and we would finally be out of the hardest part of the journey.

The wind had begun to pick up and a shrill howl echoed through the hills, sounding like the banshee I swore I heard on the first day of traveling through the area. The more time I spent here, the more I understood the reason Scottish people normally had a great, superstitious fear that supernatural creatures were thought to dwell in these parts. I was surprised that Duncan hadn't said something about supernatural beings in these parts, not that I would have believed him. Even with the foreboding feeling that the place gives off, I don't think I could come to terms with actually believing in such things. I understood how the legends came to be, yes, but truly believing in them was something I didn't think I could do. Although, whether or not they were real didn't really matter, given the strange state that all three men were found. As long as they were real in the mind, they could do the same amount of damage to one's soul.

The sound of a storm strengthening, made the horses restless, who seemed apprehensive about heading forward. It took all my strength and will to get my horse to not panic and run off. I had to keep petting her, reassuring her that everything would be alright with me guiding her through the gloomy, open area of the Highlands. Glancing back, I discovered that all my men look panicked as we kept moving forward.

"It's alright, men! It is just the wind!" I yelled back, even though I doubted they could hear me. By glancing at George and Michael's tense faces, I didn't think they did. They look afraid, and Michael wasn't one who got afraid often.

Even I somehow didn't believe what I had said. There was something haunting about these Highlands, and I wanted to get out of here as soon as we could. So, I kept pushing us forward without any slowing of our pace.

It wasn't long before the storm grew even more colossal, giant clashes of thunder began deafening our eardrums with streaks of lightning blinding our eyes. I could barely breathe, once raindrops began to falling from the darkened skies. I choked on some water as I opened my mouth for air. The rain fell harder now, and we could barely see in front of us. We weren't lost, at least not yet anyway, but if this low visibility kept up, it was a good possibility we could be stranded somewhere, at least until the storm stopped. And who knew when it would come to a halt?

We kept pushing through the chilly weather, but our earnest efforts of making it out of the highlands seemed to be in vain. The wind kept throwing us back and the road itself began to wash away. We were wet and miserable and the horses were suffering through the mud. This was almost worse than a war, being trapped between this hellish terrain and the ideal safety of our homes back in England. It played at my mind, making me want to just give up. But I couldn't, I had to be strong for not only my men, but Alice as well. I couldn't let her marry a weakling. I couldn't let her down.

I had to make a decision. I either had to keep my men's morale up, so they would keep pushing through this storm, or I had to turn them around and guide them miserably back to the inn. If we moved forward, we risked getting lost and dying in this storm. If we turned back, I risked losing some more of my men to whatever was haunting this place. In some ways, a part of me had the vaguest desire, though, to seek out the evil that killed three of my men, including Ralph, and take revenge on it. Whatever it was had killed the two youngest men in my group and I would never forgive them for that.

After much debate, I decided we should turn back. It was the lesser of two evils.

Even though the place had to have been haunted by some demonic spirit, I knew it was the safest thing to do. There was nowhere we could go in this storm other than back towards that inn. My men knew that, so we turned the horses back and started for the inn.

That's when I saw her again, on one of the hills. It was just for an instant, her white dress bright when the lightning flashed. Her white eyes stared at me as she seemed to be calling me back into the middle of the Highlands. To her home.

I took a deep breath and told myself it was just an illusion.

The McGregorys had been expecting us back when they saw the storm come in and worsen with time. They had a fire ready in the common room to dry our clothes, just as they did the first night. I asked for Duncan to bring out mattresses for all of us to stay together in the common area. He didn't question it and did as I had asked. I had my men put away their things, but explained that we would all be bunking together that night. They all agreed to it, not wanting to be alone for the night, not after what had happened the past two nights.

Duncan brought out a bottle of scotch, on the house, and my men and I finished it quickly. We didn't want to be back in this godforsaken place, not when we feared what could be coming for any of us. I bought another bottle of scotch and poured a generous amount into my glass. Based on the eagerness of the men to share in the alcoholic bounty with no restrictions, none of us seemed to want to be sober for the night that was to come. It also helped us to feel warm, something that was hard to do in such a retched place.

Darkness came eventually, but the storm did not let up. Flashes of lightning lit up the common room as we each shivered at the thought of the monster waiting for us outside. None of us seemed to want to sleep, even after riding and walking for so many wasted hours. We just wanted daylight to come so that we could get out of here, as quickly and safely as possible.

An hour passed, each of us continued taking turns cradling the second bottle of whiskey. We kept the fire burning, Duncan bringing us a good chunk of dry wood to keep it going through the night. I didn't think any of us were going to sleep that night, even though we should have gotten rest so we could travel the next day. Unfortunately, that was not going to happen. Sleep was an elusive thing to find, in the heart of highlands, especially during a storm.

Soon enough, it was near three in the morning, which some called the witching hour. I had to agree with that name, especially when that strangely beautiful, though maleficent voice of the ghostly woman made a reappearance. Her voice was melodious, just like that of a siren. I heard it call my name. I glanced around to find all the other men also looking around, with undisguised fear and incredulity

"What is that?" George questioned.

"It's her..." I whispered

She kept calling us, her voice hypnotic, though slightly disturbing.. I tried to keep from falling under the creature's spell again, but it was no use. She was stronger than me and I watched as all my men stood up, blank-faced, and headed towards the door. None of us could stop ourselves from leaving the inn, and heading outside towards her voice

Out in the middle of the unrelenting storm, she stood in the front of a large, blazing fire. I didn't know how the fire kept going in the storm, but my eyes weren't lying to me. No, I knew the truth this time and knew that other people could see her. There *was* a fire and this woman, this creature, *was* standing by it.

She called us forward with her long sharp fingers, inviting us to join her as she danced around gracefully, wearing a ghostly white dress. Her skin was pale as was her hair. She almost appeared as an angel, if her eyes didn't have such evil behind them. In my life, I had never seen a more beautiful dance, one so lovely and appearing to follow the chords from the unheard music of the night. My mind shouted at me to stop, to not give into the temptation of going out there and joining her. That was all I ever seemed to want for my life, to dance with that creature and forget all that had happened over the past few months, fighting these senseless battles.

"Henry..."

She sounded like Alice. I felt as if my heart had skipped a beat. *My dear Alice.* I blinked, my mind bringing me out of this illusion to see the truth. *That creature tried to sound like Alice in hopes I would follow her out there.* It hadn't done that before, it must have been resorting to more drastic measures, knowing I could now resist it. It was wrong, though, it couldn't trick me that way, and she was not my Alice. My Alice would never hurt me and I had to fight this fiend to be with her. I couldn't let it trick me, not when freedom with Alice and war itself felt so close, almost at arm's length.

I turned to find that my men appeared to be as lured into the siren's song as I was, they all stared at her, glassy eyed and not letting anything get in the way from joining her in her dance of death. I had to stop them before they went outside into her terrain. "Men! Wake up!" I shouted. "That creature is what killed the others, we must not go out there!"

They didn't listen, as they started out the door towards the creature in the long white dress, Their attention was focused only on the alluring woman, while she motioned for them with her long claw-like hands to come join her. I tried to pull them back in, but there were too many of them and they were each too determined to go to this siren. I grabbed at their coats but it was no use. George, Andrew, Thomas, and Michael refused to budge, or listen to reason.

"Stop!" I pulled back the last person that tried to go through the door, Jonathan. I got him to fall back. He blinked and then looked up at me.

"Captain?"

I let out a sigh of relief. "Thank goodness I was able to knock some sense into at least one of you," I brought him in and quickly shut the door. The rest were long gone, already making their way up the hill towards the dancing creature. There was no way I could bring them back now. My heart felt like it had sunk into my stomach for leaving them out there, but there wasn't really anything I could do. I tried to come up with a plan, anything, but I didn't even know what I was up against. I had tried to snap them out of it as the creature called them, but they wouldn't budge. Only Jonathan had responded and I had to make sure he didn't fall for her song again.

"What is that... that *thing*?" Jonathan asked, looking out the window in disgust.

"I don't know," I stared at the window at the creature, watching as my men walked up to her. "I don't know."

"They are called the baobhan sith."

Both Jonathan and I quickly turned around to find Duncan standing there. He looked out the window with us, his eyes tired and weary.

I grabbed him by the collar. "Why didn't you say anything?! I could have saved them! This is your fault!"

"Would you have believed me?" he choked out. I thought about his answer for a second then let him go. No, I probably wouldn't have, even though I had seen her as well. I thought my eyes were just playing tricks, I guess I was wrong.

Duncan rubbed his throat. "You saw her earlier, didn't you? You are the one who didn't say anything either. Besides, it wouldn't have mattered. They would have come for you either way."

I rubbed my face, regretting my decision ten-fold. I could have stopped this a lot sooner if I knew she were real. "I didn't think she was real. I just thought she was some kind of siren."

"That is indeed close. She calls men in the night to come dance with her, then she drinks their blood and souls when they are too weak to defend themselves," he explained as if he had witnessed it time and time again.

It sounded like a ghost story, some fable. I shook my head as I watched as she comforted my men, making them feel safe before their deaths came. *How was she keeping them under the thrall of her terrifying powers? How many had she killed previously? How many innocent lives were taken by that beast?* It couldn't be real, none of this could have been real. Creatures like this just didn't exist in the real world, they were all myths and legends, nothing to be taken seriously.

At least, that's what I had always thought.

"Why?" I asked as I turned to Duncan. "Why do they do this?"

Duncan shrugged. "That is just the story of the baobhan sith."

Jonathan watched the men in horror as well, his eyes moving back and forth rapidly. "Why aren't you affected by her call? Why was it just us?"

"That's a long story."

I placed my hand on his shoulder, in a threatening demeanor. "Well, it looks like we have all night, so tell us."

He let out a sigh. "My brother and father were both killed by those creatures when I was younger. They spared my life and had me promise not to tell a soul what had happened, or that they even existed. I also had to stay at the inn and let them take whoever they please if need be."

I grabbed him by the collar again and slammed him against the wall. I didn't want to put up with his selfishness. "So you just make sure they are fed. You kill your own kind to save your own skin. That is why you didn't tell us or warn us. You didn't want them coming for you instead. So you kept your mouth shut. It is because of you that they are dead!"

He shook his head. "No, they rarely come. I haven't seen them in years. They travel throughout the Highlands. They don't come here often."

"But when they do, you just sit back and let them take what they want! Then you just clean up the rest once they are done killing people!" I exclaimed.

"What choice did I have? They would kill my wife and I if I did anything to betray them. Do you have a wife or someone you love, Captain? Because if you do, then you know you would do the same as I to protect her."

His words resonated in my mind. Yes, I would have done the same for my Alice. She meant the world to me. With the thoughts of what evil I would do to ensure her safety, I let him go and he coughed a bit as I had put pressure against his windpipe.

I looked back out at my men. They danced around the fire, the woman making them follow her. "What about the other men in the Royal Army? Were any of them killed?"

"No, they didn't come until you showed up."

I looked back outside to find my men dancing and laughing in the storm with that creature. "Why do you keep saying 'they'? There is only the one."

"No, there are four of them," he whispered.

I watched as two more of the creatures came down from the hill, scaling the rocks as if they were no problem. Part of their long medieval dress drew up from their leg and I could see their legs being that of a goat's leg. I covered my mouth. Those were the same hoofed feet that left footprints, near Ralph's corpse, when we discovered him that morning. They had hooves so they could scale the rocks faster. It all made sense now.

"Oh, dear Lord," I said aloud.

But that only accounted for three of them. There was still one more creature out there that I did not see. *Where was she?*

I turned around to look out the other window to find her staring in at us. Her eyes were bright, almost all white like that of a blind person's eyes. Her dress was like that of a bride's, all white and pure, even with the rain coming down. It was how I imagined Alice to be in her dress when we would wed. Her hair was a golden blonde, like that of a wheat field. I had never seen anything so beautiful. I wanted to look away, to not make eye contact with her, but I couldn't stop myself.

"Henry..." I heard her call.

"Can they get in?" I questioned as I stopped Jonathan from going outside again. He wasn't as strong as I was, or at least not as determined, which made it harder for this creature to lull me into her trap. The difference probably being my hope to go home to Alice. He didn't have a love awaiting him at home, at least not one that I knew of. Love was the most powerful weapon against these beings. It had to be.

Duncan shook his head. "I haven't the faintest idea. Usually they get men to come out to them. No one has resisted their call before, until you showed up here."

"Lucky for me then that I have an angel waiting for me back home," I muttered. "Jonathan, grab any spare guns you can find. We are going to end this once and for all."

"You can't kill them," Duncan said as we started down the hallway.

I turned to him. "Excuse me?"

"Guns don't work on them. I've seen men try before."

My heart dropped. If that were true, then we were ruined. That was all I needed to hear. "Then how do we kill them?"

"You don't."

That's when the screaming began. The screams carried through the Highlands as the beasts began to attack my men. One by one, the creatures grabbed each of my men, slicing each of their throats open with their claws and slowly indulged in drinking their blood. First George, then Andrew, Thomas, and then Michael. They all screamed as the creatures licked at the red liquid that was pouring out of each of them. It was so revolting that I almost threw up. It took everything in my power not to.

"Henry..." the one woman at the window whispered. I looked at her, her light eyes staring straight back at me. The rain didn't seem to stick to her for her hair was as beautiful as ever. It appeared silky soft and I could only imagine what it smelled like. A longing made me want to know. I shook the thoughts out of my head. I only needed Alice and the sweet memory of her scent. I didn't need these creatures trying to trick me.

While being distracted by her alluring gaze, I didn't see Jonathan had gone out the door and into the death trap. The door clattered shut, as the wind-sheared rains pelted the door, sounding like the awful din of the battlefields I had fought in far too many battles way too many times. The screams, the rain, and this soft, comforting voice, promising to take it all away, were threatening to make me forget the task at hand. Bringing my men home safely.

"Jonathan!" I called out the door, fighting to keep it open against the wind. I turned to Duncan. "Why didn't you do anything?"

"I..." he began. I punched him in the jaw before he could answer. I didn't need to hear his lies. He fell down to the ground, his lip bloody. It was the least I could do to punish his silence, which had brought this living nightmare upon my comrades and I.

I grabbed my pistol. "If I make it out of this alive, I'm coming back for you."

"Don't go out there! If you want to live, don't go out there!" he called after me, but I ignored him. I had to help Jonathan, I had to at least save one of my men.

The storm had gotten stronger. I tried to shield the water from my eyes, but nothing seemed to help. Water pelted me, obscuring my sight, and prevented me from seeing where I needed to go. I coughed up the water as the rain got into my both mouth and nostrils, creating a sensation of suffocating. Of course, I might also be panicking about whether or not I'd be able to rescue Jonathan in time.

"Jonathan!" I called out, but there was no response. I kept moving forward, towards where the fire had been. I could see it now in the distance, still burning as it remained undisturbed by the sheet of rain pouring down on it. What magic was being used to create this kind of unnatural effect? I had no idea, it probably had something to do with the baobhan sith, though, and their mysterious, otherworldly abilities.

Mud had begun to accumulate more and more as the rain came down, softening the terrain and making it almost impossible to travel on. I slipped, falling to my knees, the mud covering my new clothes in the brown, sticky substance. I cursed at this night and this land. I just wanted to go home: was that too much to ask?

Gathering my strength, I pulled myself up and started climbing the hill towards the fire. I had to get there in time to save Jonathan. I could see a figure near the fire, it had to have been him.

Lightning crashed into the hillside and I could hear the eerie laughter of the baobhan sith in the near distance. Their laughter sounded hysterical, like an inhuman cackle produced only by some legion of mad beings. Only things from hell could make such a sound like that. It sent a cold shiver down my spine, but I kept pressing forward, knowing I couldn't turn back at this point. There was only moving forward into what seemed like the pits of hell itself.

I reached the fire, but saw no sign of the baobhan sith as they had retreated back into the fog. I peered around to find my men lying motionlessly around the fire, each of them as white as ghosts. I felt like stopping and sobbing for all of them, for not being a good leader, but I couldn't. I had to find Jonathan. I could have sworn he was here.

"Henry..."

I turned to find the female creature standing directly behind me, the same one who had deceived me with the voice of my betrothed. She had Jonathan's prone form in her arms, drinking the blood out of a gash on his throat until his skin was as white as her dress. Dropping him, she let him collapse to the ground with the rest of the dead bodies of my men. I stared at him, petrified that I had been too late.

He didn't move, for he was just a lifeless body now. His soul had gone off to another place, as did the rest of my men. Why did these creatures played with life like this? I didn't know. It was inhuman, evil. It made no sense and I wished to destroy them all, showing them what it was like to be on the other edge of the sword.

I should have run for my life at that point, but I didn't move an inch due to fear trapping me in this spot. I didn't want to die, not when Alice waited for me back at home, but I couldn't look away. The creature's beauty was astonishing and the fear she caused was even more powerful and beguiling.

She stepped closer and placed her hand on my chest. Her hand brought on a warmness that almost made me calm, but the thought of everything going on kept me from submitting to her completely. She leaned in closer. "What are you holding onto, dear Henry? How are you fighting this?"

Her voice wasn't as melodious as it was before, but more normal as a human's voice would have been. It caught me off guard for a moment before I was able to speak coherently.

"Because... Because I have someone waiting for me in Nottingham. I can't let her down. I survived this war, and I can finally be with her. Nothing will stop me from being with the one I love."

The creature leaned in closer, her mouth only inches from mine. Her claws dug into my chest, but they didn't break the skin. "But I could give you so much more pleasure."

She brought her lips to mine, but I pushed back. "No, I can't."

She let out a laugh. "You are a strong one, aren't you?" she brought her finger to my cheek, and gently sliced along it with her nail. I tried not to flinch from the bite of pain. "Not many can resist me, Henry."

"How do you know my name?" I asked. If this was going to be my last moment of being alive, I wanted to know the truth as to how they did all of this.

"It's simple, I can read all of your thoughts," she brought her bloody nail to her mouth and licked it. "Every last one of them."

They could read minds. I couldn't believe that was how they were so successful. They could say exactly what we wanted to hear to get us to submit to them. They were powerful, more powerful than anything I had ever known in my life.

I knelt down to my knees and looked up at the darkened sky, drops of rain falling on every inch of my face. It ran through my hair, then it dripped onto the wet, muddy ground beneath my trembling feet. I could barely see her, the fire, or my comrade's motionless bodies. But it didn't matter, this was going to be my last moment anyways. I didn't need to see with my own eyes what was going to happen to me, I just needed to accept it with resignation. "What are you going to do with me?"

She laughed gently, unlike the laughs I had heard earlier sounding like ones from Satan and his minions. "You really do love her, don't you Henry? Your dear Alice?" she asked tauntingly.

I wondered where she was going with this, and why she even cared, being the evil creature that she was. At least I knew Alice would be safe since these creatures only stayed in the Highlands and Alice would never come up here to find me. "I love her more than words could ever describe."

The baobhan sith smiled. "Well then, I'm going to give you exactly what you want, Henry," she gently placed her fingers on my eyelids, making me close them. "Just don't resist any of it."

She dug her nails into my throat. I gasped in pain, thinking that this was the end. But instead, it felt like more energy was being pushed into my body, more power in a sense. This wasn't how I thought death would feel, I imagined something a bit more energy-draining than this. Darkness started to overcome me and the last thing I remembered was the cackling laugh of the baobhan sith.

When I opened my eyes, all I saw was light. I panicked for a moment, believing temporarily that I had found myself in the afterlife. I blinked a few times, my eyes trying to adjust to the light. It didn't seem like my eyes could adjust themselves to the light. Pain burned them. After I moment, I found that I wasn't in the afterlife, but rather in some kind of room. A medical bay.

I was no longer in the Highlands. What had happened?

"Henry?" a voice called. It sent shivers down my spine. Those creatures. I couldn't get away from them. How could they have followed me? I started to panic when I felt a hand rest on my cheek.

My eyes adjusted a little better to the light coming from the window and I looked up to find my fiancé standing there, her hand gently stroking my cheek.

My Alice.

"Oh, Henry," she wrapped her arms around me. Happiness rushed through my veins. I took in a deep breath of her scent. She always smelt of raspberries and... something different, something strange I never noticed before. It smelled sweet and refreshing. The scent was oddly... satisfying.

I had no idea what this new smell was, but it made me feel complete. I was so glad to see her safe and sound. After all this time, after all the pain I had endured, I could finally be with her. I could finally enjoy the sight of her face.

She released her embrace and I took a look around. I had no idea where I was but found other cots piled around with wounded people. *Was I back home?*

"They said they didn't know when you would wake up. You had a concussion and had lost a lot of blood. You are the only one who survived."

I tried to take in what she was saying. "Survived?"

She combed her finger through my hair. "Oh, dear. You don't remember do you? Some rogue Highlanders attacked you and your men while at the inn. You are the only one who made it out alive. They rushed you to a hospital and worked on you in Glasgow and moved you here in Nottingham. You have been asleep for over a week."

An attack? I didn't recall any of that, I remembered something completely different. I remembered a storm, and those creatures. They tore up my men and drank their blood. I had witnessed it, at least I thought I had. I rubbed my head. Maybe she was right, maybe there was an attack. Everything seemed so fuzzy, but I could imagine those creatures perfectly, especially the one who called my name.

Was it all just a dream?

She embraced me again, while I was lost in my thoughts. "I was so worried, I'm so happy you are awake."

I held her tight. I didn't want to let her go of her ever again. I had lost so many people, my entire group had been killed. I wanted to forget them, I just wanted her at my side and forget all of this. I tried not to think of my men, I swore that they had died a different way, I swore a creature attacked us. But Alice wouldn't lie, maybe a rouge group did attack us. It did seem possible.

Once I wedded her and we had our pub, there would be no necessity to return to the battlefield. I wouldn't have to deal with death any longer. Whether it were creatures or men that had attacked me, I knew one thing for certain. I didn't want to wait for life any longer.

"Marry me, Alice."

She pulled back and stared at me, confused. "We already planned on it, Henry, don't you remember? We are going to have a summer wedding and..."

I shook my head. We had been planning the wedding already, but I didn't want to wait until summer to be married to her If anything, I needed to escape my haunting past. "No, marry me now. I don't want to spend another day without you. I am retiring from the Royal Army, we can start up the pub, just you and me. We can have a celebration later, but right now I just want you. Let's elope."

Alice stared at me, her eyes sparkling. Coming from a poor broken family, the thought of marriage always brought a smile to her face. She didn't want me to leave for battle, in fear that our love would be all for nothing. Now that I was back, there was nothing stopping us. Finally, she nodded her head. "Yes, Henry, let's do it! Let's get married!"

I pulled her in and kissed her hard, her lips tasting of cinnamon and sugar. If I could, I would kiss her at every moment of the day. I had missed her sweet lips for so long.

She moved back and smiled. I stroked the side of her cheek. "Now go find someone to discharge me from this hospital. Then we can go find a priest."

"Are you sure you are up for it? You were badly injured when they brought you in," she fretted, concerned about my personal welfare.

I grinned. "I feel fine now that I am with you. There is nothing to worry about, the doctors will check to make sure I am fine. Now go get them."

She nodded and did just that. The doctors checked me out to make sure I was fine before being released. To their surprise, I had healed just fine and more quickly than they had thought. I figured it was the power of love, not focusing on the strange sensation that was settling in my gut. There was pain there, even though the doctors had given me something to eat. I ignored it though, figuring it was just my nerves acting in advance of the marriage that was about to happen. The doctors dismissed me from their care, still curious as to how I had regained my strength back so fast when I had been asleep for over a week. I told them that nothing would hold me back from getting married that day.

But something in the back of my mind was telling me something different. Something told me that I had changed that night on the Highlands, but I just couldn't figure out how.

Alice and I ran to the nearest church and demanded the priest at the church to marry us that day. It was a small little church that I had been to once or twice in one of the corners of Nottingham. At the time, the church was unoccupied by any parishioners, which we were both happy for. We didn't want to have to wait until some other marriage or solemn occasion happening there that day was finished, before we got married as soon as humanly possible.

To be honest, I was a little afraid to get married. It was a big commitment after all, but it was one I was willing to take. I loved Alice with all my heart and nothing would change that. I wanted to be with her for the rest of my life. I wanted to forget everything that transpired before this moment, I wanted a new life with her, erasing everything else.

After some convincing, the priest did marry us. I told him my tale of fighting throughout the war and escaping death more than once. Given the circumstances now, marrying my beautiful Alice would be the best way to escape the past, and create a new life for the both of us. He agreed it to be a good reason to marry and, after the ceremony, I swept Alice back to my flat just down the street above a little shop, common housing in this part of the city. It wasn't just my home any longer—it was our home.

Walking through the threshold of my flat, I carried Alice and placed her on my bed. We were both ready for this, wanting to become one flesh again. Although we had gone to bed with each before I left, this was different. This felt more official.

I kissed her gently on the mouth. She tasted sweet, satisfying even. I wanted this so bad, dreaming of it the entire time I was away. I climbed on top of her, adjusting my hips between her legs. My lips moved down her cheek and then onto her neck.

Something entranced me as I brought my lips onto her neck. An internal feeling, a longing. It felt like a hunger, like I needed it to survive. The pain in my stomach grew stronger and stronger.

I bit down.

"Ow!" she exclaimed. "Henry, why did you bite me?"

I blinked, realizing what I had done. What had possessed me to do such a thing? It wasn't something I would ever dream of doing. "I'm sorry dearest," I looked into her eyes. "I didn't realize what I was doing, Alice. I just..."

Her eyes were glossy, as if in a trance.

Just like the men's eyes were on the Highlands, after those damnable creatures put them under their spell.

I gulped. "Alice?" How could have I done this, and why was this happening? It didn't make sense.

Unless something happened to me that I didn't remember. I recalled something cutting my throat. I felt my skin. There was no wound, so what had happened?

Alice didn't say a word as her eyes glossed over and she became entranced with me, not refusing any of my movements. I was about to ask what was wrong again when I glanced back down at her neck. I could feel her pulse, smell the sweet scent coming off her. Something in the back of my mind was beckoning me, something was drawing me to bring my hand to her neck. I traced my finger against her throat, feeling the blood pounding with every beat of her heart. It was pleasing, it was satisfying, as if this was what I had been longing to do since I had opened my eyes, before our impromptu wedding plans. Her skin was soft. I kissed her once more with my lips. I couldn't breathe, the haunting feeling drawing every last breath. I stroked her throat with my thumb once more as she didn't move, seeming to be put in a trance by the sound of my voice.

Then I dug my nail into her skin.

Blood came dripping out of her throat and I brought my lips to it. Alice didn't move nor scream as I drank the sweet nectar coming out of her veins. It tasted better than anything I had ever consumed. It was more intoxicating than any scotch, sweeter than any ripe fruit I had ever had. I let it take complete control over me. I didn't want it to ever end. The pain in my stomach subsided, as if this is what it had been longing for the entire time. For blood.

But something in the back of my head repeated the word: Alice.

I jumped back, blinking, coming out of the trance that I had put myself in. What was I doing? What had I done? She was my love, she was my life. I looked down at Alice. Her skin was white.

I shook her. "Alice, Alice, wake up!"

She didn't move. I shook her again but I knew she appeared white as ghost, just as Ralph and the others appeared on that horrifying day back in the Highlands, the day I wanted to forget.

She was gone. I couldn't comprehend what had happened. It was just like what those creatures of the night, back in the highlands, had done to all my men.

But this time it was me.

I laid my head down on her soft, motionless body, tears falling down from my eyes without cessation. I was shaking uncontrollably, not understanding how I could do such a thing to the woman I loved. *They* had done this to her, it was *their* fault. *They* had done this to me. I wanted my Alice back, but I knew that wasn't possible. All I wanted now was revenge, revenge for what I had done to her.

I had to get answers. I had to get away and get revenge. There was only one place I could go.

Back to the Highlands.

It took days to get back to the Highlands. I had to jump from town to town in the night, not being able to stay out in the day. The sun burnt my skin, after I had taken more blood into my system, even if the clouds hid the sun away on any given day. I stayed in inns along the way, hoping no one would take notice that I traveled out during the night instead of the day. Nothing stood out about this time, at least not that I recall. I took the blood of innocent lives on the way. Every time I drank their blood, I remembered Alice lying there, staring at me with lifeless eyes. I couldn't even think about it without driving myself insane.

As I made it to the Highlands, it was raining, as usual. I didn't know this place unless it was cold and dreary. I came upon the hills and I could hear her calling me.

"Henry..."

The voice of the devil, as I now considered her. I looked all around, but I didn't see any trace of her. I screamed out, my voice echoing through the valley. "What have you done to me?!"

She appeared in front of me, slowly caressing my face with her hand. She was as silent and beautiful as ever. I hated her beauty with a passion. I wanted to destroy it, slash her, and make something imperfect out of this seemingly perfect monstrosity. But I couldn't move, she still had a hypnotic effect on me.

She smiled. "I gave you exactly what you wanted."

I shook my head. "No, I didn't want this! You made me into a monster! You made me..." I placed a hand over my mouth and collapsed to my knees, the tears falling from my eyes quickly disappeared in the rain. I had killed her with my own hands. Nothing could make the pain go away.

My sweet Alice, what had I done?

"It was up to you who to kill, it was you who couldn't control it," she whispered in my ear. "You didn't want to live with her, you didn't want to be with her forever."

"Yes I did!" I shouted back at her. "I wanted to have a family with her! I wanted to grow old with her! To be with her forever!" I could barely choke out the rest of the sentence. "Now she's gone."

"If that were the case," she lifted my chin to look at her. Her eyes were like diamonds, glistening in moonlight. I hated their eyes so much, their beauty hiding the hideousness that was inside. "You wouldn't have killed her. You would have brought her here, knowing I could make her into the same type of creature as you, as us, and you two could have lived forever."

I stared at her. She was right, I couldn't help myself. I wanted to drink her blood so badly. My face collapsed in my hands. It was all me. My hunger. My thirst. My desire. Nothing would change that fact. Nothing could change the fact that I had killed her, not the lady I saw before me. It hit me like a wall, a wall that destroyed every emotion in my body, every caring feeling for humans. The only pain I felt was her death, which would haunt me for the rest of eternity.

"Now you are stuck living an eternity without her, because you couldn't control yourself. You should have put it together, Henry, you should have made her into what you are," she scratched my cheek and licked the blood off her finger. "Then we all could have lived happily ever after."

I shook my head. "I would never do this to her, I would never go to these lengths."

"Then you must not have loved her like you say you do. If you loved her, you would have made it so you would always be with her till the end of time."

"No, love is about putting your loved one's life above your own. I would have never done this to her without her permission, that isn't what love is about."

"To put one's life above your own is ridiculous. You won't survive out here if you live like that. And believe me, after time passes, you will begin to think the same," she let out a little laugh and disappeared into the fog.

That's what it was like, talking with these creatures. Being with these creatures. They made you realize your deepest and darkest desires. They made you do things that you never thought you would do. And why? Just to pass the time. They didn't care about who they hurt, they didn't care about who they played with. It was all just a game.

Now, as I walk the nights through Nottingham, I watch as couples look up at the stars, giving them a moment of bliss before I take away from them what was taken away from me. Their love would never last anyway, I was doing them a favor. It wouldn't work, something always would get in the way and they would get hurt. I was just ending it for them, letting them not live in torture as I had been doing for the past few centuries.

With every kill, with every human who looks up to me and begs for me to save them, I think back to the night when I pleaded with her to save my life.

I wish I had never resisted death.

A WORLD OF VAMPIRES

Strigoi

Even as I stay in this place, I can see the rapid changes occurring all throughout the land I've called home for so many years. Centuries have passed and I have watched as people, inhabitants or not, come into this land, looking for adventure or just to settle down. I was once one of those people, a young girl wanting both adventure but also a home. I must have wanted adventure more than a home because only adventure could have trapped me where I was now, dreaming of the day I can return to the real world, if that was even possible. I knew myself to be a fool for thinking that, but one could always hope.

As I look out into the world, I can see the ongoing thirst for vampire stories, both old and new, resonate through the land, and, I presume, through the world. I've watched as trucks zoomed past, logos of the newest media trend plastered on their sides. How can they believe that a creature as vile as the vampire could ever have feelings for a human being? It is a lie, they will never understand the truth of the creature who is hiding in the shadows, waiting to take another human victim as their prey. They will never understand the lies of all the stories they hear about the monsters that hide in the night. They don't sparkle, they don't have feelings or remorse. There is no stopping them from doing what they want. They will go to whatever lengths they can to survive, destroying only God knows what just to get their way.

If I could, I would leave this place and knock some sense into these humans. They don't understand the horror and pain that these creatures are usually known to cause. Every time I hear of a love story between a human and vampire, I feel like spitting out the vile taste such an idea leaves in my mouth. They aren't loving, they aren't caring. If anything, they are evil beings, who only care about themselves. And if anything, they are conniving, selfish bastards that will do anything to survive.

Even kill their own.

So I write to you this story, a telling of how untrustworthy, crafty, and cunning the strigoi, the true vampires that spawned the myth, are in reality. This tale is a cautionary tale for all girls, like myself, who could be seduced by such cunning beings. If I had known to what lengths they would go to survive, I wonder if I would have still trusted that man with my life as I had done. I probably would have, even though to this day I regret my own folly and wish I had died that night rather than suffer the consequences for eternity. But he wouldn't have let that happen, no matter how hard I tried. And now it was just too late to ponder anything in the area of "what ifs?"

It all started one evening when I was returning to my Romany camp in the wilderness in what was the 1500s (has that much time really passed already?). I had gone out to the village six miles north of camp to buy some food for my friend, Jack, who was sick. He needed some lemons for a cider recipe and our camp had been experiencing a short supply of them. It wasn't necessary for him to have these lemons, but I believed it would help him get over his sickness which had been persisting for a couple weeks now and I couldn't let him suffer any more than was necessary.

So I snuck out and gathered all the coins I could. Granted, none of the coins were mine; I had stolen them while I was in the village. Mostly, it was only from rich people in the market, showing off their jewels and fine clothing, whom I bothered stealing from. They were so pompous and arrogant that they didn't even notice as I snuck up behind them and grabbed a few coins here and there from their purses or pockets. I could have done it in my sleep, really. Some say that I was lazy to pick-pocket like this. They didn't understand that it was still hard work on my part to not get caught, even though I had become a master at it.

After successfully getting the coins I needed, I quickly made my way back through the forest before anyone in the village noticed that their precious gold and silver was missing. Madam Sonia, the leader of our camp and my mentor for becoming a Shuvani, didn't want anyone knowing about us in hopes that we could make this place in the woods our home for a while. She preferred to stay still, but with the winter months coming, it was hard to keep morale up as rations began to dwindle. We would have to move eventually for food, but not until we had to.

Thievery had been a problem in the past, but Madam Sonia made all the people in the camp promise not to go into town and cause a scene. A lot of people weren't as good as I at sneaking in a few coins here and there, ruining it for the rest of us more talented thieves. They would always get caught and the town would drive us out of the forest and our camp would have to move before we had time to really become familiarized with an area and could call it home for a long while. So, now there was a strict rule that prohibited any kind of stealing, and no one was to venture into town without obtaining proper permission from Madam Sonia. I didn't follow either of those rules and hoped that I could get away with telling her instead that I had been hunting the entire time that I had been missing from the camp.

The sky began to darken as I made my way back through the woods of Romania. It had taken longer than I had thought it would to get back to camp from the town and the moon had already begun to peek its face out for the evening. I was hoping that I would be home before night came, escaping the chance of Madam Sonia founding out where I had run off to. More importantly, people in my camp always talk about how strigoi were known to haunt these parts, not that I actually believed in such tales. Nonetheless, I would be in a lot more trouble now that it was dark and the strigoi were prowling the night, and would kill anyone they happened to chance upon.

The mother moon was full, brighter than I had ever remembered seeing it before. I smiled up at it, feeling more alive that night than I ever imagined was possible. I danced at the sound of the wind rustling through the trees, the warm summer air bringing more beauty to the forest than any person ever could create. Twigs tugged on my skirt as it twirled about but I didn't care. I loved my life as a traveler, even though we didn't travel as often as we used to when my grandmother was in charge. We got to see the world, and be free of the shackles that came with living in a town. In a town, you were expected to have to pay taxes, issue laws that the citizens don't necessarily agree with, and sometimes choose a ruler who doesn't seem to care at all for the welfare of their people. We had a leader, yes, but she loved the camp and listened to everyone who wanted to talk to her. We voted on things, making sure the majority, if not all the camp, agreed to something before we did it. It was nice being in such a small community, knowing and trusting everyone with your life, feeling safe in knowing that they would always be there for you. I would never want to give up this life.

I listened as owls began to call out into the night while bats fluttered up into the sky. I could make out their wings as they hurried off after some bugs. Most people feared bats, but I had always found them quite fascinating to watch. They seemed to have a beautiful story to tell, if only someone would just care to listen.

A couple of deer trotted ahead of me, looking for a place to rest for the night. They looked like young deer, who were braving their first night as adults. Their spots were all gone, but they had that apprehensive look in their face that seemed like it would belong to a fawn. The newly fallen leaves crunched under their hooves, as they hurried off to somewhere safe and sound to spend the remainder of the night. I wondered if anyone in the hunting party caught anything today. It would be ironic for me to see a couple of deer if they hadn't caught any.

As I danced towards my camp, I heard the sound of a violin playing in the distance. I stopped in my tracks. I had heard that music before, in my dreams. I had always thought it was someone in the camp playing that lovely instrument, or just my imagination recalling hearing it long ago in the past. Curious as to where this lovely music was coming from, I listened closely. There shouldn't have been anyone in these woods, yet it sounded as if it were really close. The sound was magnificent, the song fast and enthralling, I couldn't help but be captivated by it. In fact, there was no way I could turn away from the music, not when it was so delightful. So I headed toward it, letting it lead me to its source.

I forgot where I was and what I was doing. The music captured all my attention, leading me to drop the bag of lemons I had been carrying back from the town. I was a slave to its melody, as if I were a fly trapped in a spider's web and there was no turning back now. I couldn't snap out of it. I felt like I was in a dream, as if all the nights that I had heard it while growing up had been leading to this very climatic moment all along.

Coming to a clearing, I found myself in front of a castle. It looked old, abandoned, if not almost ready to fall apart. Something about this castle made me feel like I should have noticed it there before, but I had no memory of it. I had ventured through these woods many times before this night and I had never seen this castle until tonight. I swore that there had been a small cemetery near here, rather than a castle. I glanced around, seeing no sign of the cemetery. Had I been mistaken? Was this not where my mother brought me so many years ago to say goodbye to my father?

My heart raced as I stepped inside the castle. A swift cold wind ushered me in, causing me to wrap my arms around myself. I hadn't felt cold while walking in the woods, yet this place was sending shivers down my spine. Shrugging off any thought of turning back, I started deeper into the castle.

The castle was layered in constant shadows, with no light coming from any direction around the castle. There were a few candles scattered along the stairwell, beckoning me to follow them up towards where the music was coming from. I could see light coming from one of the doors on the upper floor. I started up the stairs, cobwebs and dust surrounding me. My heart was pounding in my chest but I couldn't stop. I just couldn't stop moving.

I swore I saw shadows moving around the stairwell, ghosts of the night. I gulped, not moving my head towards them in case they were something that I did not want to see. I just kept telling myself they were a creation of my own imagination, or shadows of the trees outside the castle moving around in the wind, not wanting to move my head towards them. But something of this world couldn't move like that, not even a shadow.

I kept creeping up these stairs, the quick-paced violin's music kept getting louder and louder. The candles led me straight to the room, as if someone had been waiting for me to come. My heart kept pounding in my chest, harder and harder. I couldn't stop though, I had to find who was creating that beautiful music that beckoned me to enter into this mirage-like castle.

I made it to the top of the stairs, the door only opened a crack as light shined from it. I slowly pushed it open, fearful for what I may find behind these doors.

The room was perfect, no dust or cobwebs in any corner. It wasn't like the rest of the castle. No, this room looked like it had been consistently well-kept. A fire burned in the fireplace, crackling as it let out heat and lit up the room, which was a deep contrast to the shadows and darkness of the other areas of the castle. By it were two leather chairs and a wood table that appeared to be worth quite a bit of money. With such refined furniture to sell, I could supply food for my camp. Although to be honest, we weren't exactly poor since we grew and hunted all of our own food. Sometimes, the crops, though, did not sustain the camp and we would have to go into the town to get some more food. It would be a lot easier if we had more money to do that. The costly rug resting near the fireplace would give us money for a year's worth of meat alone. I glanced around the room some more, finding tapestries on the walls and a mirror on the furthest wall. It was the largest mirror I had ever seen with a gold rim surrounding it. As I examined the mirror more closely from the doorway, the music suddenly stopped.

I blinked, realizing it had been the music that drew me near. I knew what was going on but it wasn't until that moment did I truly realize I had been a slave to the melody. I shouldn't be there, I had to get back to my camp. It was a mistake to have let myself be drawn in here by that song.

I turned to find the door slamming shut on me. I tried to open it, but it wouldn't budge. I tried again and again, frantically, but it was no use. I was trapped in this place.

"Where do you think you are going, Miss Amalia?" a voice said. I spun around to find the most handsome man I had ever seen standing behind me. His hair was golden, like a field of wheat, and his eyes were light like the sky on a summer morning. He was an older gentleman, who was even more handsome than many young men I've encountered through my life of traveling. A violin was cradled in his hands. He was the one making the beautiful music.

"I... I shouldn't be here, I have to get back home," I tried to pull the door open again but nothing happened.

"Shh, don't worry, you can go home. But first, you must listen to my song," he placed the violin under his chin and began to play.

I stopped trying to escape, the music captivating me once again. It was seductive, alluring, it felt almost like a love affair just by listening to it. Playful, yet soothing, I could keep listening to it until the end of time. I followed the man as he stepped back and led me towards the mirror. I was doing this, all because of being trapped in a trance. Yet, I had no means of escaping from this trance this music seemed to draw me into, as if a magic spell was being conjured by his music.

Standing in front of the mirror, I watched as he played softly, the bow moving back and forth against the string. A few in our camp knew how to play, but none played as majestically as this man did. He circled around me, but I kept my face toward the mirror.

That's when I noticed that he didn't have a reflection.

My heart began to pound in my chest. I didn't know what to do, I had heard stories around the campfire by Madam Sonia, but I never thought they were real.

The strigoi.

It was a creature of legend, one that terrorized our villages and camps for centuries. The dead that have come back to life to drink the blood of the living.

And now he stood right in front of me. His face was as gentle, and satisfying as a spider that had finally caught a fly. His eyes were full of excitement as he planned on what he was going to do with me. My heart was racing and a tear escaped the corner of my right eye, but I couldn't move. The strigoi must have noticed my fear, for he stopped playing.

But, I was still unable to move, and I was forced to continue staring at the reflection of myself without the strigoi in this room.

"What's the matter, my dear Amalia? Don't you like the music I play?" he whispered into my ear, sending shivers down my spine.

"You are..."

"A strigoi? You're a smart little girl for figuring that out."

"Who are you?" I squeaked.

He let out a brief chuckle. "Why I am Petru, ruler of all the strigoi."

"What do you want with me?" I gulped.

I suddenly felt my hair being moved away from my neck. Even though I felt his hand lifting my hair gently, the mirror showed no evidence of what was happening.

"Why, that's simple. I want revenge for the pain your camp has brought to me." With that, I felt pain in my neck. I could see blood trail down my neck, but there was no trace of him.

Then everything went dark.

I woke up to the sounds of birds tweeting in the distance.

My head was hurting so bad that I could barely think. As I opened my eyes, the light brought on even more pain. I glanced around. Where was I? What was going on? I blinked a few times to find myself in my tent.

I was back in my camp.

I bolted up out of my mattress and out of the tent to find my friends and family already up and about for the day. Both Darius and Madeline had already captured some song birds and placed them in cages to sell in the town. A group led by Marcus was getting ready to go into the woods for a hunt and some kids, including my friend's children Dan and Magda, were picking up golden leaves and pinecones that had fallen upon the ground during the night. I couldn't believe my eyes.

How did I get back here? Was everything that happened last night then just a dream?

No, it couldn't have been. I remembered the music, I remembered being bitten. I shuddered at the thought as I placed my hand on my neck but there was nothing there, not even a scratch. It must have been a dream.

I went back inside my tent and rifled through my things. In my bag, I had found the lemons that I had purchased for Jack.

But I swore I had dropped them somewhere in the woods.

Rubbing my head, I tried to recall the journey home. I remembered the woods and everything up to that point, including the strigoi, but that was it. I couldn't remember getting back to the camp. My heart was still pounding in my chest. The song he was playing in my dreams, it was a song sometimes I would hear late at night as I would fall asleep. Could it have been him all this time? No, it was probably just a dream. It couldn't have been real.

I felt sort of foolish to think that it could have been real, but every time I thought back to it, the more I felt that it had happened. I distinctly remember his touch as he moved my hair away from my neck. I shuddered again. But I was back in the camp, if that had really happened there was no way I would be back here.

Deciding I should go visit my friend to see if he was feeling better, I grabbed my sack of lemons and started towards his tent. Jack was only a couple of tents over from me. He had been sick for a while now, running a fever, sweating uncontrollably and his eyes were redder than a rose. So far, Madam Sonia hadn't figured out what was the cause of it, but since I was working under her, learning the craft of herbal medicine, I decided to try to help him myself.

And the best thing to start with was honey, garlic, and lemon.

There was a sign outside Jack's tent, explaining that Jack was ill and to stay away from the tent. We still weren't sure as to what he had and only practitioners in the medical and spiritual field, the Shuvani, were allowed to see him. Since I was both that and a close friend, I felt it was my duty to visit him as often as I could, and to do my best to cure him of whatever he had. We had grown up together, his parents dying when he was at a young age and my father the same. We felt some kind of a connection from being able to relate with that kind of shared grief over a deceased parent Therefore, we have always looked out for one another, for as long as I could remember.

I called out from the other side of his tent. "Jack, is it alright if I come in?"

I heard a faint yes and entered his tent.

There wasn't much to his tent, as our tribe were travelers by nature. We could only have what we were able to carry. Clothes were hung up along with the tent. Jack himself still didn't look good, his face covered in sweat, a cloth on his forehead to help soak up the liquid. He had some water and wine by his mattress, but it didn't look like he had touched it. He had complained that his throat and ears had started to hurt as well. His skin was pail and clammy, but he tried to keep up a smile when he saw that I was there. I doubted that smile would last long after I left.

"Hey handsome, how have you been doing?" I asked as I sat cross-legged by him. I moved a piece of his black hair out of his face for him as he started coughing.

"I've been better."

I held up the lemons. "Look what I picked up."

His eyes brightened a little. "You got some lemons? That must have cost you a fortune."

I shook my head. "No, it didn't cost *me* a fortune."

He frowned. "What have I told you about stealing? I told you I didn't want you doing that anymore. You could get caught and I don't want anything bad to happen to you, Amalia."

I twiddled my thumbs. "I know, but I didn't want something to happen to you, either. I will do whatever it takes to make you feel better, okay? Just don't worry about it, I will be careful. If you want me to stop stealing, you will have to get better. How about that?"

He grinned. "Fine, I will see what I can do."

I tried to keep up a smile, but I had heard what Madam Sonia had said to the others. She didn't think she could heal him, but I would give it everything to try and help. That was why I went to the town and got the lemons. I didn't care how long he had been sick, nor did I care that both his father and mother had suffered the same illness years ago and died when Jack was just a child. I wouldn't give up.

"I'm going to go put these in some vinegar with garlic and ginger and bring you the medicine, all right?"

He nodded his head and I left his tent to find the rest of the ingredients I needed. Fortunately, we were never in short supply of apple cider vinegar, garlic, honey, or ginger. Madam Sonia had tried a similar concoction once before, but I think adding some lemon juice could do the trick in helping Jack feel better. It had worked for Emilie, a young girl, when she got very sick last winter. Therefore, it should work for Jack, right? I had to try, at least. He was my closest friend after all.

I snuck through the camp, not wanting to get caught with the items I had stolen from the nearby town. There weren't too many people in our camp, about forty altogether, so it was easy to sneak around when you knew everyone's schedule. If I was seen with the lemons, people would suspect something and tell Madam Sonia of it right away. I made my way through the traffic of other people as they went about their day weaving clothes, feeding animals, and cooking meals. I grabbed all the other items I needed to make the concoction. It was easy, I found myself becoming a master at such sleight of hand tricks. Madam Sonia would not be pleased, but I always did it to help someone. I couldn't just let someone suffer when I knew I had the resources to help.

I found a place behind some tents where no one could see me as I began to make the concoction. I started to chop up the garlic and onion into smaller pieces.

"Where did you get those lemons?" I heard Madam Sonia's voice explode from behind me. I turned around to find her hands on her hips and one of her dark black eyebrows raised.

I gulped as I jumped up, almost knocking the garlic and ginger off the board and onto the ground. Her dark green eyes stared down at me in an accusatory fashion as she awaited my confession to my thievery. I looked down at my feet, trying to think of a good defense, but I knew I couldn't lie to her. "I went to town yesterday and bought some."

"Bought? Or do you mean steal?" she tapped her foot, awaiting my answer, as if I were just a child.

"I bought them..." I began, then sighed, knowing I couldn't lie to her, "with someone else's money."

"Amalia!"

"I couldn't let him suffer, mama," I responded quickly. "I just couldn't."

She pursed her lips. "You care for him a lot, don't you?"

I turned my head away from her, ashamed of my feelings. I didn't know why that was, but I just couldn't admit my feelings for him. We were both young and I knew that, but I felt as if I knew he was the one for me.

"My sweet Amalia," she wrapped her arms around me. The scent of jasmine came off of her, always making me feel calm when she was around, as long as I wasn't in trouble of course. "You don't have to lie to me. I can see it in your eyes that you love him. But you can't be going to town alone and stealing things. That is not our camp's way. By stealing, you put all of us in jeopardy. You know how the city peoples feel about us, we cannot be found, okay?"

I nodded my head slowly, a few tears dropping out of my eyes. I wiped them away, not wanting to appear weak, but truthfully I was scared for his life. I didn't know it was even possible to care for someone else, as much as I did for Jack. And I was sure he felt the same about me, though that might just be wishful thinking. Studying medicine and spells made me feel like I was the only one who could help him, that if he died it would be my fault, even though I wasn't allowed to perform powerful spells on my own yet. A couple more tears rolled down my cheek.

"That's a good girl. And don't worry, I will try my best to heal him, but if the spirits don't want him to live, there isn't much I can do about it. You understand?

I nodded again, sniffling away my worry. She stroked my back, hoping to give me some comfort.

"Now, finish up the concoction you are making and give it to him, but next time come to me before doing something so reckless. Once you are done with that, return to me so we can start your chores for the day."

"Yes, mama," I said as I knelt down and finished chopping up the garlic and ginger. She left to go check on the rest of the camp. Being the daughter of the lead Shuvani in the tribe had both its perks and disadvantages. It meant that I wouldn't get away with anything and that people looked to me to be the next Shuvani. Although I loved learning about herbs and the practice of medicine from her, I didn't know if I would ever be ready to lead the camp. Mama believed in me, but the problem was I didn't believe in myself.

Once I finished chopping and squeezing the juice out of the lemons, I brought the ingredients to a boil and let the concoction simmer for a while. I added a little cayenne pepper as well.

I let it cool a bit and the brought the warm concoction to Jack's tent. I could hear him having a coughing fit as I approached his tent.

"Are you all right?" I asked as I entered his tent.

He coughed a few more times. "Can't seem to get rid of this cough."

I set the concoction down and helped him sit up with the pillows. "This should help with the cough as well." I handed him the cup and he took a sip.

Nodding in agreement, "It does help, thank you."

I smiled, relieved that the medicine at least did something. "It's not a problem, Jack. I just hope it will help you feel better."

I started to leave when he grabbed my wrist. "I mean it, Amalia, you have been a great friend. Thank you."

Holding his hand for a moment, I pretended in my mind that he was better, that this would be a happy moment in my life. I wanted to pretend we were both healthy and that I could tell him how I felt. Instead I found myself worrying about his life and whether or not we would have a happy life together.

"If you need anything, just let me know," I said as I left him in his tent.

After my time with Jack, I found Madam Sonia and helped with the camp's garden and cooking. We grew all kinds of herbs and vegetables in hopes that we could make this our home without being discovered by someone from the nearest city. It was quite far away, at least a half day's travel as I had found out, and it was out of the way of any roads leading into town. I doubted anyone from the town would ever find us this time.

After working in the garden and helping start work preparing the evening's dinner, Madam Sonia gave me my daily lesson on apothecary and we went over the health and spiritual properties of each herb she had. She also told me more stories and legends, so that I may be able to retell the tales of our ancestors.

Today, she told me the story of my great-great grandmother and how she battled a powerful strigoi to keep our camp safe. My heart skipped a beat.

"A strigoi?" I asked.

She nodded. "Yes, one of the most powerful in all the land. It was a long time ago, the story has been passed down many generations. Your great-great grandmother was a very powerful woman, she was the one who learned all the methods of apothecary and different spells that I teach you today. She brought our camp to this land, fighting many guards and knights to be here. But, one night, they found out that the land was haunted by a vicious strigoi who thought it was he who ruled the land. Your great-great grandmother would not give up her right to be here, though, and knew she was the one who had to stop it."

"But weren't strigoi once humans just like us?" I asked.

"Yes, this strigoi was once a powerful ruler of the land, but his kingdom was overthrown and both him, his son, and a lot of those in the castle were slaughtered and never given a proper burial. He, along with many of the other, became strigoi and caused a lot of chaos for many villages and camps in the area. He created even more creatures like himself and it was a time of great turmoil."

"What happened?"

"Well, your great-great grandmother searched around for more priestesses like her so that together they could overcome this evil. She knew that there was power in numbers and decided they must cast a banishing spell upon the castle where the strigoi lived, so that the strigoi could never hurt another human again. They mustered up all the power they had combined, cast a circle, and called upon the spirits to put an end to the strigoi's evil."

I listened to the story, wide-eyed, my heart racing, wondering what was going to happen next. "Did they succeed?"

Madam Sonia chuckled. "We are here, aren't we? Yes, with the power of the spirits, they succeeded in banishing the strigoi from the land. Your great-great grandmother was revered throughout all the land, and many of the people in our camp now are descendants of people from other camps, wanting to follow her guidance and show their loyalty to her."

"Are the strigoi still around?" I mustered up the strength to ask the question that had been in my mind since she started telling the story.

She shook her head. "No, they haven't been seen for over a century," she smiled gently. "Don't worry, it is just a legend, but one we must remember, in order to understand the power that we carry."

Even though I was sure she was right, I couldn't help but replay the nightmare I had the night before. I had heard of strigoi before, but I never knew that one of my ancestors had been the one to defeat them. Was that what the strigoi meant by revenge before he bit me? I thought about telling Madam Sonia, but I figured I didn't want to worry her. It was probably all just part of a really bad dream anyways.

We finished up our lesson and I helped other people in the camp get ready for dinner. The hunting group brought back two deer, which would feed our camp for a couple of weeks. I was thankful to the spirits that they were able to find something this late in the season. If we were lucky, they would find something else next week as well and we could preserve it with some salt. Then we would be good through the winter. Hunting for game during the winter could be very hard, so the hunters of our camp needed to be very attentive to the needs of the camp.

Once the stew was ready, I took two bowls to Jack, one for me and one for him. Normally, Madam Sonia would take him dinner, but she was busy talking to some people and I thought I could enjoy his company over dinner. I knew how lonely he got, when having to remain cooped up in his tent all day.

"Who's ready for supper?" I asked as I opened the tent flap.

He smiled and coughed. "I didn't expect to see you again today."

"What, you don't think I would come visit my best friend?"

Laughing, Jack sat up. "You have plenty of other friends to visit. You shouldn't spend so much time here; you could catch whatever I have."

I shook my head. "I would have already caught it. Don't worry; I took all the necessary precautions. I know my medicine."

He took the bowl and started sipping some of the stew. "You don't have to stay here, go join the rest of the camp."

"No, I will stay here. You are all alone here; I would feel horrible if I left you here without anyone to talk to. ."

"Go, I insist. I don't want you to stay here when I know you could be with the rest of the camp having a good time. Please, for me?" He looked at me with his sad red eyes. Although I didn't want to leave him there, since he was the only one I wanted to be with out of all the people in the camp, I did as he asked. I couldn't say no to him, not when he seemed to want me to leave so badly.

I nodded and left him alone. As I closed the flap of the tent, I could hear him start coughing again. I wondered if that was why he wanted me to leave, because he couldn't keep up a happy face. His condition was getting worse and he didn't want me to see. I felt a tear roll down my cheek. I had really hoped the lemons would help. They still could, I knew, but my heart felt like it was going to be torn apart by sadness. I couldn't lose him, I just couldn't.

Night came and the moon was full, the peak of the mother moon. I looked up at it and recalled the dream I had the night before and wondered whether or not it was real. I knew it couldn't have been, especially since I had woken up here in the camp. If the strigoi had actually bitten me, I would have been dead.

Or worse, I would have been made into one of them.

It was silly to even think about it, to consider that any of it had actually happened. My great-great grandmother was probably a very strong woman, I didn't deny that, especially if she was anything like my mother, but I couldn't believe that she went against such mythical beings. There was no way that they could have really existed, could there? There was no castle in the woods; there was no man with a violin. It had all just been a dream.

The sound of a violin playing had been haunting my nightmares for a long time now; it was no surprise that I had a nightmare such as that one on such a majestic night as the night before. The first night of the full moon, the beginning of the fall season, and the fear of getting caught with lemons probably led me to have that nightmare. It wasn't like I had never had nightmares about creatures like that before, though those usually featured werewolves and ghouls, but this time it had seemed different. This time everything that happened in that nightmare was much clearer.

As I started to clean up for the night, a smell came wafting over to me, filling my lungs. I breathed it in and let it out slowly. It was outstanding, a beautiful scent filling me with bliss almost. Whatever it was, I wanted it.

I followed the smell through the camp, trying to find out where it originated from. Whatever it was, it smelt as sweet as fruit on a new summer's day, as fresh as lavender in a field, and it made my mouth water like specially prepared sweets. I wondered who could have been preparing such a lovely meal, especially since most people had already retired for the night.

Coming upon one of the tents, I lifted the flap to find the deer that had been killed that day to be hanging up. I watched as their hanging bodies dripped blood into the bowls beneath.

Blood.

That couldn't be what I was smelling, could it? No, it wasn't possible. Blood didn't smell like this, it was revolting. Death could never smell so sweet.

The strigoi.

Shaking my head, I tried to get the thoughts out of my head. No, it wasn't possible. That didn't happen last night. It wasn't possible.

Or was it?

My heart began to race and I felt like I couldn't breathe. There was no way I could have been bitten by that creature. There was no way I would have survived the day, at least that isn't how the legend went. My mind was racing with all the possibilities, but I couldn't think of any other reason why the smell was coming onto me like this. I glanced back down at the dripping blood. Maybe it wasn't the blood that smelled so good, maybe it was something else.

I glanced around. There was nothing in here but dead animals. I gulped when I realized that the stench of death was no longer a horrifying smell, but actually the source of the pleasing scent I was breathing in. It smelt more like life now than it did death. The thought made me nauseous, but I had to know if a true, monstrous change of some kind was taking place within me.

Holding out my hand, I let the drops from the deer's bleeding carcass fall into my palm. I slowly raised my hand to my mouth and drank the red nectar.

It was exactly what I had smelled. And it was wonderful. It tasted sweeter than candy and was more satisfying than any evening meal served up in this camp. Nothing that I had ever eaten could ever compare to this delicious liquid. The metallic taste on top of the freshness of the blood...

I stepped back from the carcass. What was I doing? Blood didn't taste like that; it all had to have been a dream, yet this incident proved that it might not have been a nightmare. The rational side of my brain, though, insisted on the fact that I couldn't have been bit by the strigoi, creatures like that weren't real. My great-great grandmother didn't actually fight them; it was just a legend to keep the unity of the camp. The strigoi were just a figment of people's imagination. Yet, I glanced down at the bowl of blood, and I knew I had to have more to satisfy the thirst.

Without thinking, I grabbed the bowl of blood and gulped down the liquid. It felt smooth as it slowly went down my throat and satisfied the hunger I never knew I had. I forgot everything around me and indulged in the moment, caring only for the liquid that stained my mouth with a red stain that would never leave my lips. I felt like I was in a daze, completely out of control. I just couldn't help myself.

Stepping back, I forced myself out of the trance. What was I doing? It was wrong and sickening. I knew I had to get out of here before this progressed even more. I had to figure out what was going on.

I stumbled out of the tent, looking for something that could help me. I didn't know what that was, but I knew I had to find it. I needed to find someone I could trust, someone who could figure out what was wrong with me. I couldn't go to Madam Sonia in fear of what she might do to me. I was a strigoi now; she would want to destroy me. I was something that the entire camp dreaded. Everyone feared that the strigoi were fated to return someday, except for me. That ignorance was probably what led me to where I was now. But I knew I had to find someone to help me out with figuring all of this bizarre stuff out. There weren't many in the camp that I trusted enough to tell them such a secret and know that they would try to help me to the best of their ability, without disturbing the peace of the camp.

Except for Jack.

Everything seemed to be in tunnel vision as I made my way to his tent. All I remembered was looking down at my feet as the moon shined down on me. Leaves and branches crunched as I stepped on them. Arriving at his tent, I stepped in.

Jack was still awake, and sat up in his makeshift camp bed when he saw me enter.

"Amalia, what are you doing here so late?" he whispered, knowing that it could be bad if someone found me in his tent at this hour. I admit, it wasn't the greatest idea, but I didn't know where else to go, who else to turn to. I didn't want to worry too much about rumors circulating about my improper behavior, when this situation set before me demanded urgent action.

"I'm not," I rubbed my head. "I'm just not feeling that great."

"Did I get you sick?" he asked.

I shook my head. "No, it's not what you have... It's something else," I sat down next to him, debating if I should tell him the truth. "Something strange happened last night to me."

"Oh, what's that?"

"I... thought I saw something, someone, in the forest."

Jack placed his hand on mine. It felt cold with sweat but I didn't mind. "Did they hurt you? Are you okay?"

"I..." I was about to answer the question when I noticed a cut on his hand. "What happened to your hand?"

"Oh, it's nothing. Just caught it on a piece of wood on my bed. You know how splinters are," he tried to smile, but started coughing instead. I stared at the cut, detecting the same scent that accompanied the blood of the deer carcass in the tent. I couldn't move my eyes away from his cut; I had to have the blood pouring freely from it. I had to consume it.

My hand slowly made its way to Jack's wrist. I stroked his skin slowly, captivated by the red blood that had begun to fall down his arm. I'm not sure at that moment if he thought I was being strange, or if he thought I was showing him affection. All I knew is that the world around me had stopped and all I could focus on was that blood giving off the most delicious scent that I had ever breathed.

"Amalia, there is something that I have been wanting to tell you…" Jack began. I wanted to look at him in the eyes, but I couldn't help but to stare at the cut, my eyes locked in place. "I just… I really care for you. I didn't want to say anything in fear that I may lose this battle against the sickness and I didn't want to place such a burden on you, but I feel like you need to know the truth. Amalia, I love you."

I wanted to tell him the same thing, which was that I truly loved him as well and I would do whatever it takes to heal him of this sickness. But I couldn't. I felt as if nothing else around me mattered except that pull inside myself, making me want to sip the blood dripping down his arm. The pain ached inside of me, and the only way I could satisfy it was to drink that blood.

I grabbed Jack's wrist and pulled the cut to my mouth.

"Amalia, what are you doing?" he asked slowly.

Without warning, I bit down on his arm, the delicious liquid trailing down my throat once more. This time it was different, though, this time it was much sweeter and much more satisfying. It brought so much energy to my veins.

Jack screamed out and tried to pull his arm away. I let go of his wrist, his yelling bringing me out of my trance. Then it hit me, I had tried to kill my best friend. I had tried to kill the person who just confessed his love to me.

"What is wrong with you? What are you?" he looked at me as if I were some monster. My heart felt like it dropped to the bottom of my stomach. How could he look at me like that when moments earlier he was happy to see me? I thought out of all the people, he would be the one who would understand. I was wrong.

The flap to the tent opened and I turned to find Madam Sonia standing there. I don't know what she saw when she looked at me but her skin turned deathly white.

"No, this can't be possible," she covered her mouth. "Strigoi... Strigoi!" she called out to the camp.

She saw what I was; I couldn't deny it any longer. The strigoi was not part of a nightmare, it had been real. And I had been turned into the creature that my village greatly feared. "No, Mama, I'm not what you think—"

"Get away from me, you demon!" she yelled.

My heart sank in my chest. My own mother couldn't look at me; she couldn't face the creature I had become. I was confused, and afraid as to what was going to happen. She was the only one who could have helped me sort this all out, but she had turned her back on me just as Jack had done. I didn't understand, I didn't want to believe it, yet here she was, calling me a demon.

I ran out of the tent in shock, and I fearfully saw the occupants of the camp begin to circle me with undisguised anger, holding up both knives and torches. All of them wanted me destroyed. I couldn't believe it, after all this time they would betray me this easily.

Madam Sonia held up her hand, but I could see the sadness in her eyes as she looked down at me. "She is a strigoi, she is an enemy of this camp."

"Mama, please," I begged. "I am still your daughter."

She shook her head and I watched as a tear left her eye. She didn't want to hurt me, but I could see that she had no other choice in order to keep the camp safe. "No, you are a curse to us. You must be burned before you hurt anyone else. I will not let this burden affect the camp. Not again. You already bit Jack, and it is only a matter of time before he turns now."

"I didn't mean to. I won't do it again, I swear," tears were running down my face. "I just want to be home and to be with my family."

She shook her head. "No, you are a demon cast upon us as a curse. You must be destroyed before *he* can get his hands on you."

"What are you talking about...?" I began as the people circling me started to come even closer to me with a more antagonistic stance. They held their torches and knives a little higher in their hands. My heart was beating fast as I looked every which way for some means of escape from them, my family. It broke my heart to think that they would turn on me like this, not letting me tell them what had happened. But the fear of the strigoi had been passed down by many generations, and I couldn't help but understand their actions, even though it hurt me inside to fathom them. But I couldn't let them catch me, nor could I let them kill me. I had an urge to survive, even though I even considered myself a monster at this point. I had to run; I had to be free of them. The only way to do that was to run straight into the woods and to never look back.

And that was exactly what I did.

I didn't know if it was the fear of them capturing me or if it had more to do with my being a strigoi now, but I felt as if I could suddenly run faster than I ever had been able to in my entire life. It was as if I was hyperaware of everything around me. This newly discovered ability was bound to be my way of guaranteed escape from being killed by my own camp. Who knew that in a short span of time that I'd go from "one of the tribe" to exiled renegade? I would mull over it later, right now I had to figure out how to get away from all the people that were after me.

In addition to my newly acquired powers, I fortunately knew these woods like the back of my hand, for I had spent a lot of the time out in the woods foraging for any berries and plants that had healing properties. I also knew all the best hiding spots—none of which they knew anything about. I would get away from them eventually; I just had to run fast enough away from them.

As I kept running, I felt something pull me back. I tried to scream but the person who had caught up with me put their hand over my mouth.

"Shh, it's alright. I won't let them hurt you," a man's voice whispered in my ear.

I kept struggling but it was no use, he was stronger than me. I watched as the hunting party ran by, not noticing us as we hid ourselves in the nearby bushes. After a few moments, they were out of sight. The man finally let go of me then. I spun around and faced him. He had dark hair and the shadows of the night masked his light-skinned face. He wasn't someone I had ever seen in the camp or in the towns I had been in, but I swore he looked familiar. Something about him made me feel calm, as if I could trust him with my life. I didn't know where it came from, but at least my heart was no longer racing and I no longer feared that the people of my camp would catch up with me. Yet, my relaxed nerves worried me even more.

I backed away from the man. "Who are you?"

"I am just like you, a strigoi on the run from humans," he explained, flashing his long canines at me. "I saw you were being chased, so I knew I had to help."

I shook my head. "No, there aren't any strigoi in these woods that weren't already driven out long ago. How could one of you still exist? I don't believe you! You are trying to trick me!"

He grabbed my arm and tried to calm me down before I could run off in the other direction. As his hand touched my arm, I felt as if my worries were driven away. "I'm not trying to trick you, I am just trying to help you. I know what it's like to be driven out of a home for becoming a monster. Just let me help you."

"How did you become a strigoi? How do I know you aren't just going to kill me?" I asked, even though it didn't feel like I was really worried about it, yet something inside of me wanted to ask those questions.

He sighed. "The same way you did, by the man with the violin."

I felt as if my heart skipped a beat. The man with the violin. Was he out there at that moment? Would he come for me and kill me? Or did he just make me a strigoi and let me out into the world, hoping I would cause havoc? I had so many unanswered questions in my head; I just didn't know what to do, nor who to trust. All I wanted was to go home, but I knew that would never happen.

"Why did he turn me? Why did he turn you? I don't understand," I muttered as I ran my hands frantically through my hair.

The man shook his head. "I'm not sure," his eyes shot over to the side. "But we should get out of here. I'm afraid they may find us. I know a safe place we can hide; it's where I stay most days."

I debated letting him take me to his hiding spot, but I really didn't have another choice. Something inside of me made me trust him and every time I started to question this feeling, something in my mind blocked the questions. There was something about him that felt almost unreal, as if I would do whatever he said without question. It made my body quiver, in fear there was something else going on, as if this was still all part of some dream. Every time my mind lingered at the thought, it seemed to just disappear into nothing and I was again faced with the dilemma of whether or not to go with him to the safe place he had. A strigoi or not, my camp wanted me dead and this man seemed to want to help. He seemed honest enough, especially since he had just saved me. He also knew what happened and for all I knew, he may have more answers as to why the man in the castle turned me.

"Fine, let's go," I said, even though I felt I would regret it later.

He led me deeper into the woods. I followed him closely, my heart jumping every time I heard a noise around us. For a moment, I was sure it was someone wanting to cut my head off and burn my body- any of my fellow tribe mates would do that without a moment of hesitation. I gulped. I couldn't believe the mess I had found myself in. I couldn't believe this was all due to some entrancing violin music, which put me under some crazy spell.

As we walked back, I replayed everything back in my mind from the night before. I did find a castle with the violin music. This man had mentioned seeing me go in the castle, so it wasn't all in my imagination after all. I couldn't believe it. The strange man, who nearly killed me the night before, was indeed real. I started shaking, not able to take it in all at once. I was a creature, a monster, and everyone I knew for so many years now wanted me dead.

Except for this man.

Why was that? Since he was also obviously a strigoi, then he wouldn't want one of his kind to be killed. Maybe he was lonely and needed a friend and just couldn't stand by and watch me die. So many questions were running through my head. I wanted to ask him the questions that were running through my mind, but I had a feeling that he didn't want me to make a sound.

The woods were eerie that night; I had never experienced them in such a way. I had never had to fear for my life while running through them before. Every wavering shadow the trees made by the moonlight felt as if it were going to attack me. I felt as if something out of nowhere would jump out of the darkness and devour me once and for all. Never had I feared for my life as much as I had that night.

As we came upon a large tree, the man I ran with began to slow down. He stopped in front of the tree that had large roots going through a rock. It didn't appear to be anything special until he stood by the rock and pushed on one of the branches. Suddenly a piece of it opened and it opened up to a large room. It was a secret cave.

He gestured towards the inside of the house. "Welcome to my humble abode!"

I stepped inside and gasped. I couldn't believe how large the interior main room was. Granted, it wasn't anything special. A chair here, a table there, and a cot for a bed, but it was a lot nicer than I had imagined, standing on the outside and seeing only a rock and tangled net of tree roots. It was also more spacious and refined than a tent, so I really wasn't one to judge.

"What is this place?" I asked as I peered around.

"Just a place where I can hide from the world. No light comes in during the day so I am able to stay out of the sun. It's great, really. I don't have to live in a grave like the stories led you to believe," he smiled.

"Do you also have to stay out of the sun?" I questioned.

He nodded as he glanced out the door once more. "You won't be able to stay in the sun any longer, now that you have had time to process the change. Usually after the first day, your body can no longer handle it and you will burn to ash from this point on. Believe me, I have tried to go out there during the day. It doesn't work, and no it doesn't just leave a really bad sunburn."

I couldn't believe what he was saying. I would never be able to enjoy the warmth of the sun again. And, I wouldn't be able to run in the woods, during the light of the day, or see either my mother or Jack again. All the times I had help healed one of my camp members, one of my family, then they turned around and treated me like a monster. I had brought so much joy to them over the years and them to me. Yet one little mistake had led me into the woods at night, and led me to follow the music of the violin. Then everything I loved was taken away from me. I felt tears begin to form in my eyes.

The strigoi must have seen how upset I was about it all, for he suddenly wrapped his arms around me to try to console me. "It's alright, don't worry. I will help you through this."

I felt strange being in this man's arms all of a sudden, not even knowing his name. Although I had always believed that the strigoi would be cold, being in his embrace made me feel warm and calm. I felt as if I could be there forever, as if all the problems I had in this moment would go away. At the same time, though, it didn't feel real and it was also not this person's arms I wanted to be in. I had hoped that Jack would see me as the same person still and help me through this, but I guess I had asked too much of him. I mean, I was asking a lot for a whole camp that uniformly despised the strigoi. As for this man, he wanted to help for some reason and I wasn't sure as to what reason he wanted to help me. "Why?"

"Why what?" he asked.

I stepped back and looked up at him. "Why would you care to help me? You don't know me."

He let out a breath. "I know more about you than you realize," he sighed again. "There is a lot to explain, but I know why you were chosen to be turned into a strigoi and why you are one of the only ones who could hear the violin at night."

Why didn't he say that in the first place? It would have made me feel a lot more sure about trusting him, but him knowing about the violin made me begin to worry as to how long he had been watching me. "What? How?"

"As I said, it's a long story. I have to start from the beginning," he gestured to the chair. "Please, take a seat."

I sat down on one of the chairs he had set out and waited for him to tell the story.

"It all started a century ago. The ancestors in your camp found a family of strigoi that lived in these woods. Long story short, the strigoi killed many in your camp and your great-great grandmother, along with other leaders, put a curse on them,"

I nodded. "Yes, my mother told me that story. But isn't that it? She banished them from this land? Why are they reappearing now?"

"She didn't banish them, she trapped them within the castle boundaries and the castle wouldn't appear to humans except on the three days of the full moon. On those three days, a human can enter the premises of the castle, but the strigoi cannot leave."

So there was more to the story than my mother had told me. Did she not know that they were simply hidden, not actually banished from the land? "Do you know how she trapped them?"

"A very dangerous spell. Are you not the daughter of a Shuvani?" he asked.

I nodded slowly.

"So when you traveled out last night, during the first night of the full moon, you stumbled upon the castle and through that, the leader, Petru, figured out who you were and turned you into one of them."

"Even if they were the stigoi that my great-great grandmother cursed, why would they turn me into one? What is the point? Wouldn't they just have wanted to kill me and be done with it, out of revenge?" I asked.

He shook his head. "No, they would want you to suffer the same as they have. They want you to understand how they felt being trapped for so long and break their curse, since only the one with the same blood as the Shuvani that cast the spell can also lift it."

So that was why they wanted me, because of what my great-great grandmother had done. She was powerful enough to bind them to that castle, and they thought that I was strong enough to break that curse. Was that why I had always heard the violin since I was a little girl? It was the strigoi calling out to me, waiting for the day I would waltz into the castle so that they could turn me and cause me the same pain that they felt? It seemed like something out of a ghost story, but I had to face the grim fact that it was true. The only problem was, I still didn't understand who this man was and why he knew all about my family and this legend.

"Who are you and how do you know this?" I asked.

"Oh, beg my pardon. I neglected to introduce myself beforehand," he stood up and bowed. "I am Radu, son of a blacksmith in Brasov. I ventured out here one night and was lured into the castle by Petru as he played the violin. He made me into the same type of creature that he was, imprisoned me inside the castle until the hunger was unbearable, and let me go out in the world. Probably just did it to watch me suffer from that little window of his in his castle."

I frowned. Something didn't seem right about his story. "I thought the castle could only appear on three nights of the month. How can he watch you?"

He seemed surprised by the question, but quickly answered it without thought. "We can't see the castle, but they can see us from it. It's like it is there, but not visible to humans."

I didn't know what to do with all this information, nor how he came to know it. I didn't know what to do about being a strigoi and I didn't know how I felt knowing how that creature could always see me from afar, from that partially invisible castle of his.

"What do I do now?"

"Well, I was actually going to talk to you about that," he leaned in closer. "When I was in the castle, I read the text of the curse that was placed on it. There is a way it can be broken, but there is also a way to destroy the castle once and for all; to kill all the strigoi inside there forever. Only you can do it."

I shook my head. "There is no way, I'm not that powerful."

"You have the power of your ancestor's blood running through your veins. I think that there is a lot you can handle, you just don't know it yet."

"You're wrong; I'm just a young girl. I don't have the kind of strength that my ancestors had. Maybe Madam Sonia..." I stopped and listened. I could hear screams from a distance, outside of this hovel. "What is that noise, and where is it coming from?"

He didn't answer, but his face was suddenly full of sorrow.

I stood up and started for the door. He grabbed my wrist. "You don't want to go out there."

"But, where is all that screaming coming from?" I whispered.

"We aren't the only strigoi in these woods that have been turned by Petru. Over the years, there have been a few who stumbled into the castle that Petru turned, for no real reason, but to maybe alleviate his sorrow, of being alone and conscious of the curse hanging over his castle."

I gasped. "The camp! My mother..."

"There isn't anything you can do. If you want revenge on the strigoi for killing your people, you must go to the source. If you can destroy the castle, you can destroy all of the strigoi once and for all."

Tears were running down my face. I thought about all of the people that were in the camp that were now gone. My mother, Jack, and all of my friends I had grown close to over the years. It was all because of me. I had to go to town and get the lemons for Jack because I wanted to heal him. I wanted to prove I was stronger and knew how to heal him. I was selfish and because of that, I had brought this curse back down upon us and destroyed everyone I had loved. I was partially responsible for inadvertently letting the legendary beasts back into the camp, by causing the village's strongest warriors to chase after me rather than defend the camp from a strigoi invasion. It was all my fault.

"Fine," I wiped away the tears. "How do we destroy the castle?"

Radu had a lot of this already planned out, well in advance of our fateful encounter. As he had explained, he had been waiting for the day Petru would find me, so I could help destroy the castle. Evidently, Radu must have been imprisoned inside the castle for a long time because he had sketched out every detail of the castle's interior. I could barely remember what it looked like inside, being under the trance and all. I followed his hand as he pointed out the rooms.

"The entrance brings you here and lets you either go upstairs where Petru awaits any unwelcome guests, or it can lead you to these three rooms. Preferably, we want to stay away from him, but I have a feeling he will see us coming. I will try to make some kind of a diversion and you can run and get the spell then."

"How do you know all of this?"

"I spent some time in the castle before I was let back into the world," he whispered.

I stared at him for a moment longer, wondering what he meant by that. Why had the strigoi been holding him there, in the first place? And, why did they ultimately let him escape? Again, I was still reeling from everything that happened in the past day, being exiled from my home and now I was finding out just how much I played into some greater plot concerning these creatures, the strigoi.

"I'm sorry, I didn't realize..." I began.

He shook his head. "No, it's fine. When I was there, I took a look around and found the scroll that contained all there was to know about the spell cast over the castle. Luckily I had been taught to read and write. From what I could tell, it seemed that your ancestor wasn't strong enough to just simply destroy them all, but knew that one day; a descendant could be trained to be strong enough. It was just a matter of time when the strigoi figured that out as well."

"My mother must have thought it was just a legend. She had told me the stories of the strigoi, but never to this detail."

He shrugged. "I guess it just had been such a long time ago they didn't believe in the legend anymore. Or they were afraid of it, but since it wasn't affecting them, they didn't care about finishing the job of destroying them. The strigoi rarely attack a camp unless they are alone, I take it your camp always stays together at night?"

I nodded.

"So they must have feared the creature, and didn't want to try and destroy it since they weren't being bothered. Why do something dangerous when doing nothing was still safe?"

I thought about it. I supposed he was right. My mother did notice that I was a strigoi right away and wanted to kill me. She knew about it and hadn't told me the full story before that day. It was ironic it was the same day that I changed into one. "They were probably afraid telling the story might release them, bring them back to life. So, they chose to just keep these locked away in the minds of the few elders that remembered the most details of this story."

He nodded. "That is probably it. As for not telling you, you were probably just too young in their eyes. They didn't want you to know the truth, especially if we're going with the theory that they were very much afraid of the possibly that it may prove true."

I let out a slight laugh. "And look where that left me. Cursed for an eternity."

"They should have told you, they should have known to prepare you in case this happened. But that isn't the case and here we are."

"How does the curse work, do you know? Do you know how I am supposed to destroy them, once and for all? Is it as easy as killing their leader?"

He shook his head. "No, unfortunately I don't. I can't remember the exact details; I just know there is a way."

"Will it kill us as well?" I asked, the true question lingering in the back of my mind.

He shrugged. "I don't know, but I think it is a chance we are willing to take."

I agreed. I didn't care if I died when I could bring down those who brought death to my entire camp. I just wanted to see them gone from this world.

"When are we going to do this?" I said.

"Tomorrow night."

My eyes widened. "Are you kidding? We have to prepare longer than just a night. I'm not strong enough. I don't even really understand the whole idea of being a strigoi yet. I'm confused, tired, and sad about my eviction from the tribe, and...I'm also very..."

"Hungry?" he asked.

I looked away from him, ashamed that I was. Ashamed I wanted to feast on even more blood, especially after the last mishap with Jack. That was still very clear in my mind, leaving me to feel nothing but self-loathing for this terrible new instinct of mine.

"Don't worry, I know exactly what you are going through," he opened the door and looked outside in the silent night. "We still have a couple of hours before sunrise. How about I take you out hunting?"

I started to shake my head.

"For animals. Not people."

"Will it satisfy this thirst? I have drank both animal blood and human blood before I ran off. The human blood..." I began, but trailed off because I just hated admitting this to myself.

"Is a lot more filling. I know what you mean. It was hard to handle at first, to only drink from animals instead of humans. But, like you, I couldn't bear to think of killing any humans, and even if we just bite them we can end up turning them into strigoi as well. Usually that doesn't happen though, but you never know, considering our not so great reputation with the self-control thing," he explained.

"Why is that?" I asked.

"Most strigoi, like us, can't stop once they start drinking the blood of a human. It overpowers them, killing the human they were drinking from. "

I thought back to Jack. Had I made him into a strigoi? Did he survive the attack? I didn't know, but I had a feeling either way that he was gone and would never ever forgive me for what I did to him. I don't think I even wanted to dare contemplate any further about what exactly happened to him. Maybe, his death would be less painful, than the more irreconcilable possibility he might have turned.

"Now, come with me," he held out his hand. "We should get some energy for tomorrow. We have to defeat Petru and the rest of the strigoi once and for all."

It was strange. I could see perfectly now in the darkness. The physical changes that came with transforming into a strigoi were continuing to take effect. The night no longer seemed quite as scary as it had just hours earlier, now I was beginning to feel as if I belonged, if that made sense. The strigoi were called the creatures of the night, and I was beginning to see why. At first I thought it would be a nightmare, but I began to understand the appeal. My senses were heightened and I could almost sense the exact location where each animal was in the dense terrain. In my mind, I could even see a clear visual of what they were up to.

Radu gestured all around. "This is all of ours. We get to drink the sweet splendor that is the night."

He seemed excited about it as he said those words and I was beginning to understand why. The night smelt so much sweeter than it had ever before, but it could have just been the heightened senses from turning into a strigoi. Although I felt better for the most part, the thought of being such a monster still ate at me. I was a blood-thirsty creature that wanted to drink the blood of my people, the blood of any human.

"What do you think?" Radu asked, as he saw I was deep in thought.

I blinked, realizing I didn't respond to his comment about the night. "Yes, it is beautiful."

"But you are wondering how being such a vile creature can be so wonderful?"

I nodded slowly.

He laughed. "I wondered the same when I was starting out, after I left the castle of course. You experience so much as a strigoi, it's incredible. Although I miss being a human, I don't know if I would be able to go back, seeing and experiencing the things I have experienced."

I watched as he stared up at the moon and stars, taking in the beauty as he probably did every night. I started to see a different side of him, a side that wasn't a monster that I feared him to be, I saw him as someone who could help me through this. Maybe that was the vibe I was getting from him all along, and that was why when I was near him, I began to calm down.

Or maybe there was something more to it.

Shaking away the thought, I tried to take in the moment and clear my head. I needed food, more specifically blood, and I would have to hunt to do so. It wasn't that I had never hunted before, I had hunted many times with my camp, but that was with weapons. This was completely different, this was one-on-one, and I didn't need to kill the animal since Radu explained to me that we couldn't kill every creature for their blood. There would be none left to survive on after a while, especially with all of Petru's other, less responsible strigoi scattered about these woods. We needed blood every night and blood from an already dead creature wasn't as satisfying as blood taken from a live animal. For some reason, it didn't turn animals into strigoi as it would a human. They had some kind of immunity to the blood curse.

I spotted a young buck as he glided through the forest, heading back to his home. I quickly approached him and with Radu's help, I knocked him onto the ground and quickly bit his neck. The warm nectar filled my mouth. I could control it this time, I didn't need more than what was needed to appease my thirst. Once I was finished, I let the creature go and it galloped away, as if nothing had happened.

Wiping the blood away from my mouth, "why don't strigoi just drink the blood of animals instead of humans? Wouldn't it be easier and not attract suspicion?"

"Humans give off a lot more energy than animals do. I am not sure why, but it is a lot more satisfying..." he seemed to let the word linger as he drifted into a thought. He shook his head. "But luckily you didn't have enough human blood to begin with."

I remembered the feeling when I took the blood from Jack. It did feel like I gathered a lot more energy from him than I had from drinking the blood of the dead carcass that was stored in the butcher tent. I didn't realize until now that there had been a difference, that Jack had given me more energy. I hoped I would never feel that again.

The night felt wonderful to be out in. I felt more alive than I had ever felt before this night. I had thought I would miss the supposed thriving life of the forest during the day, but night was far more interesting and was lively in its own unique way. At night, you were able to see more features of the forest than you could ever see during the day. Nighttime was when a lot of animals were still active and roaming about the woods—the owl, the wolf, the fox. It was a beautiful sight that I had never witnessed before this, never having the chance to really be out in the middle of the night with these profound new senses.

Radu noticed my surprise and laughed. "It is lovely, isn't it? The nights like these when there is nothing to worry about. It's just you and the life that has come out to play."

I nodded. "Yes, I could learn to love it. But..." I began and stopped.

"But you miss your family and friends?"

"Yes, I can't stop thinking about how I am the cause of all this, that their death was because..." I began and stopped before the tears came rushing back.

He placed his arm around me. "It's alright; it's not your fault. Just remember that they shouldn't have chased you away but rather helped you through this. You weren't going to harm them yet they treated you like a beast. I am here now; you can trust that I would never hurt you like they did."

He was right, I had just needed help from those in my camp, yet they took me by surprise by being prepared to kill me. The people I grew up with, the people who raised me—they would have destroyed me if I hadn't run from them and Radu hadn't helped hide me away.

It felt strange to be in Radu's arms. Even with my few hours of being with him, I felt as if I knew him. It also left an ache in my chest, that I could get this close to a man after Jack had confessed his love to me that very same day. Was I really that fickle? Or was there something different about Radu, and him being in the same situation as I, that made me feel safe and secure? Or maybe it was because Jack had turned on me so quickly when he found out I was a strigoi that it had broken my heart?

I was still the same person, I knew. I felt normal enough, besides the heightened senses. I thought I would feel a lot more different, I thought I would feel as if everything would be changed to the point of no longer being able to identify myself quite as clearly, as a rational human being. But I didn't. I felt like me.

"What was it like for you when you first were changed? When you became a strigoi?" I asked as we headed back to Radu's make-shift cave. I had more energy now that I had fed, but I still didn't feel as powerful as I did after I drank Jack's blood. I wanted more human blood, I had to admit, but I didn't think I could bring myself to drink it ever again, not after all that heartache and angst caused by that incident.

Radu shrugged. "I guess I had the same feeling as you. I was wondering what was going on, why it was happening to me. Petru, though, didn't let me go as he did you, so I had to face it, while locked away in that castle for a while. He kept me there until I was very weak and hungry so that I would attack the first person I saw, once I left the castle. He found joy in it, I suppose. But I got away in the end and have been on the run ever since."

"I'm sorry, I shouldn't have brought it up," I began.

"It's fine. I never saw my family again though, although they probably would have had the same response as your family and fellow tribe members had, not wanting to deal with me and any ilk like me. They probably would have killed me the first chance they had as well."

I nodded, recalling the scene with my mother. She wanted to kill me; to destroy what she thought was a curse on the camp. If she just listened, she would have realized it was still me. Given a little to get used to these strange new senses, I could have handled it, and maybe then, none of this would have happened. I would never have had to run into the woods and I would have never found Radu.

The sun began to rise in the distance and we quickly went back to the hideaway. Radu was right, though, none of the sunlight entered his little cave. It was pitch black, yet I could see perfectly fine, with my more nocturnal-refined eyesight

"We should probably get our rest. We must be prepared to end that bastard's life once and for all; that damn Petru" he hung up his coat. "We will attack at twilight."

I nodded and he gave me his bed while he slept on the floor. For once in my life, I felt strong enough to do something by myself.

Twilight came and we went over the plan once more. I was to get to the room with the scroll in it as Radu made a distraction to detain Petru. Easy enough, but I still wasn't sure what type of spell breaking this curse would involve. Although my mother had taught me a lot, I didn't think I was strong enough. I didn't know if it would involve any ingredients that I would need. It wouldn't be that easy to have to go back out and get those ingredients and then come back again. I didn't have anything with me and I doubted the strigoi would have any of it, especially if they thought it was all part of some concoction to kill them.

I did feel ready for this moment, as if my life up to this point was preparing me for this. It didn't seem possible and it felt out of place, but the feeling was there, as if someone was whispering just how to feel about the impending battle in my ear. It was strange, but I couldn't shake the feeling that this was all a preordained plan, and that someone was guiding me along the way. I believed it was the spirits of my ancestors helping me defeat this evil, and that is what gave me the confidence I needed.

The moon was out, bright and full once again. I knew that this was our only night to enter the castle for a month and we would have to get it right. If there was any screw ups, then the castle would never be destroyed, since I was the last in my line with any innate magic potential.

The castle was a lot eerier than I had remembered. The darkened stone, the broken and cracked windows. A couple of bats flew overhead. It was horrifying.

And almost perfect, in a way.

It felt as if someone had set it up this way to make me afraid, so it would seem like I was going into a place where I might not ever return from. I was a smart girl, at least I thought so, and I felt this strange foreboding, out-of-place feeling, suddenly, about all of this. Where was that heroic stride, of feeling like everything was preordained and that all was going to be fine?

The feeling didn't matter; I knew I had to do this. I had to get rid of the strigoi once and for all. Even if it meant my demise,

I had to try. I had to avenge my camp's death, if not to seek vengeance for the creature Petru had made me into.

So we entered the castle.

I expected to hear the violin playing, but there was no sound whatsoever, only silence haunting our every step. I looked around for the shadows that I had remembered the night before, but there were none. We seemed to be the only two in the entire place.

"Now, you remember where to go. I will distract him upstairs. Be quick or he will figure out what we are trying to do."

I nodded and started toward the room, fear making my body want to turn around and leave. But I couldn't, I had to be brave.

This was my one shot to finally subdue the leader of the strigoi. I couldn't mess this up.

The room was exactly where Radu said it would be. It was dark throughout the entire castle, but it didn't matter now. I could see perfectly fine. I was surprised that I hadn't seen anyone out yet, but I had no idea how many strigoi there were altogether. For all I knew, it could have been just Petru and no one else, while the shadows I thought I saw were simply shadows and not any strigoi skulking the corridors around where the book was to be found.

I looked all over for the book that Radu said would be there. I checked every nook and cranny of the area, but it wasn't there.

"Looking for something?" I heard a voice ask.

I spun around to find the man of the other night smiling, holding Radu by the throat. His blue eyes were full of satisfaction for he had caught us in the act. His century-old attire seemed perfect, as if he didn't even have to put up a fight against Radu, whose clothes were torn and ripped now. Even Petru's hair looked perfect, not a piece out of place.

"I'm sorry," Radu said.

I gulped. He held up the book. "Seems you were after this, weren't you?"

I didn't say a word; I was shocked into silence by the sight of Radu being strangled by this impressively-sized, rather formidable strigoi. Petru was a force to be reckoned with.

He threw the book on the table. "Funny, my son forgot to mention to you that nothing can get past me and your plot to destroy me would fail miserably no matter what you did."

Son? Did I hear him right?

He raised an eyebrow. "He didn't mention that part either, did he? This is my son Razvan, and I am his father Petru. We have been living in this castle for centuries, until a curse was placed on us by your kind, one which we have suffered through for all these emotionally-numbing centuries. It was your people who did this to me. I never wanted to be like this."

"Why?" I squeaked. "Why would they do this to you?"

"Because they didn't agree with the way we had ruled this land. They didn't want me as a ruler anymore so they cursed me and my family to roam this land for an eternity. But then they realized their mistake in doing so and trapped me in this castle. It is their fault I am this way, it is their fault that they left me no choice but to live on in this depressing castle."

I shook my head. "I won't lift the curse. I won't let you leave this place."

He pulled up his son, making his grip tighter around his neck. Razvan started to gag.

"Don't hurt him!" I exclaimed. He had been the only one to help me through all of this, even though he had lied about who he was, although I could understand why. I don't know if I could have trusted him knowing he was the son of such a horrible man. No, I felt that for once I could trust someone even though he had lied to me.

"Why would you care? He must be punished for defying me."

"No, please don't. It isn't his fault."

"Oh, I highly doubt that," he squeezed harder. Razvan looked like he was in so much pain.

"Please stop! I will look at the spell. I will see if there is a way to undo it!"

He stopped and smiled. "You would betray your entire family just to save someone who lied to you?"

"Don't do it, Amalia. Please, don't let him out of here," Razvan gasped.

Petru squeezed tighter. "Shut up, you fool. Let the girl make up her mind on her own," he turned to me. "Well, what do you say, darling?"

I glanced at Razvan. He was suffering because of me. And for once in my life, I would be able to end someone's suffering. Even if I destroyed this castle and all the strigoi in it, it wouldn't bring back my camp or my family. They were all gone and I had no one left.

Except for Razvan.

"Yes, I will, but I will need to study the writings. May we go somewhere a little nicer so I can look at them carefully?"

He nodded. "Yes, let us go up to my parlor," he gestured to the stairs. "After you, my darling."

I went up the stairs, my heart racing as it had before. I did see shadows this time, racing around me. There were others here; they were just hiding so they could capture us when we were distracted.

We made it to the top of the stairs and entered the parlor. It was exactly how I remembered it, the fireplace was going as it was before, and the furnishings were clean compared to the rest of the castle. I wondered why that was.

"Now," Petru threw down the scroll with the text of the spell on the table. "Get to reading." He still had Razvan in his grip.

"Let Razvan go."

"Not until you undo this spell," he said.

"I want to know that you won't hurt him."

"I won't unless you don't hold up your part of the bargain. Now, as I said, get to reading."

I sighed and unwound the scroll. The spell went into great detail as to what had happened years before. Petru had slaughtered so many innocent lives, and that was before he was a strigoi. After that, he had killed many more, including many in my camp and the cities surrounding it. The more I read, the more I realized I couldn't let this man live.

I had to destroy him once and for all. I found the part of the spell that went into detail as how to do that. It was simple enough; I just had to repeat one sentence three times.

That was it? I couldn't believe it, there had to have been a catch. The method of ultimately freeing him had to be harder than this. To do the spell, I had to gather a candle and a gold candle stick, chant a prayer, and pour the wax on my hand.

"Alright, I am ready," I said. "I need a candle and a gold candle stick."

Petru gave me everything needed to work the spell, so I slowly lit the candle, beginning the task of doing my first spell on my own. Although the circumstances were horrible, I did feel a sort of excitement as to see whether or not I could perform such a power spell on my own. I knew I shouldn't have felt like that, but I couldn't help myself. The power that was accumulating in the air was overwhelming.

I waited for the wax to start to slowly melt, so I could appear to be getting the spell ready. My plan was to act like I was preparing for the spell to lift the curse when at the last minute I would repeat the words to destroy the strigoi for once and for all. I presumed Petru knew what I needed to do and I had to act like I was doing it until the last moment.

Razvan looked at me sadly, wondering what I had to be thinking in order to actually pursue this. He still thought I was going to bring the barrier down so that his father could hurt the surrounding land, and wreak havoc on the villages. I couldn't let that happen.

"Cum lumina Lunei pline și Stelelor de noapte, așa peretele nu va mai fii."

That was the first step. I felt a slight breeze go through the room. Razvan was shaking his head not to do this. I gave him a wink, letting him know I had it all under control.

"Prin voința mea și viața mea, aceste creaturi vor fi praf!"

"No!" Petru shouted. "That is not what you need to be saying! Stop or I will kill him!"

"Prin voința mea și viața mea, aceste creaturi vor fi praf!" I threw the candlestick at him, but he ducked and it shattered into the mirror.

Everything went silent and darkened. I glanced around to find the room darkened with dust and decay. The mirror in front of me was shattered and I didn't understand what had happened. Nothing in the room seemed the same, but everything was ripped and shredded. The fire was no longer going and the only window in this darkened room had shattered into small pieces of broken glass.

I glanced around the room, looking for Petru and Razvan. I saw a dried carcass on the ground and screamed.

Behind me, I could hear laughter. I turned around and found Razvan standing behind me, laughing. "Well, well, this is a strange development."

I shook my head. "I don't understand, what is going on?"

He gestured to the broken mirror. "You destroyed my masterpiece of a story. You broke my mirror that I had been using to lead you to believe everything was real."

I tried to understand what he was getting at. "None of this was real?"

Razvan laughed. "No, no. It was all in your mind. The mirror gave you the illusion of everything that was happening. Just a little trick I picked up over the years. Your grandmother wasn't the only one who knew magic."

I couldn't believe it, yet it answered so many questions that were in my mind. It answered all the doubts I had about what had been going on, it was because it wasn't real. There was only one question that was still going through my mind. "Why?"

"To get you to break this stupid curse. You were supposed to repeat the lines 'Prin voința mea și viața mea, aceste creaturi vor fi praf' while holding the candle stick, just like I knew you would, and it would have broken the curse and I could have exacted vengeance on your little camp and throughout all of Romania."

I shook my head. "But everyone..."

"Is dead? No, that was all part of the trance I had you in. Seemed real didn't it?"

"So you are saying that I never went back to the camp? I never became a strigoi?" I asked.

He shook his head. "No, none of that happened. You have been here for almost three nights now. You aren't a strigoi, believe me the process is far more painful. You wouldn't have woken up not knowing."

"But..." I glanced down at the carcass. "Who is that?"

"Oh him?" he nudged the body with his foot. "That was my father, at least that part was true. We haven't had a human come in here for a very long time. I got lucky with you. Had to devour my entire family. I am the one the story in the scroll talks about, not him," he let out a slight chuckle. "Funny how I can get you to read it however I please."

We stood there in silence for a moment. So I was still human, my family was still alive, and they probably all thought I was dead, which was probably going to happen soon. After everything, I didn't know what to do. I thought I could trust him; he made me believe I could trust him. I wanted to slap him but I knew he was much stronger than me.

"What now?" I asked.

"You are going to finish breaking the curse and let me out of this prison."

"I'd rather die than help you," I shot back.

He smirked. "I'm not going to kill you. No, I have a better plan than that," he grabbed me by the throat. "If you don't help me get out of here, I will turn you into a strigoi for real this time. Then we will wait and see when you will break this curse. So, what is it? Will you save me the trouble and break it now? Or do you want to suffer my fate?"

"I won't betray my people," I gasped.

He shrugged. "If you insist," Razvan bit down into my throat. I let out a shrill scream. The pain was unbearable. Tears were running out of my eyes and down my face. I couldn't breathe. All I could do was feel the pain and feel as my body began to die, yet I was conscious for all of it. My body was dying but my spirit stayed. I screamed out more and more, but it didn't help. The pain was still there and it wasn't going away.

Finally, he let me go, and I fell down to the ground. I tried to move, but couldn't. I simply lay there, conscious of everything, but not able to do anything about the pain that still coursed through my body. I felt my heart stop, the air from my lungs go away. Blood stopped moving through my body and everything was shutting down slowly.

I was dying and I could feel it all.

Razvan sat down on his half ripped-up cushioned chair. "Gets worse as time goes by. Takes a day or two for the pain to go numb but then the body starts to get hungry and there is only one thing to satisfy it. Blood. Nothing else, not all the food in the world, nor any drink to numb the effects. That is what it is like to live with this curse every day for a hundred years. Now, you and I, we get to live through this together. Until *you* decide to end it. The longer you wait, the more it will hurt. So really, you are the only one who can save yourself now."

One last tear fell from my eye that night. The last tear I would ever shed. He was right, the pain would numb after a while, but it didn't make the hunger go away. Do you know what it is like to starve for hundreds of years? Slowly, not being able to die from it, but not being able to live with it either? It's pain beyond your wildest dreams.

Time came to pass when the world began to develop around us, but no one ever noticed the castle that came out at night. We were still deep in the woods, and the only people who came by were those traveling through the area. They never stopped or took notice. Razvan played his violin every night, but none ever came to listen. None were ever anywhere as entranced as I was on that not-so fateful day.

My camp left the area centuries ago, probably moving to some new woods. I saw them search for me, but there was nothing I could do. I didn't want them to find me in fear of what I might do to them, and what they would do to me. Of course, after years as this damned creature, I got to know more about Razvan. He was the bastard that the scroll had made him out to be. I had found so many drained strigoi through the castle; it made me sick to think that for even a moment that I felt close to him, even though it was the mirror that persuaded me. I am still surprised he hasn't killed me.

I can't imagine what he would do if I broke the curse now. There are so many people in the world now, and I don't think any of them could stop him. He is an intelligent man, even if he is beyond evil. He would figure out a way to never get caught, to never see the day of his own death. I thought about trying to kill him myself, but I would never be strong enough and I had this urge not to die. It is an internal instinct that I don't quite understand. I hate it, really.

So here I am, looking out into the world that doesn't believe we exist. A world of science and destruction, a world where people think what they don't know can't hurt them. Well, believe me, what you don't know can hurt you, and it is I who stands between you and him.

And I am beginning to think that even the smallest drop of blood would be worth leaving this place for.

A WORLD OF VAMPIRES

n inch of time is an inch of gold, but an inch of time cannot be purchased for an inch of gold. It was an old Chinese saying and, at one time, I believed that time was worth more than gold, I planned on spending what limited time that I had with my wife, my two children, and my brother, as we traveled across the seas in search of a better a life. Our adventure was supposed to bring us happiness, if not some kind of viable fortune. But to my wife and I, all that mattered was each other. She didn't care about money, just that our family could have the possibility of surviving in a new country. In that way, I had ultimately failed her. I had failed everything, leaving me to suffer for it all in the end. This all happened over a hundred and fifty years ago, and now I just wish that time would run out for good to destroy whatever guilt-ridden memories I had of what I had done to betray my wife's dreams.

I hear the rumors in the night, passing over me, that speak of people who want to become immortal, who want to become this... thing... this jiangshi that feasts on the qi, the very life force believed to occupy another living being. It makes me sick that such people can even dream of doing such things to each other, although I'm not one to talk. Greed and wrath were the cause of this curse unleashed upon me and I would never forget that one tragic choice that led to my demise. How I wish those demons were easier to battle, then maybe I could have lived a peaceful life, with a headstone saying "Hui Zhang, who lived a happy life with his family" and be buried peacefully in the grave next to my wife and kids. And my brother.

It was surprising how much things changed between the 1850s and the present day. San Francisco itself had changed so much, between the gold rush, the age of industrialism, both world wars, and the eventual suburban sprawl of the city. I watched it all happen, hidden away in the darkness, as I hunt for the qi to keep myself barely alive. I have found places to hide during the time that the sun shines, even as buildings change and people have become increasingly stricter with security. There are still areas I could find, though, where people never dare venture.

There is a saying from my native country that solemnly says, 'wū lòu piān féng lián yè yǔ', meaning 'when the roof is leaking, there will be continuous nights of rain'. I think that saying holds true for most of my life, and I have an extensive experience of life to back this up. Every part of my life seemed to fall apart. One thing after another, nothing went right at any time. And, it was all my fault.

I could blame someone else instead of myself, I knew. I could blame some evil creature or some demon for the things I did, to make myself feel better about it all, having lost everything in my life. But I knew that it wasn't true. No, it all started with one single bad decision I had made in the past and now I suffered the consequences for the remainder of eternity for it. I had created this evil inside of me and I would have to live with that fact for the rest of my unnaturally extended life.

It all started over a hundred fifty years ago, when I had decided to take my family and move to America. Back then, America was thriving. It was a beautiful country with so many possibilities, or at least, that was what was promised to anyone emigrating there. My own home country, China, had just suffered through the Opium Wars and a lot of us had decided to move to the new country of America, in order to survive and make money for our families. I was living in the providence of Fujian, just off the sea, which had very little fertile land by tail-end of the Opium Wars. Most of its physical terrain was made up of mostly water and mountain terrain, making it very hard to survive, especially when the taxes of our homeland began to increase substantially after the war. A lot of men left their families at home and sent money over for them, so that they could save up and return one day, if not bring their whole families over there once they had enough money to securely move themselves to America.

Although times were hard in Fujian, and in the rest of China, I didn't want to leave my homeland. My family had been farming lotus seeds and roots for a very long time, and I felt I would be disgracing them if I left it all behind in pursuit of carving out a new existence in a new land. I did have some cousins who were planning to take over the farm in my absence, but the guilt still ate me up inside as my older brother Ming and I sailed across the ocean with my wife Meilin and two children Li and Ruoxi. My brother had no remorse about leaving behind the rest of our family in China, including our cousins and and an elderly uncle. I promised them that I would send over some of the money I would be making, hinting to my brother that he should do the same. He ignored that hint and never promised anything along those lines.

The journey over was a tough one. We had to raise the money to pay for the boat passage and then we were on that boat for what seemed to be a very long time. Not many of the passengers talked to each other, as they were scared out of their wits by the whole notion of sailing on a ship over the world's largest body of water. More important, none of us knew what was in store for us when we arrived in America, we just hoped the rumors of plenty of higher wage jobs being available was true, making this entire daunting sea voyage worth every agonizing minute.

Out of everyone on the boat, Ming seemed to be the one that was the least worried about what awaited him on shore. It was as if he didn't have a care in the world, just wanting desperately to get to America so he could get more money from foolishly gambling away what little he had. He was selfish like that, but lazy as well. Back on our farm, he always seemed to do a lot less work than any of the other farm hands, and yet inexplicably took the same amount of money as I for much less work. He had no sense of honor or, it seemed, to want to work hard, honest labor for his earnings.

Once we arrived to America, we were met with prejudice and what almost felt like disgrace. The white men would look down at us and the jobs offered had lower salaries than those attained by the white men. White women wouldn't even make eye contact with us. At first this was hurtful, but after a while, my family and I didn't care at all for their approval. We were still earning more than we would in Fujian and there was a large community of Chinese immigrants like ourselves that we could belong to.

My brother and I got hired in the growing gold mining industry of California. We shared a small apartment within the Chinese district of San Francisco. My brother decided that he was going to live with my family, since he didn't want to pay for a place of his own. He argued that family should stick together, but I knew the real reason. He didn't want use his own money, he didn't care about family. It was a little cramped at times with even just the five of us, but we made due. He squandered most of his money, gambling, and drinking, choosing to depend on me to provide him both food and sleeping quarters with my own meagerly wages. Meilin wanted him to leave us since he was taking away our share of the money. We spent quite a few nights arguing about this matter intensely, but in the end he never left. I was too afraid to kick him out, out of fear of what his drunkenness would cause him to do. But, a day came, where all of that would change.

Ming and I were working in the mine one day; the dark lighting and dust-filled air made us choke and cough spastically during work and after work. I had noticed that some people are affected more than others. Those who were American didn't seem to have as bad of a reaction, although that could have been because they weren't sent in the same areas that we were. We were treated like animals at times, but it was something I suffered every day so that I might be able to provide for my family. There was no other way. Sometimes, I felt like the only one struggling to responsibly manage my funds, to try and make that distant dream a possibility. Although I knew my dreams to be something I probably would never achieve, it didn't mean I couldn't let them lighten my spirits time-to-time. I just had to try and keep working and believe that some day those dreams could come true.

We kept on working through the hot summer day, the heat eating away at my skin and mind. Others were suffering right along with us, as well, but the reward was well worth it in the end. As I promised, I had been sending spare money to our extended family back in China. Although it seemed circumstances kept getting rougher for them in Fujian, they kept on working as well. I told them to come to America eventually and that I could get them a job at the mining company, but they wouldn't budge. As I worked away, I could see why they wouldn't want this, even though it brought more food to the plate. It was demeaning work, but neither I nor my brother cared. So day after day, we found ourselves with a pick, shaving away the exterior rock, so we could all someday find the miraculous gold we were all searching for.

"Ming, Hui," our supervisor Charlie came over, his face covered in dirt, and his hands, even when we weren't in the mines, never seemed to be clean. "I have a job for you two boys."

"What is it, sir?" I asked with a brief sigh. Even though I hated our supervisor, I always called him sir. It was the honorable thing to do, even if he treated us horribly.

He flashed a toothless grin. "I need you two to go down as far as the tunnel goes and start digging there. Take this light with you, you two will need it. Report back here if you find anything."

I glanced down the dark tunnel. Men had been talking about how poorly made the tunnel was and how it could collapse at any time without warning. Some even said it should be condemned. "But sir..." I began.

"Are you disobeying my orders?" Charlie rolled up his sleeves. "No one disobeys my orders."

"No, no sir, I was just gonna ask if we can have another light," I explained. Ming did nothing to help the situation but stand there and wait to see how it would end. He never seemed to help in situations like this.

Charlie narrowed his eyes. "One light per group. Now go before I decide to send you somewhere else. Somewhere worse."

I nodded and hurried off with the lamp. Ming followed me as we made our way deeper into the mine, leading the two of us into a very dank part of the cave.

"I can't believe you didn't help me back there, we shouldn't be coming down here, no one should be," I mumbled to Ming.

"He was going to send us either way, just except that. They spit on us here."

"But if something happened, Meilin, Ruoxi and Li would be left alone," I worried. My heart was filled with fear every moment I was down dreading the possibility of death. The only thing that kept me going was knowing it was the only way to support our family. I just wished there was a way I could leave this job behind and make money another way, but in order to do that, I would have needed a larger sum to start out with.

"Oh, they would be fine. I would take care of them, you know that."

"If something happened to me down here, it would hurt you as well."

He shook his head. "No, we both know that I am the stronger brother. Nothing bad could ever happen to me," he laughed. I just glared at him, trying not to think about it all. He would likely spend all the money and probably leave none for my wife and children. No, I could never let anything happen to myself and leave him in charge.

We made it to the end of the corridor and my fear was confirmed. The area seemed unstable. I quickly put down the lamp and started work at the difficult task ahead, hoping that the day would go by quickly. I didn't want to be here any longer, even though we had just started this tedious job weeks ago. I doubted that there was gold down here, Charlie just wanted to mess with us. He hadn't liked us or any of the Chinese men from day one and would send a couple of the men from our group on dangerous tasks daily.

Lunch time came and my brother and I took a small break, where we worked to eat the meal Meilin had made us. She made the best steam buns on the entire planet and I was very excited to see that was what she had packed for us. It made my day a little bit better.

Ming sat down against the wall. Some pebbles rolled off the wall all because Ming showed no care when leaning back on it. I gulped as I looked up at the ceiling, which thankfully still seemed to be holding together. Meaning, no risk yet of us being caved in here.

"Hui, do you think there is anything back here or do you think our boss is just a jerk?" Ming asked as he chewed off a piece of his steam bun.

I shrugged. "We don't know that for a fact, there could be something back here. We just have to keep working diligently in order to find it."

"Yeah, well, I don't like it when he uses us as bait. This area isn't structurally sound and it is why he only sent the two of us. He doesn't ever send any of the American workers this far in."

"That' because he is a racist and doesn't care about anyone except himself. It would be easier if we were able to make enough money to leave this place. Then I could start up my own business."

Ming raised an eyebrow. "Oh? Like what kind of business?"

"Don't laugh at me, but I really want to paint. It had always been a dream of mine to paint when we were children, but I never had the money to do so. I used to watch our neighbor paint sometimes, until he shooed me away."

Ming laughed. "You are crazy to think such a thing. Unless we find a bunch of gold back here, there is no way that could happen. We are stuck in this life for the rest of our years alive, however many that might be. There is no denying that, Hui."

I sighed. Although it hurt for him to laugh, I knew he was right, there was no way I would be able to become both a painter and be able to support my family. I had to be there for them through everything, and I wasn't keen on missing the best years of their life in any way

We got back to work, knocking rock away from the side wall. It was amazing how such repetitive work began to eat away at my mind. I wanted to do so much more with my life, but I could not. I was sure I was cursed to live out my life in this place, a place I deemed worse than anywhere else imaginable

As for my brother, he didn't seem to mind this menial work as he robotically chipped away the rock. He just did the work he was supposed to and didn't seem to want to complain or do anything else for that matter. It was surprising since he was so lazy when we farmed back home. Maybe it was because here he could get caught not just by me, but by our supervisor who would hurt those who didn't work.

I couldn't believe he didn't have dreams like I did of owning a shop or exploring some other avenue of work besides mining. In Fujian, we had both been farmers, and this work wasn't much different from that other than the fact that mining didn't involve getting rained on, or the disappointing experience of a bad harvest. All we had to do was literally strike gold, smuggle it out of the mine, and we would be set for life.

The hours ticked away, and it was almost time to head out for the day. I wiped the extraneous sweat off of my forehead. I couldn't wait to get out of these stuffy mines and get some fresh air, some sunlight to remedy the depressing darkness of the mine. I just hoped that tonight would be cooler than the last. San Francisco had been having a heat streak, although it still wasn't as bad as the summers we had experienced in China.

"Well brother," Ming knocked the pick into the rock once more. "I don't think we will find anything today."

He hit it once more and the ground around us began to shake. An earthquake. My heart quickened, fear filling my senses. There was nowhere for us to take cover, so the only thing we could do was try to outrun it. I started for my brother, and we hurried down the tunnel. But, it was too late. The rock from the walls began to crumble and large rocks fell and blocked our path. We were trapped.

Both Ming and I were coughing, trying to clear our lungs of all the dust that had gotten trapped in them throughout the day. Gladly, our lamp had survived everything and we had light for at least a few more hours. We would have to dig our way out now, the rock having blocked our only means of escape.

"Are you alright, brother?" Ming asked as he patted my back, while I coughed some more.

I nodded. "I'm alright, we just need to figure out a way out of here."

"The tunnel was the only way out. I don't know how much of it collapsed, hopefully it was only this one section. We should start working it away."

"We have to get out of here, Meilin will be worried," I said as I began to move away the rock. "It doesn't seem to go that far, I think we can move all this rock within an hour before the light goes out. We will just have to work as a team."

Ming nodded, and we started digging through the rock. I had been right about it not going that far, as we began to see the other side of the tunnel within the next hour of digging.

Surprisingly, Ming worked diligently. I presumed it was because he wanted to get out and make it down to the closest bar for a drink. It seemed he would spend almost every night there, drinking and spending money on gambling. It was embarrassing to call him my brother sometimes, as those who saw him drunk in the streets late at night generally disapproved of his behavior. Sometimes I had wished I didn't have a brother, then I would never have to worry about him any longer and I could spend more money on my family.

As we kept moving the rocks away, I noticed something strange. There, lodged within the brown and grey rock was something glittery.

"What is that?" I asked as I moved away the dirt. It was a large chunk of gold, the size of an apple. I gasped. I couldn't believe what I was holding. It was a giant chunk of gold, more gold than I had seen in my entire time working there combined.

"That is gold, my dear brother!" Ming smacked his hand against my back. "Enough gold for you and I to not need to work here any longer, for a while at least. That could last a family for a long while, if not the rest of their lives. Split into two, we would be able to not have to work for a bit, at least."

It could support one family for the rest of their lives, but once it was split into two, we'd both have to return to work. Those words repeated themselves in my mind as I stared at the large piece of gold. I could stop being a miner with this gold, if I could sneak it out of the mine without my brother's notice. Then I could open up my own shop, like I had wanted to. Then all would be good with the world. But in order to do that, I needed everything that the gold provided. He had already seen it, and I wouldn't be able to take everything for it. I would have to split it.

My insides began to feel warm the more I thought about it. Ming, I knew, would waste away his share very fast, even though it would be a large amount. He was not as responsible as I was, and a very extreme part of me did not want to see him squander it so fast. Even worse. I would have to work again, and I wouldn't be able to follow my dreams to escape the doldrums of the mines. I would give anything to escape this place, all I wanted to be was happy with my family, a family that deserved everything in the world, not a brother who wasted away much needed resources.

I glanced at my brother, a dark thought slowly made its way through my mind. No one was around at this moment, and an accident was bound to happen. All that needed to happen was for a rock to hit him in the head. No one would notice, there was a ceiling collapse in the cave. No one would expect me to have done it. Better yet, with this strategy, Charlie wouldn't make sure there was any gold on me when I left. I could easily sneak it out of the mine. Then, this gold would be all mine. And I could live happily, ever after, with my family.

I shook my head. What was I thinking? I couldn't kill my own brother for a piece of gold, even if that gold meant I could live happily with my family without worry of slaving away in a mine again. The more I thought about it, the more I realized Ming didn't even need half of that gold. He only had himself to support, and no family of his own, besides me. It wouldn't be fair for him to have half of it, when I had to support both me and my wife and our two children. But he would still take half and waste it away in what? A month? A week? While if I had all of it, I would make sure it would last for the rest of my life. I shouldn't have to take care of him, he was my older brother. He should have enough responsibility to take care of himself and not take me down with him when he is acting so immature. He didn't deserve all that I had given him over the years and he didn't deserve the gold that was in my hand now.

I began to think about the happy home I could have with Meilin. We would be able to hire a teacher for the children and they would be able to become smart and get better jobs when they grew old enough. I could afford it, and Meilin would never have to worry when shopping for food about how much to spend. She would feel more confident when she walked the streets and I would be able to open a shop, and sell my paintings in it. It would be a dream come true at last.

Ming had his head turned away from me. This was my chance, I would be doing the worst evil of all, but it would bring so much to my home that I couldn't say no. Slowly, I picked up a rock and when he wasn't looking, I smacked him in the back of the head with it. He went down with only one hit. I dropped a larger rock on his head, to make sure it looked like the tunnel had collapsed on him, and to make sure he was dead.

I fumbled back, my heart quickly beating in my chest as I gasped for air. I couldn't believe what I had just done. My hands were shaking and I could barely see straight. I had just killed my one and only brother. How could I have done such a thing? It was pure evil. But the gold...

Looking back at the gold lying there on the ground, I knew it had to be done. I had to be able to support my family and not serve my duty under here every day, dying slowly inside the entire time I toiled away in the cave. No, now I could spend more time with my family and be happy for once. I deserved it and my family deserved it most of all. Ming had depended on my wealth for a while now, he had done wrong by me and it needed to change at this moment. I wouldn't let him ride off of my wealth any longer.

I picked up the gold and placed it in my pocket. There wasn't much rock to move still, so I quickly finished clearing the tunnel and dragged my dead brother out into the open air. Strangely, I didn't feel as remorseful as I thought I would, just emotionally-hardened and even a bit cold, much like the stale air of this cave. As people saw me drag my brother out of the entrance, they helped me take his body into town, and offered me their saddened faces, and remorse for what had happened.

"It was truly terrible," many said, "that such a great man could die so young."

I nodded, as if what they said was true. They didn't know him like I did. It wasn't terrible, it was a blessing. A blessing that I had brought upon myself.

The funeral was set for only a couple days after the unfortunate incident. My family and I were the only ones, who had attended as they lowered the body into the ground. He didn't have many friends, as he had many people he gambled with angry with him for never paying their dues and those who worked in the mines didn't want to take a day off, in fear of what Charlie might do to them if they did. I no longer needed to worry about that.

The grief and guilt over the fact that I had been the one to cause his death, ate at me. I felt like a traitor, as I stood in front of his grave with my wife beside me who had tears streaming down her face. It was her that I felt I was betraying the most, acting as if I was a good brother and had done everything I could in my power to keep him safe. That was a lie and it tore me up inside. But an accident could have theoretically happened as we tried to leave he still could have died without my help. This was just desperate rationalization, wasn't it?

I didn't tell anyone the truth of what had happened, instead saying that a terrible earthquake had caused a rock to fall on his head. I didn't want to go into any more detail than necessary with anyone, afraid that they may have suspected something else. I also didn't want to get lost in the details, say one thing to one person, and another thing to someone else. I wasn't a liar; I wasn't my brother who lied to many people daily. It was hard for me to lie like this, but I knew that in order to keep my family safe, I had to do it. As for Meilin, she didn't seem to suspect anything but the truth from me, which is what hurt me most. I didn't see anyone from the mine other than a few fellow workers wandering the streets time-to-time, but we didn't say much to one another besides. I never went back there, saying that my brother's death left me in such a state of deep grief that it was impossible for me to ever return. No one knew that I had taken gold out of the mine and that I was prepared to sell it to the black market now for profit. I had to wait a few days in order to do so, in order not to raise any suspicion. I wasn't sure who to trust anymore, even myself.

I had nightmares every night after the murder. I knew I would have remorse and grief, but I didn't realize that the event would play over and over in my mind at night. Some times he would come to me as a ghost in my dreams, his face covered in blood, his body decaying. He would keep repeating the word 'murderer'. I woke up in cold sweats more often than not, shaking and shivering. Meilin would ask what was the matter and I would just say it was from the horror of seeing my brother die before my eyes. It wasn't a lie.

A week had passed and I had begun to think that it would be no trouble to sell the gold. I had heard of a place deep in Chinatown that bought gold for a great sum. This man was supposedly a collector of sorts and people always did as he asked. He had quite the reputation and no one messed with him, so I knew that the gold wouldn't get tracked back to me. I just needed to tell my family a solid reason for going out.

"Meilin," I called out. She came to where I was in our little home, her beautiful smile always on her face. My wife had always been at my side through the years, doing all she could to make sure life was fine for us. I owed her everything, especially after everything she had been through with me. She needed this money in order to not have to worry any longer. "I have to go pick up some things, something Ming asked me to do before he died. I will be back later."

She nodded. "Please, be careful. I don't think I can imagine losing you after all that has happened."

"Don't worry, I will be back in time, I promise." I kissed her on the forehead and then left her standing there alone outside the house.

The nights had finally cooled off, and I was glad for it. I could feel the moonlight shinning down on me, as I walked through the streets. Not many people were out since it was so late in the night. Most that were left in the streets at this late hour were criminals or prostitutes.

I kept my head down, not wanting to bring unwanted attention to myself. I didn't want to cause trouble, I just wanted to get the money for the piece of gold and be on my merry way. I jumped at any slight sound that came near me. Most of the time it was either a cat or mouse. No one that was out seemed to notice me, which I was thankful for.

I couldn't believe my brother would travel out here every night. It was dangerous, not to mention stupid. I wondered about all the trouble he got into while he was out. Maybe I didn't want to think about it. Although, if I knew about all the shame he brought on our family name, maybe I would have felt a little better about what I had done.

Was that true? Did what he do bring shame to my family? I wasn't sure as to how he spent his nights, just that he always came back smelling of booze and his money mostly gone. It wasn't hard putting two and two together, and others had said they had seen him talking to some people with bad reputations for gambling. I just wished for once he would have thought about his actions before doing such a thing, but I was never that lucky. Even after everything, I felt tormented about killing him.

I reached the destination of a known man, who bought gold that was snuck out of the mines. The place seemed normal enough, like any other building in the area. I had never actually met the man before, but I knew my brother had done so on a few occasions, along with others working in the mine. If Charlie had ever found out, he would have whipped the men until they could no longer move. He would have been mad for having to find new workers. Charlie never seemed to think ahead when he hurt someone, how it would affect how many employees he had. He also seemed to always be angry, and hate us for no apparent reason. It didn't matter any longer, I would never have to see his ugly face again. I knocked on the door and after a few moments, was let in.

The inside was like nothing I had ever seen before, not even back in my homeland of Fujian. Ornamental Chinese paintings were sprawled out across each wall, paintings of plum blossoms, of the diverse mountain ranges that were scattered across our country. They were a sight to see, such beautiful paintings that made me nostalgic for my homeland. The place was also littered with fine jade statues all along each wall. Buddha, ancient warriors and emperor statues, he had jade statues of them all. He even had every animal of the zodiac as well. Incense was also burning in a little dragon burner, making the room smell of sandalwood and jasmine. I couldn't believe my eyes, it looked like a palace.

"Please, take a seat," an elderly man motioned to the cushion on the floor. I bowed and did as he said. "I am Mengyao, what brings you to my humble office?"

I glanced around. If this was humble, I wanted to see what a non-humble home looked like. How I wished I could live like this. Even with the gold in my pocket, I couldn't live this grand. I didn't need to, though, all I wanted was to start up my painting shop and live a happy life with my wife. "I have some gold available, if you are willing to pay."

He stared at me for a moment, smoking his pipe. "Let me see this gold."

I pulled out the apple-sized chunk that I had found in the tunnel. His eyes widened as he laid his eyes upon it.

"And you found this?" he asked. It must have been one of the largest anyone has ever brought him, which made me quite happy. It meant he might pay more than what it was worth to have such a piece.

I nodded. "Yes, how much are you willing to pay?"

He motioned for me to hand him the gold. I did as he asked, knowing that he wanted to inspect it to make sure it was the real thing. I quietly waited for a response.

"Yes, this is the real thing. I don't know how you got your hand on it, but it is indeed worth quite a pretty penny," he took another breath of his pipe. "I will give you two thousand dollars."

I about passed out from hearing the amount. It was enough to provide for my family for the rest of our lives. I didn't even need to bring money in with my painting. It wouldn't matter. I had no hesitation in answering. "I accept the offer."

He laughed. "Of course you do. Now go, before I change my mind."

I bowed in thanks and hurried off. One of his men paid for the gold and I was ready to start my life anew.

Making my way back to the house, I couldn't wait to share the news with my wife. She had been working so hard with what we had, and now I could finally provide her with everything that she needed and has ever wanted. When we first married, we didn't even have enough money for a real celebration. She made her dress out of old fabric she found and I wore one of my nicer pairs of working clothes. The ceremony took place at our home and the drink that we had provided for everyone, my brother had drank greedily, leaving barely enough for anyone else. Now, Meilin and I could finally live in peace, knowing our children wouldn't have to go through the same hardship we had gone through any longer.

As I traveled down the lonely streets, as no one was out any longer, I began to hear something behind me. *Tha-thunk. Tha-thunk. Tha-thunk.* It sounded like something hopping. I glanced back behind myself, finding nothing that could be making that strange noise. I didn't know what it could have been, but I hurried faster through the street in hopes of outrunning it. I didn't need anything taking away these happy times for me that I long deserved.

Tha-thunk. Tha-thunk.

"*Hui...*" A faint voice called.

It sounded like my brother.

My heart began to beat faster, as I was practically running towards my house now. It wasn't possible, that it could have been my brother calling to me, but I wasn't about to stop to find out. He was dead, I had seen him be ceremoniously lowered into the ground. I couldn't believe such a thing could happen, the idea that he was still alive in some tangible way. It was just my conscience playing a trick on me. I just had to get over this and realize I had saved my family from suffering in the long-run. I had to think of my children.

I made it back to the house without any more trouble. There was no more noise and there didn't seem to be anything following me. I looked outside once more before I looked the door. It must have been my imagination that I had heard my brother. There was no possible way he could be walking around. Not after what I had done to him.

Meilin was still waiting up for me, making sure that I had returned unscathed. I kissed her as she greeted me, and looked around the room. It was small, smaller than quaint. I couldn't wait to tell her the news that we could move out of this place and find someplace new to start up again. That we could live somewhere that didn't have floors covered in dirt, or walls stained with the leaking rain, and a place that had a real kitchen and enough bedrooms for everyone.

"I'm so happy you are alright," she said.

"There was nothing to worry about. I just had to find some of Ming's last assets he left us. Look," I held out my hand with the bag of cash. "He apparently had been saving up. We have enough to live on for a long while."

Her eyes lit up as she shuffled through all the cash. "He left us all of that?"

"Yes," I lied. "Apparently he had done some gambling and won a fortune. He had been keeping it away for a special occasion. Regretfully, we will never know what the exact occasion was."

Meilin looked through the cash she had grabbed from my hand. "This is impossible. I can't believe he did such a thing."

My heart felt as if it had stopped. I should have known she wouldn't believe my lie. I had been a fool. "What do you mean?"

She shrugged. "I don't know, just having lived with him for so long, I can't believe he would keep money like this without spending it. He must have been keeping it for something big."

I nodded. "Yes, I recall him mentioning he wanted to move out. I guess so he could drink more. I didn't think he would ever have enough money to do so, but I guess I was wrong."

"He didn't care much about saving, I agree," Meilin said. "He must have just recently came about it, I doubt it would have lasted long," she wrapped her arms around me. "This is great news, Hui. We can finally open that shop we have always wanted and you can paint."

I nodded. Meilin knew my passion of painting, as I had tried to practice while in Fujian. I could never get time, though, having spent most of the day out in the field and we didn't have enough money for candles or any sort of lighting at night. I squeezed her tight. "Yes, yes we can."

"We will tell the children in the morning this wonderful news," she kissed me on the lips. "We can finally afford the education we wanted to give them as well. We will finally have peace in this house."

It made me glad to hear she thought that. She looked so happy now, and it made me feel warm inside, knowing I had brought it to her. It was worth the guilt I would be suffering until the day I died. It was worth making her happy.

I glanced out the window, swearing I had seen something move by the window. I just hoped she was right about the fact that we could live in peace now.

We explained to the children what was going on, that we no longer had to live in the shack, but were able to move to a real home with more than two rooms. We also told them that I had no longer needed to work in the mines, but was able to run a shop below our home. They didn't quite understand it all, but they were happy that they now had enough food and could buy things that they all dreamed of having. They also would be getting a tutor, a woman Meilin knew from town. She said she was one of the best in the area and the woman could teach them writing, English, Mandarin, history, and American culture. I felt so proud of them, knowing they would be able to do great in this world with such a tutor.

Meilin and I purchased a shop with a home on the second floor. We would be able to sell trinkets and my paintings on the first floor and there was room for a studio in the back. There was also a room that we could use for the children to be taught by their tutor. It didn't cost much compared to what we had, and I was much thankful for that. We still had plenty left to live off of for a while.

I began my work painting, just as I had always wanted to do. I set up shop, with my fine paint brushes I could now afford, along with the rice paper I'd always dreamed of having the means to buy, and I began painting.

It took a while to get used the elegant equipment, compared to the regular make-shift brush and cheap dye I had been using when I could, which was rare, but since I had been practicing any chance I could, I picked it up quickly.

I painted many scenes from the farm I had worked on so many years ago. I painted animals, flowers, landscape, even a picture of my wife, which I kept hanged in my studio. I enjoyed working my own hours, my wife coming and watching me whenever she wanted, and Li and Ruoxi running around when they weren't studying. I let them paint some, teaching them the technique behind it. They were still too young to be interested fully, but I hoped one day they would take to it. It would only be a matter of time.

Recalling the first time I tried to paint, all I had were some sticks, grass, mud, and a scrap piece of fabric. I had seen someone painting when my father and I had gone to the market to sell some of our Lotus root and flowers. I wanted to stand there and watch the artist, but my father made me leave with him. That night, I grabbed what few things I had and tried to paint. It didn't turn out as I had envisioned it, of course, I was too young. If I remembered correctly, it was just some lines that I thought looked like a cow. My father caught me and scowled at me for ruining perfectly good fabric. I didn't do any art until later in life, when I knew I wouldn't be caught by my parents, or when Meilin and I were married. She believed in me and always supported me when I spent what little time I had trying to master the craft. Now I had all the time in the world.

We had a few customers buy the paintings which I was thankful for. I asked a relatively high price for them, but they still accepted the offer. Business kept growing and I was painting every day for as long as I could.

One night, I was working late on a painting of the mountainscape I remembered from when I was just a young boy, when I heard something in the shop. I put the brush down and stood up. It was probably just my imagination, but I had to make sure everything was fine. I was sure that I had locked up but one could never be too careful.

I quietly stepped into the main area of the shop to find everything as it was. Nothing seemed to be shifted out-of-place, but I checked around again just to make sure for my own sanity.

"Hui..."

It was him, it was my brother. My heart began to race in my chest. It couldn't be possible. I searched all around, but I didn't see any trace of him.

"Hui..."

The sound was coming from outside. I quickly raced out into the street to find only a single figure out in the night.

And it indeed was my brother.

"Ming, how is it possible?" I explained. "I buried you, how are you here?"

"My soul cannot go to the afterlife, because of you, brother. You murdered me with evil intent. I was killed wrongfully and now my soul will wander this world for thousands of years to come. And it was all because of you and your selfish greed."

I took a look at him again. His skin was pale blue, dark crusted blood running down the side of his head, leaving some of his black hair crusted with blood. His once braided hair was disheveled, strands sticking out every which way. His nails were like claws, having seemed that they had grown as his skin had shrunken back on his skin.

I couldn't believe my eyes. I knew what he was, I had heard stories growing up of people who died and came back to life. I jabbed my finger at him, petrified. "You... you are a jiangshi!"

"That is right brother, and it's all because of you!"

I shook my head. "No, it wasn't my fault. I needed to support my family, I had to take the gold for myself."

"You could have shared it with me and you know it, brother," Ming shot back, his eyes a glowing yellow, blood lines radiating from the pupils. His teeth seemed sharper as well, from what I could see as he had opened his mouth. He even seemed a bit more bloated.

"No, I had to do it, so then I would have enough to live on. There wasn't enough for all of us. You know that, you know you would have wasted it all away!" I said.

"You mean there wasn't enough for you to begin your art career. You would have been fine with just half and you knew it!"

I shook my head. "No, I had to provide for my family. You would have been selfish and tried to use mine as well!"

My brother began to move towards me, stiff-like in his steps. As his body decayed, it made it harder for the creature to move smoothly. "No, brother, I wouldn't have. Now you must pay the price!"

"What do you mean?" I gasped.

Ming started hopping towards me, as if he were going to attack. I hurried back into the shop and locked the door behind me. He tapped his long nail on the door. The sound made me shudder. My very breath felt winded by the terror of what I had just seen.

"You can run brother, but you will not get away from your destiny in the end!" he called from outside the door. I heard an eerie laughter, and then all was silent again.

I looked out the window and saw nothing on the street. He had left for now. I took a deep breath, trying to slow down my heart beat.

My brother was back from the dead, and he was going to do everything he could to destroy my life.

The night went by and I never saw any trace of my brother again. I wondered if it had really been a dream, seeing him alive as a jiangshi. I had been having nightmares about him still, haunting me. Maybe I had fallen asleep at my desk and it was all just another nightmare. I wanted to believe that to be true, but I *had* seen him. And I didn't sleep that night after. I couldn't, in fear that he would return and take his revenge out on me. I also had to stay awake and protect my wife and children. I couldn't let a beast such as that get to them.

Meilin asked why I never came to bed and I just said it was because I had to finish the painting, which still laid where I had left it when Ming came for me. I didn't work on it after he came, but curled up in the corner of the room, frightened and scared. I couldn't admit to her what had happened, she would think I was crazy and worry about me. She would also be wondering why he would even want to haunt me in the first place, and I could never tell her the truth of what I had done. No, I would have to keep this to myself, even if it killed me in the end.

I must have seemed out of it, to her, for a while, afraid that Ming would come back. But the days went by and I thought I was finally in the clear, just like the few hours after killing him were strangely tranquil and uneventful.

I had been wrong.

It was a month after his death, when I was out delivering a painting to the same man who had bought my gold weeks earlier, Mengyao. He had noticed my booming painting business and very much liked one painting that I had recently painted, depicting a dragon flying through the clouds. He bought it for twice the normal amount I would ask, as long as I personally delivered it to him that night without delay. He also wanted to speak to me about a commission of a painting that he was having trouble finding someone to paint. I tried to ask what that was, but his messenger would not tell me, but rather insisted I came that night to find out. So, knowing that I couldn't say no to such a promising project, I hurried off with my painting into the night.

The streets were quiet, as I walked through them. There wasn't a soul in sight, at least none that I could see. Lights flickered from lamps that hung outside shops and homes, keeping the streets pretty well-lit. I listened for any slight sound, still afraid that my brother would come out of the darkness and take his revenge out on me. But there was nothing.

I made it to the man's home undisturbed by my brother's reappearance, the house was still grand as ever. He had added even more decor to the home, new fountains outside with koi swimming around in them. They were large fish and probably worth quite a sum now. I wondered if he bought them at that size, or if he had them for a long while and they grew to that size. They swam around slowly, there had to be at least a dozen of them, ranging in color from black to white to orange. They were beautiful, like flowers floating in the water.

One of his servants led me into the home, and to the main room where Mengyao awaited me. He sat at the same desk, as he did when I first came here.

"Let me see the painting," he said as he stayed seated, stroking his white beard.

His servant and I unrolled the painting and showed him. He grinned widely. "Very good, spectacular. It seems good fortune has followed you, Hui."

I bowed. "Thank you sir."

Mengyao gestured to his servant to take away the painting. A little bit later, he brought me a small pouch of coins.

"Now, as for the painting I want you to do, please take a seat," he gestured to the cushion once more.

I knelt down on the cushion and awaited his specific order. I was curious as to what it could be. A mythical bird? Another dragon? The Forbidden Palace?

He smoked his pipe for a moment, as if studying me, debating whether or not I could paint what he wanted me to. I knew that I could, it was just a matter of time. I wondered what could be so difficult about what he wanted painted. "I want you to paint me a picture of a jiangshi," he said.

I gulped. How could he want such a thing, it had to be a joke. Did he know what I had done? Had he been watching? "A jiangshi?"

"Yes. I have always found the mythological creature to be fascinating, as they hop around the night, cursed to roam the earth for an eternity, or until they are destroyed. But then who knows where their souls go," he explained as if in awe. "No painter, whom I have spoken to, has wanted to indulge any further in the topic, no matter how much I offered to pay them. It is strange, really, that they fear in creating the painting that they will awaken some kind of creature, as if they really exist. Such nonsense, don't you agree?"

"Yes," I squeaked. I coughed to act as if something had gotten caught in my throat. I had the same fear, but I didn't want to admit it. I probably had more fear than other, actually having the demon haunt me through my brother. Unless the other painters had indulged in greater evils than I. "Yes, that is nonsense."

"So, do you think you will take the job?" he asked.

I was quiet for a moment. Why would the others not take it? Did they really believe that it would have brought bad luck to them if they painted such a thing? And how is it that I had an experience with the jiangshi, and now was being asked to paint the topic? Could it just be coincidence, and was my conscience just playing tricks on me now? A lot of people were interested in such topics, it was probably just that. It was a tale told to every child, it wasn't a surprise that someone would be interested in such a painting. People also painted dragons and other mythical creatures, so why not a jiangshi? Yes, it was as simple as that. There was nothing else behind it. It wasn't fate reminding me about the things I had done, it was simply a coincidence.

"Yes, I will take the job," I said finally. Although I smiled, I felt pain begin to swell in my head. It would be hard, painting this creature, I knew. But I also knew the pay would be worth the trouble, and that what had happened nights earlier was just all in my head. No such thing happened. There was no possible way.

He clasped his hands together. "Good, that is very good. Now, I will give you twice what I paid for the last painting for this, and I expect it back within four weeks, is that understood?"

I nodded, very grateful that I had such a person who would be willing to pay so much for my work. I felt honored. "Yes sir, I understand."

"Very well then, go start your work then. I will send one of my servants to check on you in a week's time," he gestured for me to leave, as that was all he wanted to say. He wasn't one for small talk, he probably was a very busy man.

I bowed and his servant led me out of the palace and back into the darkened streets.

I started on the project, as soon as I got back. Meilin wished me to come to bed for the night, but I wanted to get this project done as soon as I could. I didn't want to look at the monster that I had to create, the one that would remind me of the evil I had done. Along with that, I didn't think I would be able to sleep, not with everything that was going through my mind about the situation. I still wasn't convinced that I had been dreaming about my brother coming to me as a jiangshi. It was still hard to sleep at night and when I did, my dreams were plagued with even more nightmares.

With each stroke, I felt as if my brush and dream was betraying me, taunting me with my evil. *You did this*, the brush would say. *This is because of what you did*, the rice paper would add. Sometimes I would answer back, saying it wasn't my fault, and then I would realize that it had been all in my head and that if anyone had seen me talking to myself like this, I would have been carried away to a doctor's office. I couldn't let that happen, they wouldn't stop asking me what was wrong until I told the truth, and I could never admit that to someone.

I worked day and night, nothing could make me stop me from working on this project in such an obsessive way. Dark circles started to form around my eyes, as I had not slept for a couple of days. I worked hard on the painting; it consumed me as I worked on each and every detail. My wife kept begging me to stop, but I could not. I would not.

I had a few different versions I was working on, wanting it to be perfect. The more I painted, the more the jiangshi began to resemble my brother. I wondered if Meilin notice, for she said nothing. I didn't want her to find out, so usually when the creature began to look like Ming, I threw it out. I had to get it perfect, and I couldn't let anyone notice what had happened.

A week passed and I did finally get some well-deserved sleep, although it had been me simply falling asleep at my desk. I dreamt of my brother, in the mines, standing there with the gold, blood dripping down his face. He was holding up the piece of gold, asking if it was worth it, if it was worth his life. Such dreams never left one refreshed as dreams should. I woke up feeling even more tired and even more distraught.

Mengyao's servant, Liang, came to check on my progress one day. My wife led him to where my studio was. He seemed stricken when he saw me. Had I looked that bad after the week? Meilin had said it seemed I had aged a decade in the past week,

I just thought she had been joking, but with Liang's reaction, I wasn't entirely sure. I probably should have checked myself in a mirror before he arrived, but it was too late for that now.

"Good morning, Hui, how have you been?" he asked, slightly bowing.

I bowed. "I have been fine, thank you. And you?"

"I have been very well, thank you. How has the painting been coming?"

"Good," I gestured to the paintings. I have started a few different versions, so that you would have more to choose from. Let me know which is the best, so that I may work further on it." I hoped he thought at least one of them was what his master was looking for, I had spent so many hours working on it.

Liang studied the painting for a long moment, and then shook his head. "No, no, these won't do. This isn't what my master is looking for. None of them have the sense of a jiangshi, there needs to be more darkness around it, more evil as to why the man became a jiangshi. It must show in the painting."

I looked my paintings, feeling as if someone had stabbed me in the heart. I thought about the couple of versions I threw away, wondering if those were what he was looking for. They had reminded me of my brother and it could have been for that very reason, it had showed too much of the evil behind it all. I pushed back the tears forming in my eyes. They weren't for him, or about Liang saying they weren't good enough, but for having to deal with the anguished memories of my brother every moment I held a brush, and even when I didn't have a brush in my hand.

"I'm sorry," I said as I rubbed my eyes. "I will do my best to fix this, I promise."

He nodded. "I will be back in a week to check your progress. Have a good day."

I sighed as he left and I threw the paintings that laid there on the table off with such anger, slamming my fist on the now clean table. My wife covered her mouth, surprised by my lashing out.

"Hui, are you all right? You are so worked up about this," she tried to comfort me, thinking it was simply the painting that had me agitated. It was so much more.

I shook my head. "I'm fine, I just have a lot more work to do. It will be fine though, I will get it done for Mengyao."

She rubbed my back. "If it is too much for you to do, just say so. I am sure he would understand. I don't like seeing you this worked up."

I shrugged her off. "It's fine. I can do it. I just need to focus more. Get me something to eat, would you please?"

She nodded, a little happy that I had asked for food since I had been eating light for the past couple of days. I figured maybe I could focus better if I had more energy. Or maybe it would help me feel less guilty about it all.

A couple more days passed and my wife began to worry more about me, begging me to take a break. I told her I couldn't, that I had to finish the painting in order to finally be free of the burden that was on my shoulders. Not just of the painting, but about my brother as well. If I finished this, I felt as if I could have a clear conscience.

The painting was coming along, I thought. I had been able to add the evil element that Mengyao had requested. I thought about what evil the demon could have done to deserve such a punishment and from there I was able to create such a disturbing creature. Even to me it felt eerie, as if I didn't know where it had come from, although deep down I did. I had created the evil in myself and let it manifest itself onto the paper. I didn't want to admit that to be true, but knew it was.

As I worked compulsively on my painting one night, I began to hear the same thumping noise that I had heard weeks earlier. I stopped painting and listened closely, my heart racing and my hands shaking. At first there was nothing, I could just hear the usual city noises coming from the street. I hoped that was what I heard, and that my worry had made it seem like before.

Tha-thump. Tha-thump. Tha-thump.

No, it was the noise. It was exactly like before.

"Hui..."

He was back. The evil that haunted my thoughts was back. I was shaking as I grabbed my coat to go outside and check whether or not it was a figment of my imagination or if it was really him. I had to know at this point, I had to if he was real or not. I couldn't stand it any longer. I had to see it with my own two eyes once more.

I stepped outside. It was dark and the air was starting to get cool for the autumn season. I looked around, seeing only a few people out during the night. I didn't see any sign of my brother. It had all been in my head, just as I had suspected. The sound must have come from a creak in the house.

Sighing, I went back into my shop. It was just my imagination, as I had been painting too much. I should have known such lack of sleep and food was bad for the mind. I decided it would be best for my sanity, if I did go to bed for the night. I headed upstairs and climbed in bed with my wife. Her warm body brought me back to this work and it seemed my fears left me even for just a brief moment. I just wished I could stay there forever, and not face my own demons that awaited me down the stairs.

I heard my wife scream in panic, bringing me out of a dream filled with dust, blood, and fear. At first, I didn't think it was real, just some kind of lingering memory of the dream I just had. After a few seconds, I realized it was real and that I had to make sure she was fine. Did Ming come back for revenge? No, jiangshi can't come out during the day. It had to have been something else, although in the back of my mind I still feared the worst. I wouldn't be able to handle it if something happened to her, it was the last thing I ever wanted. I quickly got up, and went down the stairs to find her standing in front of my painting.

"What is it, Meilin?" I asked, as she turned, showing a face struck with terror.

Hands trembling, she pointed at the painting. I looked at what it was.

And there, in my painting, was my brother as the jiangshi with red paint surrounding him, as if it were blood leaking from his mutilated corpse. I stared at it, not remembering it looking anything like that the night before. I remembered it being less traumatic, less... real.

"It's your brother," my wife exclaimed, still staring at the painting as if I had done something horrible, as if she knew what I had done. "Why does it look like him?"

Truly I didn't have an answer. I hadn't remembered it looking like that and I definitely didn't remember using that much red. Had I done that? Had I really painted my brother? Had my conscience controlled what I was doing? I thought I had heard him last night, I guess it could have something to do with this. Maybe that is why I thought I had heard him, because I had painted him and everything was getting to my mind. I rubbed my face, hoping that last night's rest would make all my problems go away now, that I wouldn't let my subconscious take over my body. I would straighten this out and everything will be fine. I didn't have to keep the painting and it was probably exactly what Mengyao wanted.

"It's not him," I dismissed her accusations, although they were true, more than she knew. "It's a jiangshi and my brother is not a jiangshi."

"But it looks exactly like him," she whispered. It hurt for me to lie to her, to tell her she was seeing things, but I didn't need her reminding me of the same thing I saw, my deceased brother.

"You are speaking nonsense, now go start breakfast and let me work on my painting in peace," I gestured for her to hurry on. She did as I asked, but I couldn't help but stare at the painting a moment longer, wondering how it had happened this way. How it could look so much like him without me noticing.

Deciding, though, that it was probably what Mengyao wanted, I kept working on it. He would take it off my hands soon enough, and his body already haunted my nightmares. Now they would haunt my dreams as well.

"This is looking excellent, keep at it," Liang exclaimed as he came to check on my progress. "My master will be very pleased once he sees your finished work. It looks exactly how he wants it now, I'm glad to see you were able to make those changes. When do you expect it to be done?"

I examined the painting. It was still in the beginning stages, I still had to add quite an amount of detail before it was finished.

It was my first attempt at such a type of painting, but I felt I was doing quite well. "Give me two more weeks and it should be done."

He nodded. "Right so, I will be back in a week's time to check on your progress. I will tell Mengyao the great news about the painting. He has yet to find a man to make him such an exquisite painting."

He bowed and left me to return back to my work. I sighed as I looked back at the painting. It still seemed to appear as my brother no matter how hard I tried to change it. I had worked on his face for such a long period of time, yet it still looked the same. I kept the red below it, knowing it would please Mengyao, bringing out the dark element he wanted.

As I sat there staring at the painting, I heard the shop door open and close. I got up to greet whomever it was that just entered my shop.

"Hello?" I called out. There was no response. "Is anyone there?"

The sun had just set and I wondered who would come to my shop at such an hour. Maybe it was Liang, maybe he forgot something. There didn't seem to be anyone in the shop, but I looked around some more.

After finding no trace of anyone, I dismissed it to be just the wind, or a replay of my nightmare, caused by my chronic insomnia over the past couple of weeks. The filter of rationality in my brain didn't always work then, as well. I headed back to my studio, when I saw a figure standing in the doorway between where I was and the studio.

"Ming!" I exclaimed. There, in front of me, stood my brother. I couldn't believe my eyes. His skin was a lighter blue than before, with dark crusted blood running down from the top of his head, where I had hit him with the rock. His clothes were matted with the same blood and covered in mud. He stared at me with dark eyes, red with evil. His arms stuck straight out at an awkward angle, as his body had begun to stiffen with death and his nails were growing into long, rake-like claws.

"You are a murderer, brother, now you must pay the price!" he called out to me. As he opened his mouth, I could see his decaying teeth, even more sharpened than the last time I'd seen him. He had been growing more and more into a truly bewildering creature. He looked exactly like my painting, I couldn't believe it. The blood, the color of his skin. I still wasn't sure if he was a figment of my imagination or if he were real. I didn't want to stay any longer to find out.

I turned around and ran out of the shop, but I could hear my brother hopping towards me, his body stiff-like with rigor mortis. *Tha-thump. Tha-thump. Tha-thump.*

My heart was racing as I looked quickly for somewhere to hide. I couldn't find anything as everything had closed for the night. I hurried further away from my house, hoping I would find someone to help me.

"Please! Anyone, help!" I called out into the night. There was no response. Why was there no one there when I needed them! I felt as if the world had abandoned me to face my evil head on, that there was no longer anything that could help me. I could run back to the shop, but that was where Meilin was and I didn't want to bring this evil to her. I had to get as far away from the shop as I could.

"Hui! You are a murderer!" my brother called as he hopped after me. I looked back to see that he was no longer in the street, but hoping from roof to roof, along the buildings I had dashed away from. He was gaining distance on me. "You murdered me and made it look like an accident! You will pay the price and misfortune will be cast upon you!"

I had nowhere to go, Rationally, I knew I should just face the consequences of what I had done, but fear seizing my body with panic kept me from doing that. I had to get away, I couldn't leave my children fatherless, and leave Meilin alone to raise them. Sure she probably had enough money to hire someone to help her, or even marry someone that would take care of her better than I have. Marry someone who wouldn't murder their brother for gold.

Running down the streets, I kept trying to get away from my brother but no matter how fast nor matter how far I ran, he was still behind me, hopping after. It would have looked strange, if not otherworldly to someone if they had seen this chase. Ming jumped from building to building, ground to ground, as if it were no problem. He was like a monkey or a squirrel, yet still a lot like himself in his movements. I didn't know how he could have such strength in his movements, it had to have been something demonic.

Thoughts of things he could do to me ran through my head. Would he simply kill me? Or would he make me suffer like I had inadvertently done to him? Would he go after my wife afterwords? Or my children? No, I couldn't let that happen, I could not let him do that to my children.

Rounding a corner, I found a group of men surrounding a fire. I felt relieved that I had finally found someone to help. I ran towards them. "Help me! Please!"

The men ran off as they saw the creature jumping from building to building behind me. As I turned back to face my brother, my brother landed right in front of me. The fire behind me lit up his whitened face, making him look even more dreadful than he had only moments earlier.

"You must pay the price, brother. You must die!"

"No! Ming, I am sorry, I am sorry I did this! It wasn't my fault, if you had just been less lazy and more honorable, I would have never have done this to you. Can't you see? You were a drunkard and a gambler. You were hurting my family, I had to make it stop!"

"You didn't know me like you thought you did, brother! I was sobering up! I was going to move out with that money! I was going to start life anew! But you didn't wait that long, you are more evil than I could have ever been!"

I shook my head. "No, it was a mistake, I know, but a mistake I would make again for my family's sake!"

"And after I take care of you, I will go after them!"

"No!" I screamed as he started for me. He attacked me with his claws, scratching away at my arms. I had to fight back, I didn't want to die, for I had both my wife and children to think about back at home. Dwelling on the futile hope of both my safety and theirs, I grabbed him by the arms and hurled him into the fire behind me.

My brother screamed as the fire covered every inch of him, destroying both his body and soul forever. I watched as he turned into ash, knowing now he could no longer hurt me. He reached out for me, his glowing eyes the last thing I could see before he completely disappeared into nothing. I felt the burden of my evil life lift then from my shoulders and I felt I could live in peace, knowing he could no longer hurt me.

I looked down at my arms. He only shredded my sleeves, getting a little cut on my arms. I was thankful for that. I wouldn't have to worry about seeing a doctor, as it had been only a minor scratch. I could take care of it myself. Taking a deep breath, thinking my battle was finally over, I headed back to my shop.

I worked peacefully, once I was back at my shop. My wife noted how I no longer seemed worried and stressed, but rather seemed happy and more joyful compared with the last few weeks. And it was true, I felt a large burden be lifted off of me, as if destroying my brother's body once and for all left me feeling as if nothing could stop me. I told her I must have had some kind of sickness, and that I was beginning to feel better. She was glad for it, and I was able to resume work on the painting and spend time with my family without the fear that my brother would try to seek revenge.

Days went by, and I began to notice something different about myself. Even though I no longer had worries, I began to feel dreary during the day and felt livelier at night. I figured it must have been because of my habit of staying up for the last few weeks. So, I stayed up during the night and began to rest during the daytime. Meilin didn't want me to do such a thing, but I told her I didn't feel right during the day and she finally stopped bothering me about it.

Mengyao's servant Liang came to check on my progress one last time, before I would be done. I invited him in and he studied my painting carefully as he did the other two times.

"Yes, I believe it is going in the right direction. You are a great painter, Hui. I am glad my master has finally found someone whose art he enjoys, he had been searching for someone like you for such a long time."

"Thank you, you are too kind," I said. I felt my limbs start to ache. They had been sore for almost a week now, and I wasn't sure as to why. I had taken a lot of turmeric, but it didn't seem to help my joints at all. I probably would have to see a doctor after the painting was finished, and also get some much needed rest.

As I looked at Liang, I suddenly felt a curious urge come over me, imploring me to feast on his qi. I didn't know what the longing meant, but as I raised my hands towards him, I noticed my skin was a lot lighter than normal, almost...

Like Ming's.

It couldn't be possible, I knew. It was strange that such a thing could happen. How could I be a jiangshi, wanting to feast on his qi so that I could be stronger in effect? And why did it take such a slow time to happen? Was it because I slowly died whereas Ming had been killed first? I pondered on these thoughts. Liang didn't notice as I stood there, fighting with myself, wanting to kill him. He simply admired the painting.

"Although," he said. "I don't understand why my master is so interested in such a creature. It isn't like they really exist or anything. He is a very superstitious man, but at least he pays well."

I couldn't hold myself back any longer. I went straight for his throat with my long sharp nails and cut his neck. Blood drained out of his body and I felt the qi enter my body, as I let it pour into my open mouth. It felt refreshing to drink his blood, as if having a meal after days of not eating.

As his blood covered my hands, it hit me. I had killed another man. I had killed a man that I hardly knew. And why did I do that? Because I had become a jiangshi. How was it possible? How did I become such a thing? Evil had truly taken over me.

I remembered. My brother had scratched me before his fated destruction. Was it possible to become a jiangshi with just a little scratch? I peered in the mirror to find no reflection of myself. So it was true, I had become what my brother had been. A monster. What I had always been.

The sound of a woman screaming caused me to spin around. I found my wife standing there, her eyes wide as she found me like this. I looked down at the body. There was nothing I could say that could make this better. I took one last look at her, her eyes stricken with fear, with remorse, and with shame that I could have done such a thing. It would be the last time I would see her face, and it would be a look of fear and disgust. I didn't know what to say, I couldn't do anything to explain, she wouldn't understand and call me a monster. She would try to kill me, to protect our children, and I wouldn't have blamed her. Quickly, I hopped out of the shop and disappeared into the darkness.

I never saw my wife, or my children, again. I always thought about going back and seeing how they were, but I feared I would be seen by them and I couldn't bear to see the looks on their faces as they saw what I had become. A monster.

I don't know if Mengyao ever received my painting, or if he ever found out about what had befallen his servant. I tried to stay clear of him, in case he wanted me dead. Although I didn't want to be this creature any longer, neither did I want to die.

So I stayed in the darkness, hiding in the night as the city of San Francisco grew more and more as the years followed. I was amazed by how much changed and how much people began to forget the tales of creatures like me, even though I was still there, haunting those who traveled in the night so that I might live.

Over the years, I tried to blame others for my misfortune: my brother, the gold, my country for causing me to come to America. But I knew that there was only one person to blame for all that had happened. It was only one person's decision that was at fault, it was only one person's wrong doing, their evil, that had cause all this bad luck to fall upon my life.

And that person was me.

Acknowledgements

I just want to say thank you to everyone who has supported me in writing and in this story. A special thank you to Desiree DeOrto and Justin Boyer for helping me edit and make this story so much stronger, Daniel Somerville for the amazing covers, and Marcy Rachel for formatting and getting the novella ready to publish. I also would like to thank my friends and cousin Earlene for helping me create this series and letting me bounce ideas back and forth with them. Lastly, I would like to thank my parents and my husband for always supporting me and helping me out when everything feels overwhelming. I love you all!

About the Author

Dani Hoots is a graduate from Arizona State University with a Bachelor's in Anthropology who loves anything with a story. She travels around the west coast working at comic conventions and selling her stories and murder mystery party kits. Currently she lives in Arizona with her husband and two cats.

Check out her website
http://www.DaniHoots.com

Follow her on Facebook and Twitter
http://www.facebook.com/DaniHootsAuthor
http://www.twitter.com/DaniHootsAuthor

Made in the USA
Charleston, SC
05 April 2015